YELLOW VENGEANCE

Also by the author

Red Rover
Oranges and Lemons

A CALLI BARNOW MYSTERY
YELLOW VENGEANCE
LIZ BUGG

INSOMNIAC PRESS

Copyright © 2013 by Liz Bugg

All rights reserved. No part of this publication may be reproduced, stored in a retrieval system or transmitted, in any form or by any means, without the prior written permission of the publisher or, in case of photocopying or other reprographic copying, a license from Access Copyright, 1 Yonge Street, Suite 1900, Toronto, Ontario, Canada, M5E 1E5.

Library and Archives Canada Cataloguing in Publication

Bugg, Liz, 1949-

Bugg, Liz, 1949-
Yellow vengeance / Liz Bugg.

"A Calli Barnow mystery".
ISBN 978-1-55483-102-9

I. Title.

PS8603.U524Y44 2013   C813'.6   C2013-901469-1

The publisher gratefully acknowledges the support of the Canada Council, the Ontario Arts Council and the Department of Canadian Heritage through the Book Publishing Industry Development Program.

Printed and bound in Canada

Insomniac Press
520 Princess Avenue, London, Ontario, Canada, N6B 2B8
www.insomniacpress.com

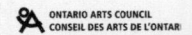

'Twas the "Vengeance of the Little Yellow God."

— J. Milton Hayes (1911)

Yellow is the colour of the third stripe on the Pride Flag and represents sunshine.

For mothers everywhere

Acknowledgements

Because my stories evolve with no outline, I am always indebted to the people I meet and the things I experience from day to day. I never know when an idea might present itself and become an integral part of the plot or a character's life.

There are, however, some individuals I would like specifically to thank in relation to this book. My agent, Curtis Russell of PS Literary Agency, gave me invaluable feedback on my early drafts. Farzana Doctor shone a light on points I might have otherwise overlooked. My editor, Gillian Rodgerson, as usual pushed me to the next level and brought the manuscript to its polished state. My fellow writers, Anthony Bidulka, Robin Spano, Shawn Syms, and Farzana Doctor generously put aside their own work to read a draft of mine and write a blurb about it. I am so grateful to all of you.

Thanks also to Glad Day Bookshop, The Sleuth of Baker Street, Crime Writers of Canada, The Writers' Union of Canada, The Word on the Street, Brockton Writers, The 49th Shelf, and Open Book for providing visibility and support not only for my work but for that of other Canadian writers.

My gratitude also goes to my family members for continuing to cheer me on, Insomniac Press for publishing The Calli Barnow Series, and the readers for making the whole endeavour worthwhile.

CHAPTER ONE

"Calli? Calli Barnow, is that you?"

My eyes flew open, and I struggled to focus through smeared sunglasses in the direction of the woman's voice, without moving my head.

"Oh my god, it is," the voice continued.

"Maybe you could have your reunion a little later," my dentist snarled as he applied the drill to my frozen tooth with more force than I thought was necessary.

The voice disappeared, and I was left to ponder the identity of its owner for the next hour and a half, while my sullen torturer worked on the first stage of my root canal. The pondering was preferable to what my mind would have been doing otherwise. I am not a big fan of dentists. It's not that I'm afraid of pain exactly. My wife, Jess, says it's part of my control thing.

My *control thing* goes like this: if I'm not in control of a situation, or at least in control of myself within a situation, I get very anxious, which is the last thing I want to do. I used to battle a full-blown anxiety disorder. Over the years, with the help of people, pills, and punching bags I have more or less brought that under control, but it still takes a lot out of me to lie helpless for a couple of hours in the dentist's chair.

By the time the sunglasses were removed and I was returned to a sitting position, my pondering hadn't produced any ideas about the disembodied voice. I tried to rinse, but between the four shots of anaesthetic and the unnatural position into which my jaw had been forced, I only managed to soak my paper bib and part of my shirt. My short hair is fairly indestructible, but after two hours upside down and immobilized, even it wasn't looking its best. Now I had a wet spot the size of a baseball right over my heart. What if the voice belonged to an old flame! Surely not. Surely I would have recognized it, if that were the case.

I attempted to flatten the cowlick that gloats on the crown of my head, gave my tingling legs a shake, and left the torture chamber in search of the mystery voice. There were two women and three children in the waiting room, but all remained absorbed in the cartoon that was playing on the TV. Maybe the voice had grown tired of waiting and left.

I knew I had another appointment for my tooth, but I'd lost the information, so I put on my apologetic face, frozen though it was, and approached the reception desk.

"All done for today?" the cheery secretary asked, as if I'd just spent two hours in a spa.

"Yeth," I managed to say, and nodded my head, just in case she didn't understand. Of course, she was probably quite skilled at deciphering dental speech impediments. This realization gave me courage to continue. "Whenth by neckth app—"

"You're due back next Tuesday at two," she said, and smiled at being able to help me out.

I responded with a one-cornered smile as she handed me an appointment card. In my effort to communicate, I had forgotten about the voice.

"Calli!"

I spun around, and there at the far end of the hall was a woman in a white medical coat, her hand raised in greeting.

I waved back. I had no idea who she was. She looked like a dentist, or perhaps a technician of some kind. My eyesight's pretty keen for a forty-four year old, but that didn't help. The woman was about my age, average looking, and South Asian. Not a lot to go on. As she bustled toward me, I was none the wiser.

"Calli, it's so good to see you," she said and placed her hand on my arm.

Once more I tried to smile. "Hi," was all I said, examining her face, as I searched my mental list of ex-lovers and long-lost friends for a clue.

"You don't recognize me." She paused and let go of my arm.

I gave another lopsided smile and checked to see how close I was to the exit.

"But of course you don't. There's no reason why you should. I wouldn't have recognized you either, but I saw your name on the appointment list."

The fist that had been tightening on my gut let go.

"I'm Sashi Singh. I *was* Sashi Mehta."

I glanced at the torture chamber where I'd spent the better part of the morning.

"Yes, that's my husband. We're also partners in the practice. I used to work exclusively out of our other office in Mississauga, but offered to help out here when Bill—Dr. Sanchez—moved to Port Huron."

This was all news to me, news I didn't care about. What I really wanted to know was how my dentist's wife fit into my past. If talking weren't such an ordeal, I would have asked outright. Fortunately she didn't leave me to wonder for long.

"We went to school together. Well, not exactly together. You were two years ahead of me, so it's no wonder you don't remember me. I remember you, though. I used to watch you play field hockey. I think I probably had a bit of a crush on you."

My frozen face flushed pink. I'd been too busy watching all the other girls on the field to pay attention to anyone in the stands.

"I read about you in the papers last winter, when you were involved in that fraud case. And all the murders! Oh my god!"

The two women in the waiting area became our audience. Sashi didn't notice, or didn't care.

"Your life must be so exciting! I just spend my days inside people's mouths. Don't get me wrong, I love being a dentist, but it's kind of predictable."

I nodded again. I'd given up on smiling.

"Listen, Calli, I'm in the middle of something right now, and I know you can't talk very well anyway, but I would like to get together with you sometime soon."

She must have noticed my apprehension, even though I was trying to hide it.

"Don't worry," she chuckled, "I'm not after you. As it turned out, I prefer men."

Although the waiting patients had lost interest in us around the time Sashi had started talking about work, they were now all ears. Listening to their dentist discuss her sexual preferences was far more exciting than watching their children watch cartoons.

Sashi noticed the women and lowered her voice. "The reason I want to talk to you is because I'm thinking of hiring a private investigator."

At last an escape was in sight. I reached into my back pocket and retrieved one of my business cards. "Call me, and we'll thet up an app—"

"I'll do that," she took the card. "Nice seeing you, Calli."

Sashi Singh arrived at my Kensington Market office five minutes early. "I hope this isn't inconvenient for you, Calli, but when I saw you yesterday, it was as if my prayers had been answered."

"It's not inconvenient, Sashi; it's my job." I was just glad to be able to speak to the woman without slobbering. I was also delighted at the prospect of work. Although business had been brisk over the winter and into the spring thanks to my media exposure, I'd had a fair bit of time on my hands since June. The hot weather must have turned people's minds to more important things than spying on cheating spouses or discovering who has a hand in the till. Of course, I could totally understand that. I would much rather be soaking up the sun at my cottage, if I had one, than discovering the nasty truth about someone. "What can I do for you?" I was already enjoying the irony of Sashi Singh's case paying for her husband's exorbitant root canal fees.

"My mother died recently," she said.

That wasn't what I had expected her to say, so an automatic response flew out of my mouth. "I'm very sorry to hear that."

"Thanks. I miss her every day." Sashi's eyes teared up. "But that's just me being selfish; it was actually a blessing for her. She'd only been with us in body for the last four years."

Despite the window air conditioner, I began to sweat.

"Alzheimer's?" I asked. My own mother forgot

things from time to time and repeated herself on occasion. I sometimes caught myself getting impatient with her. I couldn't imagine what it must be like to see your mom sitting there looking like herself, but totally disconnected from you mentally.

"No. She'd been in a vegetative state," Sashi replied, then paused in response to my shock.

I was finally able to speak, inadequate as my words were. "Oh, Sashi…I'm…"

"Thanks, Calli. Yes, it's been really hard. You'd think it might be easier to finally lose her under those circumstances, but…." The tears raced down her cheeks, as she hunted through her purse for a tissue.

"I don't suppose it's ever easy when you love someone." I had no idea if I was saying the right thing, but I felt I needed to say something.

Sashi wiped her face and explained, "It began as a trauma induced coma, but she never woke up."

"Oh, I see." What I really saw, or rather heard, was the bitterness that tinged Sashi's words. I didn't have a clue where she was going with this, and to tell the truth I didn't really want to find out. Unless Sashi just needed a sympathetic ear, which I doubted, she wanted me to do something for her that related somehow to her mother's death. I didn't want to appear cold-hearted, but I also didn't want to be too encouraging. In the end I tried for a middle-of-the-road approach. "I'm not sure what I can do to help."

There was no middle ground for Sashi. She nailed me to my chair with the look in her wet eyes and hammered her words home. "You can find the son of a bitch who did it to her."

"Did what to her?"

"Put her into that coma to begin with."

"Slow down, Sashi. What exactly happened to your mother?"

Sashi took a deep breath and waited to calm a little before she continued. "Four years ago, my mother was attacked on the street. Her purse wasn't stolen, but it looked as if someone had been through it, so the police believed it was a mugging. Do you know the success rate of finding a mugger, let alone trying and convicting him?"

"Probably not too good," I said.

"Right. The police did put some effort into the investigation, because she was so badly injured, but there wasn't much of anything for them to go on. Eventually they stopped."

"That must have been hard for you," I said.

"It was, but I was so focussed on my mother's condition at the time that I just accepted it. In those days we were still hopeful that she'd make a full recovery, or at least wake up. Then she might have been able to tell us what happened."

"Of course." My interest had been piqued, so I added, "Was anything taken from her purse?"

"Probably cash. That's how she paid for everything, and there was only change left in the purse."

"But nothing was taken that could be traced."

"No."

When Sashi didn't continue, I asked, "How has your mother's death changed any of that? I don't understand."

Astonishment flashed across Sashi's face, but by the time she answered me, she was calm and logical. "Well, I went back to the police. I thought that now it would be considered a homicide, they'd reopen the case."

"Ah, of course." I tried to temper the insensitivity I feared I'd been exhibiting. "I gather you were disappointed."

"Apparently it would be pointless. My mother was an old lady. It couldn't be proved that she had died as a result of the initial attack. Even if they found the guy, which after four years is highly unlikely since they couldn't find him to begin with, the most they could do is charge him with robbery and aggravated assault."

"And they don't have the resources to do it. Other cases are more pressing." I knew that Sashi wouldn't have gotten very far with her request. It's not that the police wouldn't like to be able to catch the guy, but there are other murders to solve, murders with leads and suspects and an undisputed victim.

"Exactly."

"So you want me to look for this person?" I hoped I was wrong.

I'm not big on attempting the impossible, but a crying woman will get me every time.

"Yes, I do, Calli." Her face pleaded, even though her words didn't.

My only hope was to make Sashi come to her senses and withdraw her request. "What makes you think I would be any more successful than the police were when they tried?"

"I don't have an answer for that. Maybe you wouldn't." Desperation was beginning to erode her features.

"*Probably* I wouldn't. After four years, the chances are slim to none that I could find out anything. You would just be spending your money on a lost cause." Although I didn't want this case, at the same time I couldn't believe I was trying to talk someone out of giving me a paycheque.

"That's why I'm here. I don't think anyone else would even try. But we have a history."

I thought she was embellishing our past a bit, but her description made me smile.

"Please, Calli. I can afford it. And even if you don't discover anything, just knowing I did everything I could do will give me a little peace of mind."

Sashi had said two things that struck a chord with me: If something like that happened to my mother, I knew I would do anything I could to get justice. Sashi could more than afford it, and my dental work was costing me a fortune.

"All right, I'll try, but don't get your hopes up." I was being honest, but I had to admit to myself I sounded more optimistic than I felt; doubt and the anticipation of failure were already taking up residence in my gut.

CHAPTER TWO

The boardwalk in the Beach was more crowded than usual for a late summer evening. Young couples pushing expensive strollers, old couples wearing Tilley hats, and scantily clad teenagers of both sexes formed an eclectic parade. After a short search, Jess and I managed to find a bench with a view of the lake through the half-naked bodies at the volleyball nets. As a rule, we don't stray far from home on weekday evenings, but Jess had just been promoted, and although her new position was more demanding in some ways, it didn't include working late as often, or trips out of town. We were enjoying these times together, especially since we hadn't had a honeymoon after our wedding two months ago.

Today I'd driven down to Woodbine Beach after my meeting with Sashi. When Jess finished work, she'd hopped in a cab and joined me. We'd had dinner at our favourite spot in the neighbourhood: the hotdog stand. Now we had the rest of the evening ahead of us, and what an evening it was. The humidity of July had vanished and the cooler evenings of late August blessed us. The slant of the sun held the promise of a beautiful autumn. Life was good.

As we watched the flow of humanity, Jess laid her hand on mine. A simple and spontaneous connection that made me smile. "I love you, Jessica Chang," I said to myself. It didn't matter if she heard.

"I've been thinking," she said, still admiring the view.

I shot her a look, hoping for some indication of what was going through her mind. Whenever Jess said those words, it meant that a monumental change was coming. Last time I heard them, it was the beginning of our wedding plans. In the old days, my reaction was to immediately put on the brakes, pick a fight, sabotage her plans, and stop things before she got carried away. The wedding had taught me to relax a bit, let her take the lead, and not overreact to her ideas. By the time we finally tied the knot, I was so happy with everything that you would have thought it was my idea in the first place.

Now instead of throwing up interference by offering to buy her another hotdog or switching to another subject, I took a deep breath and told myself not to be such a wuss. After all, there could be nothing any bigger than getting married. "Thinking about what?" I asked, trying to sound nonchalant.

"Don't worry, Calli, I'm not going to push you into anything you don't want." She stroked my hand

and leaned against my shoulder, looking up at me with her big coffee-coloured eyes. She knows full well that making physical contact lowers my resistance. At least we were in public; that would help.

I gave a half-hearted smile and said, "Shoot."

"Well…"

A pause meant trouble.

"Have you thought any more about children?"

"Children?"

"You know, Calli." She flashed her thousand-watt smile. "Those small people who like teddy bears and get excited about the park and the zoo."

Her choice of topic took me by surprise. The playground full of little ones we'd passed on our walk around the park must have prompted it. Whatever the reason, I decided to play along. "You mean those small people who wake you up at night and produce a lot of laundry and need braces and tuition?"

"Oh Calli, don't be such a curmudgeon."

"Well they do. You know I'm not a kid person." In my mind, some things are just a given, and the cost and inconvenience of children are two of them.

As if Jess had arranged it for my benefit, at that very moment a woman walked past, bliss oozing from every feature on her face. Tethered to her chest in a kangaroo pouch was a sleeping infant.

Jess watched her until she disappeared behind a throng of swaggering teens. "I know." She sighed loud enough to make sure I heard. "But haven't you ever thought it might be nice to maybe have one?"

"Ha...have one?" Suddenly it felt as if the dental freezing had returned. "You mean like being a parent?"

"You make it sound as if I'd just suggested you cut off your head." She moved away from me, as her voice edged toward defensive.

I made my "you think?" face that was actually a pretty mild version of what was going on in my head, which for the time being was still firmly attached to my body. I was determined to have it remain there.

Jess thought for a moment, before changing tactics. "You're great with kids. I've seen you."

"Being great with someone else's kids is way different from having your own. You can relax and enjoy them, because you know you're going to give them back to their parents." Despite the twilight drop in temperature, my forehead was moist.

"Are you serious, Calli? I know we've talked about this before, but I didn't realize you felt so strongly. You mean you've never even considered having your own children?" Jess's dark eyes shot out sparks through the half-light.

"Maybe for two seconds, before deciding it was a bad idea."

"I just don't understand you! I've been with you for four years. How could I not know you're so pig-headed?" She retrieved her hand.

"'Whoa, slow down. What's to understand? I'm the one who has been consistent. I've always said I didn't want kids. The last time we talked about this you didn't want them either."

The wind had risen and the cooling lake lapped against the sandy beach.

"I know, Calli, but lately I've been thinking that maybe I was wrong. That I would actually like to be a mother." She cast me a sideways glance.

"Why?"

"Tracy."

Of course! I should have seen this coming. When Jess's sister gave birth to her daughter, Tracy, Jess had worried she wouldn't be a good aunt. She'd been terrified of babies and all that went with them. But before long she'd blossomed into the most maternal creature I could imagine. I'd watched in fascination for the last two years; in fact, I'd found it attractive. Now it was backfiring on me. "You know it's not the same. Having your own is a huge responsibility. Twenty-four hours a day. Having fun as an aunt is not the same as being a mother."

"It's more than just fun that I want, Calli. How can I explain this to you, if you don't feel it? There's something inside me that wasn't there before. I don't know—it's a need."

We sat, silent, eyes locked on the rhythm of the water that was now clearly visible through the vacant volleyball courts.

There were so many things I wanted to say. I wanted to remind her we had just been married. Why couldn't we settle into it for a while? I wanted to remind her that our living accommodations were not suitable. How could we raise a child in a walk-up apartment over a bong shop in Kensington Market? What if Jess wanted to be a stay-at-home mom? How could we afford to raise a child with my sporadic income? All I could see were insurmountable obstacles. I knew, however, that if I were to voice any or all of them, she would have answers, logical answers. And I would be sunk. Besides, how can you argue with a *need*?

And then of course there was the biggest obstacle of all. It was really the only thing in this that mattered to me. I didn't want a child. I'd never seen this as a problem, but that's what it had the potential of becoming—a huge problem. The sort that can eat away at a relationship until there's nothing left. I couldn't let that happen to us, but at the same time, under the circumstances, it would be crazy to agree, to pretend I wanted this. I'd been blaming my hot dog for the feeling that had been growing inside me. Now I realized that the gnawing in my gut was fear.

When the fear and silence became unbearable, I said the only thing that came to mind. "Give me some time to think about it." What I really hoped was that Jess would think about it and come to her senses. I knew that was a long shot; up until now, she'd rarely changed her mind about anything. At least some extra time would give me space to formulate an idea, some solution that might help me avoid upsetting Jess, without having to go down the path of parenthood against my will.

I'd come to my office early. I admit it was an avoidance manoeuvre on my part. Instead of having my morning coffee with Jess, I'd picked it up next door at Joe's. For good measure, I'd also bought a mammoth oatmeal breakfast cookie. Joe had given me a quizzical look, because he knows my routines almost as well as I do, but he'd been tactful enough not to ask about the change. Normally I might have offered an explanation, but I didn't want to get into it. Besides, it was no one's business.

The walk down Baldwin Street had cheered me up a bit. Early morning is a busy time in the Market, and it's hard to remain gloomy amidst the swirl of life. Mrs. Lombardi had just wrestled her bags through the door of the produce shop on the corner when I arrived. "You should try the Macs," she said. "They're just in. You look like you need some vitamins."

For some reason, I'd taken her advice. A shiny McIntosh apple now sat on my desk beside my oatmeal cookie and coffee. My father's old oak desk and my wooden banker's chair are the only things I hung onto when I was forced to redecorate my office. New floor, new filing cabinets, and new paint on the walls gave the small space overlooking Augusta Avenue a fresh, if not exactly cheery, feel. I looked around and considered my next move. I could sit there and brood all day about my personal problems, but I'd come to my office at what to me was the crack of dawn to steer clear of baby talk. Work is always a good distraction for me. So, work it would be.

I usually have a pretty good idea where to start with a new case, but this time I didn't have a clue. When in doubt, I figure, try Google.

Once I'd made that monumental decision, I felt somewhat better. Better enough to need a breakfast break. The coffee and cookie were beckoning, and who was I to say no? To convince myself I wasn't a complete sloth, I checked for phone messages and read my email while I ate. I even managed a quick visit to my Farmville property on Facebook. Ah, the joys of being self-employed.

I love Google. Within fifteen minutes of getting back to work, I'd found the news reports on Sashi's mother and saved them to a new folder on my desktop. Five more minutes and I'd made a note of some names and addresses that might get me started. The speed with which I accomplished these preliminaries was not, however, a good thing. What it meant was, I still had very little to go on.

My second "when in doubt" default is to phone June, my good friend and ex-lover. She also happens to work with the Homicide Squad.

"Detective Sergeant Thompson." June is a morning person. Even the way she answers the phone proves it.

I cleared my throat, hoping I wouldn't sound like a sleepy frog. "Hi, June. It's Calli."

"What's the problem, Barnow?" June knows I wouldn't be calling her this early in the morning at work for a friendly chat. That means I'm either in trouble, which I am on occasion, or I need some help with a case. If June weren't such a good friend, I would be embarrassed about asking for help so often. In fact, if June weren't such a good friend, I wouldn't be asking for help at all. I would just have to muddle through.

"Not exactly a problem," I said.

"Well, that's a relief." She didn't believe me.

"Do you have access to information on cold cases?"

"I have access, but you know I can't just hand over details from an investigation, cold or otherwise." June is a stickler for the rules, and although it makes my life harder at times, I love her for it.

"Of course I know that. I just need the status on a cold case. I want to know if my client gave me the correct information. She was a bit confused, which is understandable. It's an emotional subject for her."

"Okay, Calli, why don't you just tell me the details?" A sigh escaped into her phone. "I'll see what I can find out, and if there's anything I can tell you."

"You're a doll, June."

"Don't I know it! What's the name?"

"Mehta. Indira Mehta. She was attacked and robbed four years ago, and ended up in a coma. She died recently."

"And what is it that your client wants?" June's voice was tinged with skepticism.

"My client is Mrs. Mehta's daughter, Sashi. She believes that the attack was the reason for her death.

She apparently went to the police and wanted them to investigate the case now as a homicide."

"I see," said June. The line was silent, and I wondered if we'd been cut off. Then June's voice returned. "I've brought up the computer file. I see that Mrs. Mehta was elderly, so under the circumstances, I can guess at the response your client received. There are in fact very few details about the attack. It was investigated, but that led nowhere. Not surprising."

I was the one who now sighed.

"Whatever made you agree to take this case, Calli? Are you really that hard up for work?"

"Not quite. Sashi's an old school friend."

"That's even worse. Now you're going to let down someone you know."

"Thanks for the vote of confidence, June."

"I'm only being realistic, Calli."

"As always. I know. And I wouldn't want you any other way. I explained to Sashi that it was a long shot, and if I wasn't sure she could easily afford to hire me, I would have turned her down."

"Just don't spend too much time on it. Believe me, it really isn't worth it."

"I hear you, June. Is there anything you can—"

"Wait a minute. Someone here took pity on your client."

"What do you mean?" I gave myself permission to nurse a hopeful thought.

"They've listed Mrs. Mehta's case on our website—on the Homicide Cold Case page."

"I didn't know there was such a thing."

"Unfortunately, most people don't."

"Does it do any good?"

"Once in a while. Anyway, check it out, Calli; it has all the available information."

"I will, June. And thanks."

"You might want to curb your appreciation until you've seen how little you have to work with."

"Thanks anyway."

"How about thanking me by going a couple of rounds in the gloves after work?"

A couple of years ago June had convinced me to take up boxing as a way to stay in shape and fight stress. It had been good for me, but recently I'd been growing lazy. "Not today, June. But soon."

"Sure, Barnow."

"I promise. And thanks again."

She clicked off, knowing better than to try and pin me down.

It didn't take long to find the Toronto Police Service website and to click on the Homicide Cold Case page. Any hope I'd had was dashed when I saw the length of the list. I scrolled down and found that the earliest date was sometime in 1997. I skimmed through the entries, clicking open a few just to see what types of details were included. Then I found Indira Mehta. When her case notes appeared on the screen, they were skimpier than others I had looked at. June was right as usual. What had I gotten myself into? Where on earth was I going to start?

I did what any sensible private investigator does when faced with such a dilemma. I switched off my computer and grabbed food.

As I stepped out of the cab on Church Street, Dewey was coming down the steps from Mauve, the boutique where he works. We'd arranged to meet for lunch in the heart of Toronto's gay village and talk about Mrs. Mehta. Dewey is my best friend and occasional colleague. When he's not making steady money by selling up-scale wine decanters and decorative accessories, or entertaining clubbers as Lady Dee, he provides me with invaluable assistance on my cases. If anyone could get me started on a path of some sort, it was Dewey. Even so, I had a feeling that for the present we would be doing a lot more eating than working.

"Calli!" He paused two steps from the bottom and spread his arms in a grand gesture. "You're looking..." His beaming face mutated to one of concern, as he rethought the compliment. "Tired," he said.

"Thanks, Dew. You always know how to sweet talk a lady." His hug made up for the truth of his statement.

"Of course I do, babe. And I also know how to make one feel better. Auntie Dwight is taking Calli for a nice lunch."

I opened my mouth to protest, but before I could speak, he gripped my hand and headed toward the street. People in Toronto like to jaywalk, but Dewey had refined it to an art form. He held up his free hand to stop the traffic, looked directly at the drivers, and pranced across the asphalt, dragging me like a reluctant puppy. This action was accompanied by a screech of tires, a horn blast, and a wolf whistle. Once we reached the other side, Dewey turned back to the street and with a flourish, took a deep bow. Dewey is not only an accomplished drag queen, but also the star with a capital S in his own life story.

My heart was still pounding as we entered Dorothy's. I didn't recognize any of the waiters, but Dewey did, of course. A young man named Jason took great pleasure in showing us to the best spot on the patio. I was glad to take my seat under the umbrella, but Dewey and Jason struck up a conversation. Besides feeling invisible, I was also afraid I might starve to death. I was eventually rescued by a voice from inside the restaurant that summoned Jason back to his duties.

Dewey smoothed his t-shirt over his six-pack as he sat down across from me.

"You used to date him, right?"

Dewey grinned at me. "In my misspent youth."

"Last year?"

"Mmm, maybe the year before that. Briefly." His dimples appeared on his dark cheeks.

"Okay then. Let's order, shall we?" I buried my head in the menu. My eyes had made it half way down the burger selections, when I realized that Dewey was studying me. "What?"

"Are you okay, Calli?" Dewey has the capacity to switch from flippant to deadly serious at the blink of an eye. If I didn't know that he is completely genuine at all times, I might doubt his sincerity.

"Yes, I'm okay, Dew. I just have a few things on my mind. Didn't sleep well."

"Trouble at home?" His shapely brows headed toward each other.

"No, not trouble."

"But?"

"Well...don't say anything to Jess. I'm supposed to be thinking this over, not discussing it with people."

"I'm not people, Calli." He clasped his hand to his heart in mock affront, but both he and I knew he was right.

Ten years ago Dewey had arrived in Toronto alone and frightened. He was only nineteen, and he'd fled Jamaica in search of acceptance. I was a volunteer for a youth outreach group at the time. Over the months that I helped him put his life back together, we became friends, and then we became family.

I gave him a smile, the kind I don't give out to *people*, and said, "Jess is making baby noises."

"I beg your pardon?"

"You know. She's talking about having a child."

Dewey's mouth fell open, but no sound escaped. He still looked at me, but I knew that for a moment at least, it was not me he was seeing.

I waited, regretting I hadn't kept quiet, or at least approached the subject with more finesse. I know that when Dewey is caught off guard on the subject of family, it can bring up some painful memories. Sometimes all it takes is a word, or the sight of a child with his parent, and it reminds him of his own parents whom he adored. His own parents who turned their backs on him when he needed them. His own parents who disowned him for being who he is. Most of the time he manages to live his life as if his psychological scars didn't exist. But now and then I can see the hurt that still lurks just below his carefully rehearsed surface. It was too late for me to withdraw the subject this time, so I just had to let Dewey deal with it and come back to me when he was ready.

It didn't take long. His face transformed once more. Now it was sparkling with mischief. "What's the problem, Calli? I think I'd make a wonderful aunt to a little Barnow-Chang, or Chang-Barnow, or Changow, or Barang."

"Dewey!"

"Steady, girl. I'm serious. I would love it."

"I know you would. It's not you I'm worried about," I said.

"Ah. So Calli doesn't know if she's cut out to be a mama."

"It's not a matter of being cut out to be a mama; Calli doesn't *want* to be one," I corrected.

"But Jess wants this."

"So she says."

"And so it must be considered," he added.

"I told her I'd think about it, Dew. I've never

wanted a kid...but you should have seen the look in her eyes...first when she started to talk about it...and then when I balked...I just don't want to mess things up over this."

"Whoa! Slow down, Calli. You two can figure it out. Can't you?"

"I don't know. I hope so." People at the other tables on the patio were starting to look at me. I lowered my voice. "What am I going to do?" I was twisting the life out of my paper table napkin.

Dewey reached across the table and took it from me. "First: breathe." He smoothed out the mangled paper and refolded it to more or less its original shape.

I did.

"Now listen, Calli. Nothing is going to happen overnight. It sounds to me as if part of the problem is that this came out of left field. You did the right thing by telling her you'd think about it."

"But—"

Dewey raised his hand to silence me. "And that's what you're going to do. You're going to give yourself time to consider everything, not the least of which is your own feelings. You know, sometimes people change their minds, even about important things. In fact, I've even seen Calli Barnow change her mind." He placed my napkin back on my side of the table with a warning look.

I managed a weak smile. "How did you get so wise?"

He shrugged and held me with his eyes. "I guess

I had a good teacher."

I was ready to move on to another topic, but Dewey had other plans. "Just out of interest, where would the baby, if there were a baby, come from?"

"Come from?" He'd lost me.

"Have you thought about this at all, Calli?" Dewey left me with that question, as he ordered us tea and our favourite sandwiches. He didn't even bother to ask me if I wanted something different. Ordinarily that would have bothered me. Today I was only too glad I didn't have to make a decision. "Well?" he came back at me.

"No," I had to admit. "Well, I mean, I've thought about how it would change our lives. In fact, most of what I've thought about is how it would change my life, and not for the better."

He shook his head. "As I said before, you've got time, but you'd better drag yourself out of that poor me rut, and think about some other things. Like Jess, for example."

"I know, I know. She's getting to that biological clock time of life. I don't remember ever feeling that way, but that doesn't mean anything."

"So Jess wants to give birth?"

I shrugged. Dewey was right. Not only had I not thought about important issues, but also since I had temporarily put a hold on things, Jess and I hadn't discussed them, so I had no idea what she wanted. "Well, *I'm* not going to give birth," I finally said.

"That never crossed my mind, Calli." His eyes

widened in horror at the thought.

I didn't know whether to defend myself or be pleased.

He didn't give me time to decide, but ploughed ahead, making sure that when I did think about anything, I would think about everything. "So if Jess wants to have a baby, what about a father? Would it be a sperm bank, or someone you know?"

Our eyes met across the table. But instead of seeing Dewey, I had the vision of a little person with Jess's eyes and Dewey's dimples. Before Dewey could read my mind, I said. "You're right. I need to think about it. And Jess and I need to discuss details. I don't think I'll change how I feel about being a parent, but...you never know."

Dewey was about to reply, but I cut him off. "Right now I want to talk to you about something else. I just got a new case, and if you're free after lunch, I'd like you to go with me to Yorkville. Check out the scene of the crime. Maybe talk to a witness."

"Nice evasion, Calli."

CHAPTER THREE

Since it was another beautiful day, Dewey and I walked the short distance from Church and Wellesley to Yorkville. The neighbourhood is only a few streets and avenues nestled in the northwest right angle of Yonge and Bloor, but per square foot, it's one of the most expensive areas in North America. In the sixties it was Toronto's hippie central; its coffee houses home to fledgling writers and artists, as well as musicians like Gordon Lightfoot and Neil Young. I wasn't old enough to partake in its pleasures, and my parents were just a bit too old. They, along with my grandparents and others in their social circle, looked down on the area and all it stood for with disgust and growing horror. I think I would have really liked the old Yorkville. Now, however, the neighbourhood exhales high style and money.

Dewey of course was in his element: fashion, good food, and beautiful people. I, on the other hand, looked as if I was there in search of a makeover. After my recent undercover experience*, however, the very thought of a transformation terrified me.

"Where to first, babe?"

The obvious place to start would be the location of the attack, but obvious is not always expedient. "I'd like to talk to the man who found Mrs. Mehta. He works in the hair salon just ahead. At least he used to."

We climbed the steps to Waves. On the other side of the heavy glass door the pong of peroxide assaulted us, but a violin concerto assured us we were in a place of refinement and taste. Only a large bouquet of sunflowers warmed the stainless steel and glass décor. Almost hidden behind it a young stick of a woman perched on a stool from which she commanded the front counter. Her face gave Dewey an automatic smile, but it faded at the sight of me.

"Take it away, Dew," I said out of the corner of my mouth, and handed him a piece of paper with the name of the man we were seeking.

Without appearing to take his eyes off the young woman, he glanced at the paper and said in his most charming voice, "We're looking for Lucas Anasetti. Does he still work here?"

The woman flipped her stick-straight hair over her bony shoulder and blinked. "Uh, no."

So much for our first lead.

The girl then leaned toward Dewey and put her elbows on the counter. "Why would he work here? He

---

Oranges and Lemons (Insomniac Press, 2012)

owns the place."

I tried not to roll my eyes.

Dewey upped his charm, but I knew a tirade against smart-ass receptionists was in progress inside his head. "That's great," he said. "Oh my god, is that a Kelly Wearstler?" He ogled her top.

His change in tactics worked. Stick Woman smiled, and for the first time looked slightly pleasant. "Yeah. I just got it." She primped.

"I *love* it. And the colour is perfect with your eyes."

I thought his compliment a bit thin, since the top was a dull grey, but Stick Woman was lapping it up.

"You have such good taste," he gushed.

By this time she was putty in Dewey's hands, and he knew it.

"I know you're really busy, but I wonder if you could do us a favour." He leaned against the counter, as if he were about to share a secret with the wraith. "We really need to see Lucas Anasetti, and I know that you can help us with that."

Stick Woman looked stricken. "Oh dear. He's not here right now. He only drops by from time to time."

Undeterred, Dewey continued. "But I bet someone in a position of importance, such as yourself, would know how we could get in touch with him."

I was on the verge of taking a front row seat, but it looked as if the performance were about to end.

"Of course I do." She withdrew an embossed business card from a drawer and held it up. "Here's his phone number." She pointed a long nail at the line of numbers.

Dewey glanced at the card, then back at the holder of it. He wrinkled his nose in the way only Dewey can, making him look twice as adorable. "I know I'm asking a lot," he purred, "but you see, Lucas is an old friend of mine. I just got back in town and I have a surprise for him. If I phone first, it will spoil the surprise. I don't suppose you know his address? He told me what it was when he moved there, but I misplaced it. Stupid, I know."

The woman was defenceless against Dewey's charm. She referred to something in a drawer, picked up a silver-plated pen and scrawled the address on the back. "There you go. Don't lose it this time," she teased.

Dewey made a zipper motion in front of his grin and accepted the card like a precious gift. Before we left he promised to return if he needed something done to his hair before he went back to the islands.

At the bottom of the steps I said the only thing that came to mind. "I love you, Dew."

According to Sashi's description, the information in the news reports, and in the cold case notes, Mrs. Mehta had left the Cumberland Cinema after the early evening show on January fifteenth. She said good-bye to her companion, Fatima Nassar, and headed east on Cumberland, before turning north on Old York Lane. Where the lane ends at Yorkville Avenue she'd crossed the street and continued north on Hazelton to Scollard, where she'd parked her car. Mrs. Mehta never reached her vehicle. She'd been attacked just three metres west of it, on the sidewalk in front of a construction site.

Dewey and I retraced Mrs. Mehta's footsteps. I tried to imagine what it would have been like four years ago, on a dark evening, a cold winter wind blowing between the buildings. I shivered, and wondered if Mrs. Mehta had felt in the least apprehensive.

Dewey trotted along beside me, his mind focussed on checking out the people we passed, not on mentally recreating a crime scene.

"This must be it. Somewhere around here," I said, stopping in front of a row of immaculate brick and cement townhouses that appeared newer than many other structures on the street. Of course, there was really nothing to see—nothing but a perfectly innocent-looking street with perfectly innocent-looking buildings. There were no sinister alleys, no ominous dumpsters, and no nosy old lady peering out from behind a filthy lace curtain on a second floor walk-up. Mrs. Mehta had probably travelled this street a hundred times after shopping trips or evenings out with friends. Maybe her car was parked in her favourite spot. Scollard is one of the few places in the neighbourhood that allows street parking. Of course none of these probables or maybes mattered in the least. None of them would help me find answers to my questions.

"Now what, babe?"

"Now we try to see Lucas Anasetti."

Dewey wrestled the card out of his back pocket and read the address. "It's down at Harbourfront. Must be one of those condos."

"Well, it's a nice day for a stroll by the lake. Do you have to go back to work?"

"No, Adrian will cover for me."

Despite the attraction of arriving at Anasetti's place and finding him not in, forcing us to enjoy ourselves at the waterfront, I opted for a more sensible course of action. The lake wasn't going anywhere, but I had to make some progress on the case.

Anasetti picked up after three rings, using his name as a salutation.

"Mr. Anasetti, my name is Calli Barnow. I'm a private investigator working on the Indira Mehta mugging case from four years ago. Am I correct in believing that you are the Lucas Anasetti who found Mrs. Mehta?"

There was a pause, then, "Yes."

"I'm sorry to bother you after all this time, but Mrs. Mehta has just passed away."

"That's too bad, but what do you want with me?"

"Her daughter has asked me to re-examine what happened, because she believes that her mother's death is a direct result of the attack."

"I still don't know why you're contacting me." Anasetti's responses were more clipped each time he spoke.

I didn't give up. "Would it be possible for me to spend a few minutes with you this afternoon? I don't have much to go on, and a meeting could be very helpful."

There was silence on the other end of the phone. Finally Lucas Anasetti replied. "Can't we do this over the phone?"

"It would be better if we did it in person." I waited.

"I'm going out at three. If you can get here soon, I'll see you for a few minutes."

"That's perfect, Mr. Anasetti. What's your address?"

Dewey stifled a laugh as Lucas Anasetti dictated the address that was on the back of the card. I made encouraging sounds, as if I were writing it down.

"We should be there in about fifteen minutes. Thanks."

The cab dropped us in front of the Queen's Quay Terminal building. Like many of the old buildings on the waterfront, it had originally been used as a warehouse for Great Lakes commerce. Now several floors are filled with boutiques, restaurants, and offices, as well as an art museum and a dance theatre. The top floors, which were added during renovations, house expensive condominiums.

I made a beeline up the steps and through the circular marble lobby to the long information desk. Behind it sat two uniformed security guards. "Are those the elevators to the condos?" I asked, pointing to my left.

"No ma'am," was the response from the younger man. "You need to go past those elevators, through the glass doors, turn right, go outside, and then turn right again. You get to the condos from out there." He grinned at me. "It's a totally separate entrance. Different address too."

"Thanks," I said, feeling more than just a little foolish for not being more observant. I had been given Anasetti's address twice, and I'm sure that there were street numbers clearly visible at the front of the building, but I hadn't looked.

Dewey was already through the glass doors by the time I had thanked the young man. I raced to catch up with him, but when I entered the main part of the building he had sped past the upscale fast food restaurant and turned down the line of shops on the left. I finally reconnected with him in the atrium.

"Dewey, where are you going?" I kept my voice low, for fear it would echo through the multi-story space.

He looked sheepish. "I thought we could just have a peek at the Inuit Gallery."

"Not now, Dew. We have to see Anasetti before he leaves at three. He won't wait for us."

Shoulders sagging, Dewey accompanied me back through the building and out the side entrance.

Lucas Anasetti opened the door to his penthouse

without making us wait too long. He was dressed to go out, and he looked like he'd stepped from the cover of *GQ*. I could feel Dewey drooling behind me.

"Come," he ordered, and walked away, leaving us to shut the door and make our own way through the chandeliered foyer to the living room.

Dewey made a *can you believe him* face, which reflected my feelings exactly.

Anasetti was already seated in a white leather chair when we rounded the corner into the living room. No invitation was forthcoming, so Dewey and I occupied the matching sofa with lake view. One thing was clear: Lucas Anasetti and his surroundings were a perfect match. Expensive and cold.

"This won't take long," I said, almost wishing I'd opted for a phone interview.

"Good. As I told you, I have to go out."

I whipped out my notebook to indicate I meant business and said, "You were the person who found Mrs. Mehta on the night she was attacked."

"That's right."

"Could you just take us through what happened?"

"It was years ago," he said, while lighting a long cigarette with a crystal table lighter.

"I understand, Mr. Anasetti, but anything you can remember will be very useful to us."

He drew the smoke deep inside his lungs, as if he were trying to suck back the memories. When he finally finished exhaling, he began his story. "It was my night to close the salon. I was late leaving, because I'd been on the phone with my mother." A faint grimace momentarily tinged his dispassionate features. "I'd arranged to go to a friend's house up on Davenport, otherwise I wouldn't have been walking in that direction. It was cold out, and the street was deserted. At least I thought it was, until I nearly tripped over the woman. She was unconscious, but still alive, so I phoned nine-one-one. I knocked on the door of the closest house, and they gave me a blanket to put over her."

"During all that time, you didn't see anyone else on the street?"

"No. Of course I wasn't really looking. I was more concerned with the woman. While I was talking to the man in the house a car parked farther up the street did drive away. The police said it was likely just a coincidence and nothing to do with what had happened."

"Was Mrs. Mehta unconscious the whole time?"

"Yes."

"Was there anything to indicate that she'd been robbed?"

"I told the police everything before," Anasetti said, flicking a speck of ash from his black pant leg onto the white carpet.

"I appreciate that, Mr. Anasetti, but I'm not the police. I'm just trying to help the family." I tried to appeal to any soft spot that might be hiding inside his stony exterior.

He took another drag. "She still had her purse. It was around her wrist, I believe, and she had landed on the handle when she fell. It was open, but I guess that could have happened when she went down. I didn't look inside. I've always assumed she was robbed, because the police called it a robbery."

He had a point. Most robbers would have taken the purse somewhere safe, though, not gone through it at the scene of the crime. The way Mrs. Mehta fell and the timing of Anasetti's appearance must account for its presence. "How long before the ambulance or police arrived?"

"The police showed up about five minutes after I called, and the ambulance a few minutes after that. They questioned me, and I left."

So far all I'd written down was two words: neighbour and purse. "Do you remember which house you went to?"

"The street was mostly commercial at the time, but there was a private house beside a construction site. That's where I went."

I was about to thank Anasetti and escape into the warmth of the outside world, when Dewey piped up. "Did you often walk along that street to visit your friend?"

"About once a week." He blinked at Dewey in surprise and annoyance.

I could see that this was a line of questioning the police might not have pursued.

"Was anything that night different from other nights?" Dewey continued.

Anasetti stubbed out his half-smoked cigarette, then immediately removed another from the silver container on the table. He didn't rush to light it, but once he had he said, "Nothing except that I was later than usual, as I told you."

Dewey wasn't about to give up. "Was there normally much traffic on that street at night? Cars or pedestrians?"

"Not much. I guess it would depend. Probably more in summer. But as I said, it was cold." Anasetti checked his Rolex.

Dewey ignored the signal. "And was there much light, from streetlights or buildings?"

"I couldn't say for sure, but as far as I remember it wasn't terribly well lit. It's just a side street."

"Were there many cars parked on the street?"

"I really don't remember. Maybe." His jaw tightened with each successive answer Dewey pried out of him.

"So someone might have been hiding behind a car, while you were tending to Mrs. Mehta." Dewey had slid forward on the slick leather, and was leaning toward Anasetti.

"It's possible, but I didn't see anyone." He blew smoke directly at Dewey.

Without so much as blinking, Dewey continued, "Where exactly did you say your friend lived?"

"I didn't." Anasetti glared at him.

Dewey just cocked his head and kept his eyes glued to Anasetti's reddening face.

"I don't remember the number, but as I said it was on Davenport, the south side, just west of Hazelton."

"And his name?" Dewey asked.

There was a pause where there shouldn't have been one. Then Anasetti said, "Phillip."

"Phillip what?" Dewey persisted.

Anasetti looked at the tip of his cigarette. "Sloan or Strong or Smith. I don't know, something like that."

"I thought he was a good friend." Dewey couldn't quite manage to hide the gloat that was growing inside him.

Through clenched teeth came Anasetti's reply. "I haven't kept in touch. His name was Phillip. His last name started with an S. You can check, if you like. I'm sure such top-notch private investigators won't have any trouble finding out." Anasetti stood up. He was through with hints; he was through with us.

I put my hand on Dewey's knee and squeezed, just in case he had another question up his sleeve. "Thank you, Mr. Anasetti." I tried to sound grateful and apologetic, but didn't succeed in smoothing his ruffled feathers.

His back was already towards us.

Dewey didn't need to be told to follow me to the door. Even he knew we'd outstayed our welcome.

CHAPTER FOUR

After her heart attack last winter my mother moved into a retirement residence. She had resisted as only a stubborn woman who has lived in the same five-bedroom house for forty-five years can resist. How on earth could she get used to living in a shoebox? What would she do with all her things? She'd never see her friends. She wasn't ready to be put out to pasture. Every day she'd managed to come up with a new concern.

I had done my best to calm her fears by countering each of her objections. She was far from ready to be put out to pasture. She could still drive and so could most of her friends, so she'd continue to have a social life. No one was asking her to get rid of all her things. Nothing in her life needed to change except the place she called home. Although I hated to do it, I even played the health card. She needed to be somewhere with help readily available in case she suffered another medical crisis.

At the same time, however, the little girl inside me had wanted to beg her not to abandon the house where I had grown up. My selfish self still wanted to be able to go through the front door and breathe in the home smell and hear the creaking floorboards I had learned to avoid in my late night escapades. Even though I had run away from the oppression that was embodied by that house when my father was alive, every brick was a part of me. And so it was that no matter how sensible my words had sounded, it's possible that my mother had heard the pleading of my heart.

Needless to say, I hadn't been the one to finally convince her to make the move. Our doctor, no spring chicken himself, had talked some sense into her. Once the door of possibility had been nudged open, we were able to look around and find a beautiful spot that even my mother could not fault. Fortunately my father had left her with no money worries, and the sale of the house added a nice lump sum to her nest egg. She was in the enviable position of not having to consider a government-subsidized facility; she could choose from the best there was available.

The timing couldn't have been better. Just as she was about to be discharged from the rehabilitation centre, a new seniors' residence had opened. It was close to her old neighbourhood, the suites were nothing like shoeboxes, and the communal facilities were fantastic. After three months in Worthington Estates my mother appeared to be thriving both physically and mentally.

"Calli," the treble voice chimed from the administration office just inside the front entrance of the residence complex.

I backtracked and popped my head around the doorjamb. Marlene was seated behind her big desk, elbow deep in papers. I'd rarely seen her anywhere else. Her husband was the one who did most of the legwork at Worthington.

"I just wanted to save you a trip upstairs, Calli. Your mother's in the rec room. There's a presentation on package holidays by a travel agent, and she and some of her friends are watching it."

"Oh, good," I said, my voice betraying surprise.

"You don't need to worry about her, Calli. She's adjusting very well."

I was relieved to hear my feelings confirmed, but at the same time Marlene's report didn't put a smile on my face. I wondered if my kindergarten teacher had said something like that about me to my mother. More and more it was evident that our roles were reversing. I might not like it, but at least I didn't resent it. I'd heard people complain about the demands of their ageing parents, but I just feel lucky to still have my mom. I know we have an ideal situation, but I'd like to think that I would never consider her a burden, no matter what. She's the only close relative I have.

"She's quite the woman, Calli," Marlene continued. "She never ceases to surprise me. You know, at first I thought she was timid and might not really like it here, but I couldn't have been more wrong."

I knew my mother was capable of such surprises. She'd astounded me on a few occasions over the years. The biggest change had been after my father died. Once she'd come to terms with losing him, the distant, self-absorbed woman I'd grown up with was gradually replaced by a vibrant, gregarious go-getter who was involved in more committees and social groups than I could keep track of.

"Thanks. That's good to hear," I said and headed toward the rec room at the back of the main floor. The lights were out and a film on Thailand was playing on the built-in screen. The audience was mostly women, and from the back it was hard to tell which one was my mother. Then the woman at the end of the back row turned to whisper at the person next to her, and I recognized the familiar profile.

I touched her shoulder and squatted next to her chair.

She greeted me with a smile.

"I can wait in your suite," I whispered.

"Nonsense," she whispered back. "I was hoping for an excuse to leave."

We sat at her little kitchen table, cups of steaming tea bonding us. We'd talked about Thailand, while I devoured the digestive biscuits she'd arranged on the Royal Albert tea plate. I found I was relieved that she had no intention of "traipsing around Thailand" as she'd put it. My relief was short-lived, however, when she announced that she wouldn't mind going on a trip somewhere else, like Russia. Then from out of the blue came her question, "What's bothering you, dear?"

"Are you sure you want to go to Russia?" I asked.

"Forget Russia." She added a couple of wrinkles to her brow. "I'm talking about whatever has been on your mind since you arrived."

"Why do you think I have something on my mind?" I could feel myself beginning to blink more than was necessary.

"Well...." She looked at me as if I should know the answer to my question without her having to put it into words. When I said nothing, she continued, "You never just drop in on me unannounced, unless you have a good reason."

True.

"And if that reason isn't that something is bothering you, you would have told me by now."

Also true.

"So what's wrong, Calli?"

"Nothing," I said, not daring to look her in the eye.

"Calli, the corner of your mouth is twitching. It only does that when you're trying not to tell me something that you really want to tell me."

So that was it. I would have to keep an eye on my mouth, if I hoped to keep my moods and thoughts private in future.

I hadn't really planned to visit my mother, but

somehow once I was behind the wheel, I found myself heading in her direction. I also hadn't planned to discuss with her what I knew was going to come out of my mouth the next time I opened it. The butterflies in my stomach were urging me to get the hell out of there. I ignored them and spoke. "Did you want to have children?"

My mother's eyes widened behind her bifocals. After what felt like an eternity, she spoke. "Of course I did, Calli. Why do you ask?"

I had hoped she would keep talking, tell me one of her stories about motherhood, but instead she had put the ball firmly back in my court. I could have made up a reason for my question, but she probably would have seen right through it. I chose the truth.

"Jess wants to be a parent."

The sentence hung in the air like a tightrope walker who had slipped and was about to plummet to earth. Neither of us jumped to the rescue.

Eventually my mother spoke, quite rightly putting focus on the real problem. "And you?" Her lips puckered ever so slightly.

"I don't think so. It's something I never really considered."

"It would be hard on the child," she said.

Her shift from me to the child threw me for a moment, but I came up with what I considered a good recovery. "Well, I'm sure I would love a child, if I had one." My defensiveness surprised me but didn't faze Mom.

"That's not what I meant, Calli." She poured us each more tea, perhaps waiting for the penny to drop.

It didn't.

"Oh, Calli," she continued. "Growing up is hard enough without having two mothers and no father. Being a parent is hard enough without having to justify to the world your right to be one."

She might as well have slapped me. What really hurt though was the truth in what she said. I had been so busy worrying about how a child would affect me personally and how it would affect my relationship with Jess that I hadn't looked at the bigger picture. I hadn't thought of the child. I hadn't thought of the world.

Because of my initial reticence, I should have been glad that my mother was providing me with ammunition to use against Jess. To my astonishment, it was having the opposite effect. I might not want to be a parent, but how dare she say I shouldn't be one? At the moment, however, I had nothing to argue with. None of my friends had children, and since I supposedly didn't want them either, I was woefully ignorant on the subject. Until I knew what I was talking about I would just have to keep my mouth shut.

"I didn't mean to upset you, dear. I'm sure that you and Jess would make wonderful parents, and goodness knows, I would love to be a grandmother, but sometimes you have to put the child's welfare first."

Even if I'd been capable of or wanted to put up a

feeble argument, there was something about my mother's manner that would have stopped me. She was stroking the side of her teacup, and her thoughts were only partially at the table with us. I wanted to ask what was bothering her, but something inside me didn't want to know. I wasn't sure I could handle any more serious talk just then. My silence was enough of an invitation.

"I should know," was all she said.

Silence was no longer an option. "What do you mean?"

"Oh, Calli." She gave me a look laced with love and worry. "I have something to tell you."

Although I no longer wanted to talk about my qualifications for parenthood, I didn't like the direction our conversation was taking. I knew that whatever words my mother spoke, they would create one of those moments you remember for the rest of your life, and all I wanted to do was run out the door before it was too late. Without warning, let alone my consent, she'd switched topics. She was going to tell me she was dying. I wasn't ready for that.

"There's no easy way to say this." She reached across the table and took my hand.

I stopped breathing.

I couldn't escape.

I was going to hear it.

"You're not an only child."

I took in just enough breath for one word. "What?"

She gave my hand a squeeze and then let go.

Somewhere in the back of my mind a little voice was cheering, "She's not dying!" But it was being drowned out by a cascade of confusion.

"I'm so sorry, Calli. I should have told you years ago." Tears snuck down the creases in her cheeks, but she ignored them.

I wanted to help her, make her struggle easier, but I was mute. How could I help, when her words made no sense to me? Despite my lack of understanding, something began to gnaw at my core—could it be a sense of betrayal?

"You have a brother, an older brother. A half-brother." She took a deep breath and looked at her tea.

I sat, a silent and inadequate player in the drama that was unfolding around the little table which bravely held her second-best tea service.

When it was obvious I had nothing to contribute, she continued, "I had a baby five years before you were born. Long before I met your father." She checked her teacup once more but didn't drink. "No one was ever supposed to find out. I went to an unwed mother's home in Ottawa where I stayed until the baby was born. That's what lots of girls in trouble did in those days. He was put up for adoption." The last sentence was barely audible.

But I had heard it.

"Oh, Mom," I finally managed to whisper.

Now she was silent.

I fought the urge to curse. I forced myself to stay

seated. I willed myself to look at the grey-haired woman I had known all my life. And yet obviously not known. She needed me to say something, to do something, but I wasn't sure what exactly. I just knew she was counting on me to…if not do the right thing…at least not do something to hurt her even more. I chose my words with care. "That must have been awful."

She looked up at me, and I could see her relief. She had taken the leap, dragging her reluctant daughter by the hand. And somehow we'd made it safely to the other side of the abyss. Now we could move forward.

"It was the hardest thing I've ever done," she said.

I had no way of knowing how hard it must have been, but the truth of her words even now was visible in her trembling muscles and ragged breath. Not knowing where to go next, I chose something to which I could relate. "Did you tell Dad?"

"Oh yes. I told him before we were married." She visibly relaxed; she too realized we'd survived the crossing. "I thought it was only fair. But then when we never had the son he so wanted, I felt even guiltier. Like I'd let him down twice. I know it's probably silly, but that's how I felt. It was a topic we just avoided."

Having known my father, I could imagine his stoic martyrdom, and how he would have used it as a weapon against my poor mother. No wonder she had withdrawn into a world of her own for all those years.

"What happened to the baby's father?" I'm not sure why I wanted to know, why it mattered to me, but it did.

"Sid was killed in a car accident, before I had the opportunity to tell him." The gentleness with which she relayed this information gave me comfort. She had cared for Sid. A great deal.

"Oh my god. How terrible for you." My words were coming more easily now. Somehow I had managed to distance myself to the point where it was like watching a movie or TV show starring two people who looked remarkably like my mother and me. "So he was your boyfriend?"

"Yes, we'd only been dating for about six months and I was crazy about him. I didn't find out I was pregnant until after he died, so I'm not sure how he would have reacted. Whether he would have wanted to marry me or not; we'd never discussed the future. So, although I was devastated by his death, at least I didn't have to deal with the possibility of him rejecting the baby and me. Or spend my life with a man who'd felt trapped into marriage."

Even though I was watching *the Calli and Mom Show*, I was still present enough to realize that this was the first time I'd ever thought about my mother as anything other than a mother. Sure, I'd seen pictures of her growing up, but they were just that—flat faded images taken on someone's Brownie or Instamatic camera. I'd certainly never considered her to be a young, sexual woman with desires and fears and weaknesses. To me she'd always seemed old. Old, and, although no longer completely predictable, at least comfortably dependable.

How could she have carried such an important part of her past around inside her all these years without my guessing that there was something wrong? If she'd kept that hidden, what else didn't I know? The more I considered the possibilities, the less able I was to ward off my emotional reactions. Yes, she'd had a terrible experience—but shit! I had a right to know about my brother. If I'd known, maybe I would have understood my mother. Maybe I could have had a better relationship with my dad. How could she have done this to me? I felt as if the woman I'd grown up with didn't exist anymore. My cheeks were burning, and I forced myself to breathe in to a silent count of three.

"I'm so sorry, Calli," she whispered.

I opened my mouth, but nothing came out.

She attempted a hopeful smile.

Finally a mumble emerged from somewhere inside me. "You have nothing to apologize to me for." I voiced what I knew I should be feeling.

"No, you had a right to know about your brother, even if you couldn't grow up with him. I should have thought about how you would feel, not being told. I should have found a time to tell you, before now."

I shrugged and looked at my cold tea. "If it was so hard to give him up, why didn't you keep him?"

"I wanted to. You have no idea how much I

wanted to. But giving him up was the best thing I could do for him at the time, and for his future. A good family adopted him apparently. They gave him the life I couldn't have on my own. Even nowadays being a single mother isn't easy, but in those days there was also a big stigma attached to giving birth out of wedlock. Your granny and granddad didn't want to look after me and an illegitimate child. What would the neighbours say?" She forced a feeble smile in an attempt to downplay what must have been another painful layer in her personal tragedy.

I tried to smile back, but instead remembered all the times that same sentiment had been held over my head by the woman now trying to joke about it.

She was serious once more, as she continued. "It would have been a hard life for both of us. I didn't know what else to do. I wish it could have been different, but it wasn't."

I had asked the question, but was starting to regret it. None of the information about the expectations and experiences of women in my mother's generation was news to me, but having it personalized, seeing my mother and grandparents cast in the roles of people to which I had previously paid little attention and shown even less understanding made me uneasy. I retreated to the present; it might not be comfortable, but it was preferable to the past. "And you're telling me this now because of Jess wanting a baby?" I asked.

"Partly. Your news gave me a little push. I've been meaning to tell you for a while now."

"Why now after all this time?"

She looked at me and I knew what she was going to say before the words came out. "Because I'm going to see him."

I took a gulp of my cold tea and counted the roses on the tabletop, as past and present collided. "When?"

"Next week. He'll be in Toronto."

I looked up to see the anticipation radiating from my mother's weary face. "How did he find you? Wasn't secrecy the whole point of what you did?"

"You wouldn't have paid any attention to this, Calli, but in 2009 the Ontario Adoption Records were opened. After that I often thought of trying to find him, but never had the courage. Then last winter out of the blue I got a phone call."

I couldn't keep the bite out of my voice. "When last winter?" The hairs on the back of my neck stood up as I waited for her answer.

"Yes, it was just before my heart attack. But don't blame him, Calli," she pleaded. "Even though we didn't know it, my heart was in rough shape. If it hadn't been the call, it would have been something else." She could see she wasn't making any headway with me, so she said what she knew I couldn't argue against. "You probably can't understand this, but I would have gladly died just to hear his voice and know he's okay."

I didn't understand, but I said nothing. What could I say? I didn't even know what to think. I had no idea what it felt like to have a child, let alone lose one. I also had no idea what it felt like to have a sibling, so

I'd never experienced sibling rivalry. Now at the age of forty-four I didn't want to start. Despite my desire, I feared that was exactly what I was feeling.

This news also provided possible explanations for things I never understood during my childhood. My mother was so opposed to my wanting to run around in jeans and t-shirts. I tried to rebel. I still remember the arguments. She would try to reason with me. Try to convince me that I didn't want to look like a boy. And I would cry and try to convince her that I didn't care. I had no hope of winning those arguments of course, so my tomboy self was hidden inside frilly dresses and pink terry short sets. I hated the way I looked. I hated the way I felt. It was like wearing a costume every day of my little life.

When I was finally allowed to go shopping for my own clothes, the first thing I bought was a pair of Lee jeans. They made me feel like a new person, and that new person was *me*. I remember looking at myself in the change room at Eaton's. I'd put my hands on my hips, smiled at my reflection and said, "Well, hello Calli Barnow."

My mother of course wanted me to return the jeans. She burst into tears and left my father to deal with it. Ironically, he took my side, and managed to convince my mother that it wasn't the end of the world. I had to agree to wear clothes she approved of for church and social events, but those jeans did wonders for me, even when I wasn't wearing them. I walked down the hallways of my school, my kilt swinging with my new swagger. As I sat in the church pew on Sundays the congregation saw the Barnows' well-dressed daughter, but when I looked down at my knees, I saw my Lees, and instead of feeling the colour-coordinated tights on my legs, I felt the rough flat seems of my beloved jeans.

My mother was waiting for my response.

"I'm happy for you, Mom. I'm worried too. But I'm happy." I managed a weak smile.

"Thank you, Calli. I hope you know that he won't take your place. Ken. That's what they named him. He may be my son, but he's a stranger to me. He may never be any more than a stranger. I don't know what will happen. I just know I have to see him. At least once." My mother dabbed her nose with the tissue she always kept in her cardigan pocket.

"I know." My own baby problem suddenly didn't seem so important.

CHAPTER FIVE

Mrs. Nassar lived with her daughter in Brampton, a city held fast to the northwest corner of Toronto by a non-stop stream of commuters. She was Mrs. Mehta's oldest friend, and she'd been with the unfortunate woman on the night of her attack.

I slipped off the highway and onto a residential street where large brick houses stood shoulder to shoulder behind tiny lawns and double driveways. As I searched for the address, I realized my chances of discovering anything new or pertinent about Mrs. Mehta were as scrawny as the saplings that lined the avenue. Nevertheless, once I found the house, I was anxious to at least try.

The heavy front door squeaked open, seemingly on its own. I was trying to figure out whether I should enter the house or ring the bell again, when a small voice said, "Hello." From behind the door, lower than the level of the handle, a small face peeked up at me.

"Hello there," I said. "Is Mrs. Nassar here?"

The small head shook no.

"Is your grandmother here?" I guessed.

The small head tilted to one side, the big eyes flashing question marks.

"Yann, who is it, dear?" The singsong of a woman's voice reached the step.

"No one, Daa-dee-maa," the small person called back.

I was about to develop a complex, when the door swung open. "Hello, Ms. Barnow, I'm Yasmine Nassar," the short, saree-clad woman said, and smiled in welcome, before ushering me inside the two storey foyer. "Yann, you go and play while Ms. Barnow and I have coffee."

The little boy scurried up the curved staircase leaving Mrs. Nassar and me to get settled in the large living room where a low table displayed an ornate coffee service. She'd baked delicious-looking cookies, and I was glad I'd made the trip.

"I am very sad about Indira's death," she said. "She was my best friend, for years. We were like family. Our children grew up together. I feel her loss like she was my own sister." She placed her hand on her chest and closed her eyes for a moment before pouring me a cup of coffee and making an offer of cream, sugar, and cookies. "But as you know, we really lost her a few years ago."

"Yes," I said, "It was a terrible situation. I can't even imagine what it must have been like. Sashi is very upset...understandably. You and...everyone who…" Mrs. Nassar looked so small in the big living room. When I'd spoken to her on the phone, I'd had no reservations about asking her for information. Now that I was sitting across from her, seeing her pain, I wasn't sure I could or should add to it. "Mrs. Nassar, I…"

"What is it, dear?"

"I don't want to make this harder for you, but as I said on the phone, I'm looking for answers about Mrs. Mehta's attack. Would you be up to answering some questions about that evening? I know you told the police everything at the time, but it would be useful to hear it from you."

"Of course. Anything I can do to help. I'll be upset whether or not I talk to you about it."

We shared a quiet moment before I began. "I believe you spent the evening with Mrs. Mehta and parted just before she was attacked."

"That's right. We used to see a film together about once a month. We'd go out for dinner first, then we'd go to the movie theatre. Usually we'd travel together. I lived in Toronto at the time, not far from Indira."

"But that day you went separately?"

"That's right. We met at the restaurant. Indira had some things to do beforehand. She went to the beauty parlour, and I think there was some banking or something like that. I can't really remember—some sort of business or other. Her husband hadn't been well for quite some time and he'd recently become worse, so she had taken over some of the household tasks that he would have normally done. I'm sorry I can't be more specific. Anyway, I took a taxi down, and then my husband—he was alive at the time—picked me up on his way home from a late meeting."

"I see."

"I've always thought that if I had just been with Indira, she would never have been attacked."

I looked at the little woman sitting across from me, her grey hair scraped back in a bun. "On the other hand, both of you might have been hurt."

Unwilling to relinquish her guilt, she picked up the plate and offered me another cookie.

"Do you know where Mrs. Mehta had her hair done, or where she banked?"

"No. I may have at the time. Downtown somewhere, possibly Yorkville."

"Did Mrs. Mehta always park on one of the side streets when she was in Yorkville?"

"She did, if she could find a space. She didn't like parking garages. Although she was a brave woman, she felt they weren't safe."

We let the irony settle in silence. I concentrated on my coffee and considered my next line of questioning.

Mrs. Nassar didn't wait for me. "As I said, she was a very brave woman. Too brave. Some people might have even called her foolhardy. I told her she should stay with me until my husband came, and we could drive her to her car, but she wouldn't. She was anxious to get home. As I said, her husband was ill.

She told me I was just being silly worrying about her. What could possibly happen to an old woman in a neighbourhood like Yorkville? She was also very stubborn and didn't like to put people out."

"Other than the change in routine, was there anything else unusual? Did Mrs. Mehta seem worried about anything, or preoccupied?" I asked.

Mrs. Nassar thought for a moment and then slowly shook her head. "I really can't remember any other details. I think everything, including Indira, was very normal. She was concerned about her husband of course, but I'm sure I'd remember if she'd been upset about something else. I would have asked her about it."

"Do you know if she had a lot of cash with her that day? I understand she never used a credit card."

"That's right. She didn't believe in credit. But I don't know how much money she had with her. It was my turn to pay for dinner, and I believe we were still using some movie passes our children had given us for gifts on our birthdays. They were only three days apart." Remembrance darkened her already dark eyes.

"It sounds like a wonderful friendship," I said, wishing I could leave her with that thought. "I don't know if the police asked this at the time, but I was just wondering, is there anyone you can think of who might have targeted Mrs. Mehta for any reason?"

Without hesitation, Mrs. Nassar responded, "Oh no, absolutely not. She was an angel. What would someone get from hurting her? Nothing!"

"I'm sorry, Mrs. Nassar. I had to ask. Especially since her husband was ill, and she was taking care of some things for him."

"I understand, dear. You're just doing your job, trying to help."

"What about Mr. Mehta? I know he passed away not long after the attack, but I don't know much about him. He was in the importing business, I believe."

"Yes, that's right. Imports from India, Pakistan, Sri Lanka. He did very well. He was a good man and a good businessman. Everyone respected him and trusted him. Indira wouldn't have been doing anything for the store. That was Ravi's, Mr. Mehta's, world. He also had trusted employees. Indira was responsible for their home and family."

"I see. So the mugger theory does seem the most plausible."

"I'm sure it would be easier to find the person responsible if there were a link of some kind to Indira, but I wouldn't want to believe that anyone who knew her would deliberately hurt her. I just couldn't bear that."

I'd arranged to meet Dewey for a late lunch at a restaurant in Little India or, as it's properly called, the Gerrard India Bazaar. I hadn't been to the neighbourhood for years, and although there were still dozens of restaurants, groceries, and South Asian clothing shops, I noticed that it wasn't quite as vibrant as I remembered it from the eighties. Expanding suburbs must have forced some businesses to relocate, and that might make my quest even more difficult.

Dewey had done some research, and suggested we meet at a narrow cafe sandwiched between a jewellery store and a vendor of housewares. I was almost drooling on the sidewalk from the aromas of cumin and coriander by the time Dewey hopped off the streetcar and bolted across Gerrard to join me. We were just in time for the end of the lunch buffet, and once we loaded our plates, I was so busy devouring my pile of biryani and tandoori chicken that I completely ignored Dewey.

When both of us had nothing left but our lime sodas he asked, "Why are we here?"

"I wish I could tell you. I'm just following any tiny lead I can get. This may not even be a lead. But I don't know what else to do."

"At least we're getting a good meal out of it." Despite Dewey's flamboyance and ability to enjoy life, he also has a very practical side to him. One aspect of that is his dislike of wasted time.

I drained my glass and tried to give him a more satisfactory answer. "When I was talking to Mrs. Nassar about Mrs. Mehta, we also discussed Mrs. Mehta's husband."

"Why?"

"Only because the day she was attacked she was doing something for him. Mrs. Nassar was certain it would have had nothing to do with his work, and she's probably right. But since I have no other areas of investigation at the moment, I thought I'd check into his business."

"Well, I like the hairdresser for the attack."

"You what?"

"Come on, babe, you watch TV. That's what they're saying on all the crime shows now: 'I like so and so for it.' Means they think the guy is the perp."

"Gotcha. So why do you like the hairdresser for it?"

"He's too slick. He's also heartless, just the type who would attack an old woman. Maybe she had something in her purse that was worth a lot of money. He took it and that's how he managed to buy the salon. I mean, think about it, babe. He just worked there at the time. You don't get filthy rich cutting hair, even in Yorkville, unless some sort of big break comes along."

He had a point. "But why wouldn't he have just left the scene? Why would he have hung around and summoned help?"

"I don't know. Maybe he was about to be discovered." He frowned, and I knew he was about to become impatient with himself for not having the answers to any questions raised by his theory.

"We need to interview the guy from the house on Scollard. Can you do that? And can you track down Anasetti's old friend on Davenport?"

Dewey's face brightened with my request. "Consider it done."

"It's too bad Sashi didn't know more about her

late father's business. I feel as if we may be chasing our tails."

"So why are we here? Exactly, I mean. Are we going to Mr. Mehta's store or what?"

"That was my original plan, but Sashi did know enough to tell me it no longer exists. Mr. Mehta died very soon after his wife's attack, Sashi inherited his share of the store, and then his partner bought her out. He dissolved the business a couple of years later."

"I know I'm repeating myself, Calli, but why are we here? If there's no business, then there's nowhere to go."

"Not quite. In an area like this people know each other. Even though things have changed over the years, I'd be surprised if no one remembered Mr. Mehta, or at least some of the people who used to work for him. It wasn't that long ago. With any luck we may be able to locate some former employees."

"So we're going to do a door to door?" Dewey groaned.

"Something like that." I tried to sound positive.

Dewey dabbed his mouth with his napkin and folded it back to its original shape. "I've enjoyed the meal, Calli, but will it really take two of us to follow this dead end?"

"You're my moral support. We'll start with the clothing store that's now at Mehta's old location. Maybe someone there can steer us in the right direction. If necessary, we'll split up and cover the rest of the area."

Dewey groaned again.

"Well at least we've had a meeting to discuss the case, right? You've shared your hairdresser theories, and I've brought you up to date on my progress, or lack thereof. And we've had a delicious lunch."

Dewey couldn't disagree.

"Well then, let's get going."

A block east on Gerrard we found the former import store. It looked pretty much as it had on Google Street View, except for the window display. Instead of the selection of everyday sarees and shalwar kameez that had filled the space at the time of the Google picture, now only one mannequin looked out at us. She was dressed in an elaborate wedding saree that glittered red and gold and white. When Dewey made no move to stop ogling it, I suggested that there were more treasures for him inside.

The bell over the door tinkled as we entered, and a faint odour of sandalwood greeted us. The walls were draped with lengths of shimmering silk in rich yellows, reds, and blues. Some changed hue if you moved your head, giving the whole place an organic feel. A mannequin stood in one corner, wearing an example of what was hanging on the circular rack beside it, a kind of loose top with heavy embroidery around the neck and cuffs. The sign on the top of the rack said, *Kurtis*. In another corner a mannequin displayed a saree of turquoise and gold, the pattern intricate and classic. Even I had to admit that western fashion paled in comparison to what surrounded us.

A young woman in traditional dress appeared through the beaded curtain at the back of the store. Her long black hair disappeared behind her shoulders, and when she smiled at us, she looked like the heroine in a Bollywood movie, though she sounded as local as Tim Hortons. "May I help you?" She showed no surprise at her two unlikely visitors.

I left Dewey to admire the tables loaded with printed satin, Japanese cotton, and shalwar kameez, while I gave my attention to the girl. "I hope so," I said, "but probably not." I did a mental calculation of her age in relation to when Mr. Mehta's store would have been in operation. "We're hoping that someone who works here might know about the store that used to be at this location, or about any of its employees. You probably wouldn't, but do you happen to know anyone here or in the neighbourhood who would have been around four or five years ago?"

"I don't really work here all the time. I only come in occasionally to help out my grandmother. She's been here like forever though. Do you want to talk to her?"

"That would be great."

Before I could ask for information regarding her grandmother's whereabouts, the young woman disappeared through the beaded doorway. I heard murmurs from the back room, and could just make out that they weren't in English.

I was beginning to wonder whether the young

woman had intended for me to follow her, when the beads parted and she reappeared. "This is my grandmother, Mrs. Kumar," she said, and disappeared once more into the back. A wizened version of the young woman took her place. She shuffled up to me and waited.

"I'm Calli Barnow, a private investigator, and I'm trying to find someone who might have information on a Mr. Mehta who used to have a business on these premises a number of years ago. Or even information on anyone who used to work for him."

The old woman's face softened to a smile that dropped twenty years from her age. "Ah, yes, yes, Ravi," she said and nodded with enthusiasm.

"You knew him?" For the first time all day my hopes crawled out of a pit.

"He was such a good man. Such a good boss."

"You worked for him?" Even before she gave an answer, I was doing a victory dance in my head.

"Yes. Yes, I worked for him. It was such a beautiful store. This place is nothing. Piff!" She waved her hand at our surroundings.

"Yes, I've heard wonderful things about him."

"So sad, so sad about his wife. It broke his heart. I say it killed him."

"Did you hear that she died recently?"

"Oh my, no, no. Poor woman. Poor woman." She fiddled with the folds of silk that hung over her round belly.

"That's why I'm here actually. I'm trying to find

out more information about the attack on her."

"After all these years?"

"Yes. Her daughter asked me." I was counting on the mention of family to further my cause.

"Ah. I see. I see. I will help, if I can. But I know nothing of the attack. And I'm only an old woman." She stirred the air with her head movements.

"I understand. I just need to ask you a couple of questions about the business. Perhaps you could help me with that."

"Of course. I will try."

I wanted to hug the old woman, but instead, I took my notebook from my back pocket. "Was the business doing well at the time Mrs. Mehta was attacked?"

"Oh yes. It was doing very well. Ravi Mehta was an excellent businessman. Knew what people wanted, and sold it to them at a fair price. Always quality merchandise. Customers always came first with Ravi. Not like that other one."

"Your present boss?"

"No. No. Ravi Mehta's partner. The other owner."

"Ah, I see."

"Piff!" She sliced the air with both hands. "He cared for no one but himself. Ravi only worked with him because of family. An old connection of some sort. We didn't see him much."

"And why was that?"

"He did the travelling, looked after the business of finding imports. That sort of thing. Dear Ravi looked after the store."

"What was this partner's name?"

"Sanderson." The corners of her thin lips turned down.

The old woman saw my surprise.

"Prabhakar Sanderson. His father was Scottish. A bad man."

I was starting to see that the old woman's judgement of Sanderson might be coming from some sort of racial or cultural bias, but I carried on. "Were the two men friendly? Did they work well together?" I asked, while I scribbled the name.

"I know nothing of friendship. For work, they made money. The store prospered. Ravi Mehta lived small. He was a simple man. The other one, all show and flash. I never saw any friendship, and towards the end, more and more, they did not agree. Over the years dear Ravi's heath suffered. I blame the other one. Ravi worried too much."

The old woman appeared to be growing even older from reliving her past. Her granddaughter, who had been standing in the beaded doorway, stepped into the room. "I think she's told you all she can for today. It's not good for her to get over-excited."

"I understand," I said to the young woman, then addressed her grandmother. "Please tell me though if you know what happened to Sanderson."

"I don't. He sold the store and was gone, like that." She waved her hand one last time.

I'd sent Dewey off to follow the faint trails of Lucas Anasetti's friend on Davenport and the man in the house next to where Mrs. Mehta had been attacked. Instead of pounding the pavement on Gerrard, I intended to spend the afternoon in my office looking for information on Prabhakar Sanderson.

I'd just logged into my Canada People Search account, when the phone rang.

"Calli." It was June. "I had a few minutes this morning, so I had a look back at some records from around the time of Mrs. Mehta's attack, just to see if anything popped out at me, and something did. Several months after your woman was mugged, similar attacks were reported. The guy was actually caught. A vagrant. He'd been going after women in and around Yorkville. He admitted to attacking two of them, after they found him in possession of certain items. No mention is made of Mrs. Mehta. Anyway, he spent some time in jail for the attacks. Thought you might be interested in knowing. Unless you've already solved your case that is." June's sarcasm hit its mark.

I replied in kind. "How can you even ask? When has it taken me more than two days to wrap up a case? And this one—a four-year-old cold case—piece of cake."

"I thought you might be thankful for a lead. So here's the name."

"Are you allowed to tell me this?" I joked.

"Barnow, it's public record."

"Of course it is. Okay, fire away." I grabbed my pen and a Post-it Note.

"Borisav Belic. B-e-l-i-c. He was thirty-one at the time he was sentenced to eighteen months in Mimico Correctional Centre. It wasn't his first run-in with the police, but as far as I can see he hasn't been in trouble since. If he's still around, you may be able to find him. It's not a common name."

"I owe you, June." I made loud kissing noises into the phone.

"Save it, Barnow. Catch you later."

I spent the next hour and a half searching for any traces of Sanderson and Belic on the Internet. After the sale of the Gerrard import business, Prabhakar Sanderson appeared to vanish. Of course there were thousands of Sandersons in Toronto and hundreds whose first name began with P. None of them was connected to the South Asian community and none of them was connected to importing. I focussed on small businesses and anything that hinted at an entrepreneurial endeavour. There was a P. Sanderson who had started a flight school, another named in connection with a private adoption agency that had shut down in 2002, and a third who had briefly run a print shop, but my Sanderson was nowhere to be found. Then a Sanderson obituary caught my eye. It wasn't for Prabhakar, but for Pradhi. What were the odds of there being more than one Sanderson family in Toronto with South Asian first names? I had no idea, but I assumed it was unlikely. I was right. Listed as a survivor was the deceased's brother, Prabhakar, still living in the city at the time of the death, a year and a half ago.

I thought Belic would be impossible to track down, but he had been surprisingly easy to locate. That is, if it was the same Borisav Belic, and if he hadn't already moved on. It would appear that he had turned over a new leaf in prison, for he was listed as a staff member for one of the homeless shelters downtown.

There was nothing more I could do today; or rather, there was nothing more I wanted to do that involved work. The evening beckoned with the promise of relaxation and good entertainment.

CHAPTER SIX

Jess and I had agreed to meet at Dorothy's before heading down to Studs for the show. Although I try to attend every performance Dewey gives, Jess hadn't seen his Lady Dee for a couple of years. She'd been out of town when he almost won the Queen Diva Contest, and other commitments had somehow prevented her from being there to cheer him on at his subsequent performances. As a result, she was glowing with anticipation.

We'd scored a spot near the back of the restaurant, tucked away from most of the bustle. The candle in the middle of the table flickered through its cut glass container causing ripples of light and shadow to dance across the plush wallpaper. Everything was perfect. There I was in my favourite restaurant with my beautiful wife, about to spend a wonderful evening surrounded by our people, watching the best drag queen in the city, who just happened to be my best friend.

Then, part way through our main course, Jess put

down her knife and fork and looked at me. "So, Calli, have you been thinking about it?"

Nine times out of ten when she asked if I'd been thinking about *it* I wouldn't have a clue what she was referring to. This time, however, there was no question in my mind. "Yes, I have," I said, and concentrated on my bacon mushroom burger.

"Well?"

I swallowed, but held onto my bun. "Actually, I think we need to talk about some very important issues before we can even think about making a decision."

"Wow!"

"Wow?"

"You *have* been thinking about this. I'm impressed, Calli."

"I do sometimes think, you know." I could feel my hackles go up, probably due to my view on the subject and the fact that regardless of what I had just said to her, I didn't want to talk about it at all, and especially at that moment.

"Of course you do. I was just teasing. I didn't mean to upset you." When I didn't respond she walked her fingers across the table and stroked the back of my hand.

"I'm not upset," I said, more to convince myself than her.

"Okay. So, what do we need to discuss?" Leaning back against the bench seat she made herself comfortable and waited.

I almost began to elaborate on my previous self-defence, giving myriad examples to prove I think about all sorts of things. I knew such a move would result in a disagreement that would pre-empt our talk. I also knew it would just be a temporary postponement. It wasn't worth it, and besides, we were in a public place and we'd promised to attend Dewey's performance. I decided to make the best of it. "Well, for example, do you want to physically have a baby, or do you want to adopt?"

I could tell by the slight lift of her eyebrows that Jess was surprised at the depth of my thinking and the clarity with which I expressed it. This time she paused before answering. "I'm not sure. It would be nice to give birth, have a child who is biologically part of me. But for us it isn't straightforward. I don't know how I'd feel about choosing the father out of a catalogue. That's so impersonal. But if we asked someone we know, then it's another person to consider—in everything."

I was glad she couldn't give me a pat answer. If she was unsure about these basic decisions, maybe it wasn't too late to put the kibosh on the whole crazy idea and get back to our previous state of marital harmony. I decided to throw it back at her, and I hoped it could remain there. "Since you're the one who would be carrying the child and going through the whole birth thing," I made it sound as distasteful as possible, "you would need to be really comfortable with whatever was decided." Burger juice ran down my thumbs, forcing me to put it down and clean myself up.

"But Calli, I want to hear more about how *you* feel. I know you never said you wanted children; in fact, you said quite the opposite. But that's how you felt about getting married and now look at us. Sometimes people just need time to get used to an idea. You said you've thought about it even though initially you hadn't considered it a possibility. Do you now?"

"I hadn't. And I can't properly consider it now, unless I know what it would involve. A big part of that is where the child would be coming from." I could feel the glow of satisfaction growing inside me. Rarely did I sound so logical, especially when discussing an important issue with Jess. "I still can't picture myself as a parent, but I said I'd think about it, so that's what I'm going to continue doing. I need to think about *everything* though, and to do that we need to look at all the possibilities. I mean, it could be like our wedding; the choice at the top of the list might not be feasible for some reason."

Jess turned pale. "That's true," she said in a small voice. "Oh, Calli, I hate this. I wish we could just wake up some morning and the baby would be there, or we'd know it was on its way. This is all so clinical. So…I don't know—cold. And I wish you and I could have a baby. You know, one that's part of both of us. That's what I really want. Why should I be the only one that's linked genetically?"

Although I was deeply touched by her wish, instead of agreeing, I tried to lighten the mood. "That's kind of how it works, when a couple's missing half the required parts." My attempt failed, and I swallowed my smile when I saw that Jess was on the verge of tears.

"I know," she murmured and grabbed her fork.

I watched her stab a piece of lettuce and carry it with purpose to her mouth. In the candlelight I could just make out the quivering of her chin, as she chewed and continued to stare at the remnants of her salad. I desperately wanted to make her feel better, but I was a huge part of the problem. I swallowed and opened my mouth, trusting that some words of comfort would escape. "If we adopted, then we'd be equal in every way." Holy shit! Where did that come from?

"Is that what you want, Calli?" She looked up at me, hopeful.

My burger was growing cold, but not as cold as the chill that was running down my spine. I had been putting forward arguments that sounded remarkably like I was gung-ho about the whole child thing. "All I want is…." What did I want? How could I tell Jess, when I didn't know in my own mind? At least she seemed confused too. But she was crystal clear on one point: she definitely wanted to be a parent. "All I want is for us to be sure about whatever it is we decide. And I want you to be happy. I want us both to be happy."

My burger had lost its appeal, but Jess seemed satisfied, at least for the time being.

Studs was throbbing with music and laughter and the camaraderie that is typical of a gay bar in the Village. The owners had found that providing mid-week entertainment from time to time boosted liquor sales and got the ball rolling for the weekends. It also brought in new clientele. That's why they'd asked Dewey to do a set tonight, but he had a more personal reason for accepting. His drag act was increasingly popular, and he was playing bigger bars, but he liked to return to his roots from time to time and grace the tiny stage along the back wall of the establishment where he'd given his first performance.

Jess and I wove our way toward the bar where I ordered a beer for me and a cooler for her. "Enjoy this while you can," I said and winked. Only when Jess blessed me with her smile did I realize my mistake. I had sounded like a future parent, no question about it. Jess continued to beam at me as she clinked her bottle on mine.

A hand landed on my shoulder. I turned to find Mandy, an old friend from my brief stint at university. Her hair had started to turn grey, but the toothy grin hadn't changed. "Calli, it's so good to see you. I can't believe it's been so long."

"It must be at least what...six, seven years?" I replied. "Mandy, this is my wife, Jess."

They greeted each other. Then Mandy turned and drew another woman into our circle. "This is *my* wife, Gabby." Mandy tightened her arm around the woman by her side.

The four of us nabbed the only table that was vacant and attempted to carry on a conversation over the growing din.

"I hear you're a P.I. now," said Mandy. "What on earth ever possessed you? I thought you wanted to be a vet."

"Yeah, well, I didn't fancy spending my youth hitting the books. I tried a few different jobs, but nothing stuck. Last time I saw you I think I was just getting fed up with construction work. Not long after that I got into investigations, and I've been doing it ever since."

"Seven years sounds about right," said Mandy. "I was in Vancouver for a few of those years. That's where I met Gabby." She leaned over and planted a kiss on the cheek of her adoring wife, before continuing the conversation. "Seems to me you were hobbling around after dropping something heavy on your foot."

"Yeah, that's what finally made me go into a safer line of work," I explained.

"You must be joking, Calli." Jess had been listening quietly up to this point. "Her line of work is anything but safe. She keeps getting herself into situations where she's lucky to come out alive."

"Then nothing much has changed," said Mandy. "When I knew this woman," she explained to Gabby, "I could never guess what part of her body was going to be in a cast or bandaged up from one day to the next."

"Actually, I've slowed down a lot. I take better care of myself now."

"Well that wouldn't be hard," said Mandy.

"So, Mandy, what have you been up to?" Being the centre of attention is bad enough, but not knowing what might surface while being the focus is even worse. There were lots of things from my past I didn't feel like having to explain to Jess. Not tonight.

"I'm still in accounting. I know—b-o-r-i-n-g."

"I would say stable," I added.

She grinned agreement. "We live in Riverdale, and we have a kid."

I could feel Jess's eyes light up, as she moved closer to the table.

"Congratulations." I looked at both proud parents and asked what I thought proud parents might like to be asked, "How old? Boy? Girl?"

Gabby, who had been silent up to that point, leaped into the conversation. "A little boy. Michael. He's amazing." Even in the dim lighting of the bar I could see a red rash of pleasure creep up her neck.

Mandy was already searching through her phone for the latest picture. "He's two," she added. "Had his birthday on July twenty-second." What looked like an adorable little face filled the touch screen, but she held it too close for me to clearly focus.

Jess moved my arm so she could see better, her eyes devouring the image.

Mandy gave me an understanding look. "I can give you the details of our adoption agency, if you're interested. Call me." She handed over her business card, which I slid toward Jess.

Before I could respond, the lights dimmed and Bruce, one of the owners of Studs, took the stage. "I hope your glasses are full, 'cause you'll need a drink."

"Hey, Bruce, you trying to scare us or what?" A slightly inebriated audience member in white spandex shorts shouted.

"If your wardrobe doesn't scare you, honey, nothing will," Bruce responded directly at the drunk.

The crowd laughed.

The man adjusted the glittery suspenders that were attached to the shorts and vamped for anyone who was looking.

"Okay now, settle down, girls. You're gonna need a drink for a couple a reasons. In a minute someone's gonna be on this stage who'll raise the room temperature to hot, hot, hot." Bruce hadn't advertised who the performer for tonight would be.

Hoots and wolf whistles rattled the glasses on the shelves.

"And you're gonna be cheerin' and pantin' so much that you'll need that drink to revive you."

Applause cut him off.

Raising his voice, Bruce announced, "Back by popular demand, give a down-homo welcome to Lady Deeeeee!"

The walls shook with shouts, cheers, and stomping feet.

Bruce left the stage.

The ruckus continued.

After making the crowd wait just long enough, Dewey oozed through the door and onto the platform. Well, it wasn't really Dewey at all; it was the astonishing Lady Dee.

I wouldn't have thought it possible, but at the sight of her the volume of the crowd increased.

Lady Dee was wearing a new gown, styled just for her from gold lamé. It looked remarkably similar to the material Dewey had been drooling over during our visit to Fabric Fun last winter. Whoever had designed and sewn the dress had hit the mark. Lady Dee was more gorgeous than ever. When she finally managed to calm down the fans, she began with one of her standards, Aretha's "Respect." By the end, she had everyone panting, as Bruce had predicted.

"Now boys and girls, I'm going to sing something new tonight. And it's dedicated to two very dear friends." She looked directly at our table, and just in case there was any doubt, she gestured with a long-gloved arm first toward Jess and then toward me. She followed that by blowing us a noisy kiss.

I had no idea what to expect, and when the opening notes of the introduction began, I was still in the dark. Then Bette Midler's voice channelled through Lady Dee, as every ear in the place softened to the sweetness of "Baby Mine."

Jess took my hand and held on tight.

I didn't need to look at her to know she was crying. My own eyes were tearing up at the sentimental message and the beauty of Dewey's performance. Without my lifting a finger, I knew we'd just moved a step closer to parenthood.

Dewey would be sleeping in after his previous night's work, so I decided to visit the homeless shelter on my own. Even if Borisav Belic no longer worked there, I hoped to speak with someone who might have known him, someone who could point me in his direction.

It was a beautiful day, the kind that shouts at you to make the most of it, because in a couple of short months you'll be freezing your buns off. I'd taken the streetcar across downtown, but got off a stop early, so I could walk through St. James Park. At that time of the morning, the cathedral was quiet and the park benches weren't yet filled with the lunch crowd. Only the pigeons joined me as I strolled through the formal garden, past the fountain and gazebo and on in the direction I needed to go.

Across the street from the park is the shelter. The brick and cement building makes no attempt to be esthetically appealing; survival doesn't need to be pretty. A few men slouched near the battered door smoking. I smiled a greeting in their direction, but they ignored me as I headed inside.

I'd never had occasion to visit any of the homeless shelters in the city, so I wasn't sure what to expect. The smell struck me just beyond the entrance. A faint whiff of disinfectant lingered under the aroma of bacon, and my mouth watered. A glassed-in office with a half-door was on the right. Inside, a burly man in a sleeveless denim jacket had his back to me, so I knocked.

The man turned, revealing an unshaven but kindly face. "Yes. May I help you?"

"I hope so." I introduced myself and why I was there.

"Boris is a friend of mine. You're not going to make trouble for him, are you?" The man seemed to grow in size, making it clear he wouldn't let me cause a problem.

"Absolutely not," I assured him. "I just need to talk to Boris about something from a few years ago. I need his help."

The man gave me the once-over, while he considered my request. He must have come to the conclusion I was harmless, because I was ushered into the office and given a chair, before he went to find Borisav Belic. After a few minutes a slender man wearing a chef's apron joined me. He was of indeterminate age, his eyes deep-set and haunted, his skin tight and colourless.

"Mr. Belic?" I stood and offered my hand.

He wiped his hand on his apron, before giving my hand a tentative shake.

"I'm Calli Barnow."

"Ya, Jack said. What you want?"

"You work here, right?"

He gave me an unexpected smile, revealing his

lack of dental care. "Sure do. Two years almost."

"You obviously like it." I smiled back.

He didn't contradict me. "So what you want?"

There wasn't going to be any beating around the bush. "I need your help." I knew I had to approach this as delicately as possible. "You're not in any trouble. Honestly."

"Okay." He didn't sound convinced.

"I know you served some time for—"

The panic in his eyes cut me off. His face grew pinched as he shoulder-checked to make sure we were alone.

"It's okay, Mr. Belic." I pumped as much assurance as I could into my voice. I was afraid he might take off, leave me with no answers.

"I serve my time," he whispered. "I now have job. No more trouble. I cook."

"I can see that, Mr. Belic. You've done very well. I'm not here to cause you problems. As I said, I just need your help."

"I have to get back to work. No time to talk."

"Just one question. Please."

He hesitated.

I plunged ahead. "I don't think the police ever investigated you for this, and I'm not saying you were involved. But maybe you heard something from someone, or knew someone...I know it's going to sound like a strange question, especially now...but do you know anything about a woman who was attacked in Yorkville on Scollard in the winter of two thousand eight? I'm trying to tie up some loose ends on a cold case."

Borisav jerked away, as if I'd hit him in the face. "I pay my debt. Not guilty of this."

I wanted to reach out and touch his arm, just to assure him I meant no harm, but feared his reaction to physical contact. "As I said, I'm not accusing you, Mr. Belic. But please tell me, if you know anything. Anything at all. You can't be charged now, anyway. It's too long ago." I hoped he was like most people I knew and based his knowledge of the Canadian legal system on American TV shows.

The look in his eyes made me want to sink into the floor. "I know nothing. I told you. Not me. Maybe I not remember many things from past. But that I know. I live with mother. I have good job cleaning. She die. I sick in hospital. Nearly die too. A month. You check. When I get out, no place to live. No money. Then I rob women." His spray of saliva had reached me with each of his emphatic consonants. He swallowed and looked at his scuffed shoes.

"Thank you, Mr. Belic. You've been a big help. I appreciate it. I won't keep you from your job any longer. Here's my card. Just in case." I knew he was telling the truth. I didn't need to check.

My mother had phoned not long after I'd left the shelter. She wondered if I had the time to drop by for a few minutes in the afternoon. She wouldn't say why.

It wasn't like my mother to ask me for anything, and although it *was* like her to avoid answering direct questions, this felt different. I knew something was up, and I was afraid she was going to deliver another bombshell, maybe bad news about her heart condition.

I fought to swallow the lump in my throat, as I parked at Worthington Estates and pushed through the big front door. A few people were still sitting at the circular tables in the dining room, but my mother wasn't one of them, so I rushed down the berber-carpeted hallway to her suite. The door was closed, so I knocked.

"Come in, dear." I managed to make out her words through the door. She sounded okay, and the lump in my throat shrank.

Just inside the entrance to her suite is the small kitchenette where we'd had our difficult conversation during my last visit. My mother wasn't in there, but as I slipped off my Birkenstocks, she called to me. "I'm in the living room, Calli. Come through."

I turned the corner into what is more like a compact seating area than a real living room. Despite its size, my mother has no complaints with it, since she does most of her socializing in the common areas. Today the space seemed crowded, although there were only two people—two people plus me.

I felt like an intruder.

My mother didn't need to make the introduction. She spoke anyway. "Calli, this is Ken. Your brother."

The man with greying hair and eyes like mine stood and stepped toward me.

I put my hand out, but he clutched me in a hug.

I let him.

And it was all right.

We sat on either side of our mother, while she smiled and wiped her eyes.

For a long time no one spoke.

There was no need.

CHAPTER SEVEN

I hadn't slept very well after meeting Ken. I'd tossed and turned and disturbed Jess to the point where she'd mumbled concern about my well-being, but I wasn't ready to tell her what had happened. Not that anything had really happened. The three of us had sat together and shared our lives with one another in words. Almost fifty years condensed into ninety minutes. No big deal. But although that's the version my mind was hanging onto, some other part of me was starting to see it as the kind of event that gets carved into the granite of your life with a delicate chisel. And then one day you realize that it's become one of the building blocks for the rest of your existence.

When I had time to sort out my feelings, then I'd be able to talk to Jess about them, and to my mother. I knew I couldn't put it off for long though, because although Jess had no idea what was going on, my mother would want to not only hear what I had to say, but would also want to share her side of it. If I were a really good daughter, I'd be contacting her at the first opportunity to see how she was. Maybe I'd call her later.

Thanks to a helpful neighbour, Dewey had managed to track down Phillip, Lucas Anasetti's friend who lived on Davenport. His last name turned out to be Straun. He no longer lived on Davenport of course, but at least he existed, and that put a crack in Dewey's theory about Anasetti's being the attacker.

I was in need of company, someone who could take my mind off myself, so when Dewey sent me a text and asked if I wanted to join him when he went to see Straun, I jumped at the chance.

Dewey was leaning against the front of a big box store when I pulled into the parking lot. White wires ran from his ears to his shirt pocket. His eyes were closed and his face was the definition of bliss. By the time I'd parked and threaded my way through the lot, the only thing that had changed was the addition of a slight head bob in rhythm to whatever he was hearing.

I stood directly in front of him, weighing my options. Should I go for maximum effect and tickle his ribs or maybe step on his toe? Or should I be more subtle? I chose the latter. A miniature version of my cat, Sherlock, is attached to my keys next to my little Swiss Army knife. Holding my keys and knife firmly in the palm of my hand, I let the cat dangle by its thin chain. I then slowly raised my arm, and ever so gently let the cat touch the top of Dewey's head

He fell into my trap. Thinking it was an insect, he

waved his hand over his cornrows, eyes still shut.

I had withdrawn my assault weapon in time and was ready for another attack. After he settled back into his reverie, I lowered the little feline onto the tip of his nose.

Dewey sprang from the wall and grabbed his face. Then he saw me standing there grinning, guilt dripping from every inch of me.

"Oh, Calli! Ya vex mi, gurl!"

I couldn't stifle my laugh any longer. He's so adorable when he does a parody of himself.

"Do you have any idea what you interrupted?" He glared at me.

He was clearly not in a joking mood, so I tried to look repentant.

"Of course you don't. Diana Damrau as Queen of the Night."

I was a blank.

"Only this century's definitive performance of Mozart's most challenging aria in his best opera."

"Oh?"

"*The Magic Flute?*"

"Ah."

"I give up." He ripped the ear buds from his ears and marched through the automatic doors.

This wasn't the first time that Dewey had abandoned an attempt to educate me in the finer things of life, and it wouldn't be the last. It didn't really matter. I knew he'd never give up on *me*.

I followed him into the store, not exactly sure

where we were headed, but secure in the knowledge that Dewey was. We passed the TVs, what remained of the once thriving CD section, and on to the back of the store, where rows of laptops secured to metal shelves begged to be booted up. Dewey often gets sidetracked when we go places, but this time it was I who was distracted. A sexy Mac caught my eye. Ever since spending some time in an advertising agency on a case last winter I'd wanted a Mac of my own.

Dewey found an employee and was busy talking about something, as I stroked the sleek white body and tried to ignore the price tag. I tested the keypad, lowered the top, and ran my finger around the edge of the Apple logo. I'm sure I heard "You Are So Beautiful" being played somewhere.

"Come on." Dewey took my arm and dragged me away from my new crush. It was clear he hadn't quite forgiven me for my practical joke and subsequent ignorance about his Queen of the whatever song. He propelled me toward a well-groomed man, mid-thirties, dressed in a red employee shirt. He was crouched down, filling a bin with discount flash drives.

"Excuse me," Dewey said, "are you Phillip Straun?"

The man looked up at us. "Yes," he said and pointed to his name tag.

"Would it be all right if we ask you a few questions?"

The man gave a relieved smile and stood up. "That's why I'm here."

"Not about computers," Dewey explained. "I'm Dwight Brande, and this is Calli Barnow, a private investigator. We're working on a case that involves Lucas Anasetti."

It felt good to let Dewey take the lead. He'd come a long way since the first time I'd asked for his help with a case, and my confidence in him was growing daily.

"Who?" Straun asked.

Dewey and I exchanged a quick glance.

"Lucas Anasetti. He was a friend of yours four or five years ago, when you lived on Davenport."

Straun looked perplexed. "I remember living on Davenport, obviously. But…. What's his name again?"

"Anasetti. Lucas Anasetti."

"He worked at a salon in Yorkville," I added.

Straun thought some more. "Oh, him." The light went on, but it was dim. "I wouldn't say he was a friend exactly." He gave Dewey the once over, then continued. "We hooked up a couple of times. That's all."

"So he didn't make a habit of dropping by your place once a week after work?"

"God no. Like I said, I hardly knew the guy."

"Do you remember when it was you spent time with him?" I asked. "What year or month?"

Straun hesitated before saying, "I met him in winter. At a bar on Church. We went back to my place. Had a good time. But I probably would have forgotten all about him except he kept calling me Prince Phillip.

You know, joking around. Anyway, that's the only time he was ever there."

"You're sure?" Dewey asked.

"Positive. The next time I saw him, several months later, he was flashing bills around, buying everyone drinks. We went to the back room together, but he left the bar with some other guy. I think he figured he was out of my league or something. I saw him around a couple of times after that, but he didn't even say hello."

"Do you know what year that would have been?" Dewey was going for the details we needed.

"Yeah, I do. I mean I don't keep track of my dates with guys or anything, but I remember because I'd just moved to Davenport late that fall. Then I went away for a month, just came back in time for Christmas. In fact, I met him at a New Year's Eve party at the bar. We brought in two thousand eight together."

"You've been a lot of help," I said. "Thanks."

"Hey, you're welcome. And we've got a great deal on the new HP laptop, if you're interested."

"Not today," said Dewey.

"But I might come back some time and have a look at a Mac," I added.

Straun must have seen the computer lust in my eyes. "You do that. I'll give you a good deal."

Tucked away in a less affluent residential neighbourhood of North York was a one story brick building

- 108 -

with a sign on the lawn that said The Hampstead Nursing Home. It wasn't where I had expected to be at that moment, but it's where the trail had led me. After getting back from the visit with Straun I'd looked up the funeral home that had listed Prabhakar Sanderson as next of kin. My old computer, sad and dated though it now appeared to me, didn't seem to hold a grudge after my brief flirtation with the Mac, but the funeral director on the other end of the phone was less cooperative. He had refused to give me any information on relatives of the departed.

My next move had been to read through the online condolences for Pradhi Sanderson. They were the usual heartfelt statements of admiration for the deceased and sympathy for the relatives. About halfway down the page I struck gold. The message itself was much like the others, but it was specifically directed to Prabhakar, and signed from his very dear friends at The Hampstead Nursing Home.

And so there I was, weaving through the cratered parking lot of what looked like a former elementary school from the sixties. On the other side of the home a low-rise apartment building occupied what must have been the playground, but otherwise it appeared that not much about the property had changed since its previous life.

I'd phoned the facility just to make sure I wasn't mistaken, or that Mr. Sanderson hadn't died or moved. Sure enough Prabhakar was still a resident there, and from the sound of it, they would be overjoyed to have me visit him. If he was as neglected as the flower bed I passed on my way to the front door, I could understand their enthusiasm.

As at my mother's retirement home, there was a reception area just inside the entrance, but that's where the similarities ended. No one greeted me, and the air was unwelcoming. It was heavy with the famous nursing home odour, which I had assumed was a thing of the past. The décor was spartan and everything looked as if it could use a fresh coat of paint.

There were a few emaciated residents propped in a row of armchairs in a common area. One weary plant wilted by the window, but no one was looking at it. No one was looking at anything, as far as I could tell. And it was eerily quiet.

By the time I'd wandered down a couple of hallways without finding someone to help me, I was thoroughly depressed and had decided I would leave. Based on the condolence message and phone call, this was not what I'd been expecting.

Just as I was heading for the door a voice stopped me. "Hello?"

I turned to find a middle-aged woman in a white uniform. "I'm here to see Prabhakar Sanderson," I said.

"That's nice. Do you know where his room is?"

"No, I don't."

She didn't bother to find out who I was, but said, "Go down to the end." She pointed toward the hall where I'd just been. "Then turn right. About halfway down is room forty-two. That's him."

Before I could ask her anything, she turned on her heel and headed in the opposite direction.

Now I had no excuse, aside from my queasy stomach, so I aimed my Birkenstocks in the direction she'd indicated. I passed an empty dining hall and the doors to lavatories and tub rooms. As soon as I turned right, I was in a hallway lined on both sides with residents' quarters. Most had open doors and what I could see looked remarkably similar to stripped down hospital rooms. On one side of the hall the rooms were large and held four beds. Those on the other side were smaller, and housed two people.

Most of the beds were occupied by skeletal beings, either asleep or awake and staring. I heard the occasional moan and intermittent babble. A worker passed me pushing a woman who was slumped awkwardly in a wheelchair, but neither of them acknowledged my presence.

I overshot my destination, and had to backtrack to find number forty-two. It was one of the smaller rooms, and I was thankful for that. Both beds were empty, but I could see the top of a bald head just above the back of a chair that was facing the window. I knocked, but received no response. I called Mr. Sanderson's name, but still nothing.

I wasn't exactly sure what nursing home etiquette was, but since I'd tried everything I could think of with no luck, I entered and made straight for the chair.

The old man wasn't looking out the window, not

that I could blame him. The view consisted of the back of the next door apartment building. He was sound asleep. Once again I was faced with a dilemma. Should I wake him? Should I leave? Should I wait until he woke up? He looked quite frail, the blue veins on his temples bulging through his thin skin. I didn't want to startle him, but on the other hand, once I left this place, I had no intention of ever returning.

My problem was solved when a young man strolled through the door. Based on the scrubs he was wearing, he must be an employee of some sort. Apart from his attire, he looked more like a bouncer at a bottom-of-the-line nightspot. A backwards baseball cap covered his shaved head, and intricate tattoos played on his muscular arms. The water glass and paper pill holder all but disappeared in his dangerous-looking hands.

He paid no attention to me, as he took up a position on the other side of the chair. "Yo, Mr. S.," he said, none too gently.

Mr. S. slept on.

"Yo, Mr. Sanderson. Wakey, wakey." He kicked the leg of the chair. "I ain't got all day. It's time for your happy pills."

I bristled and was about to intervene, when Mr. Sanderson began to rouse.

"Here ya go, Prabby, chug this down. It'll keep ya breathin' for another day." He thrust the paper pill holder into one of Mr. Sanderson's shaking hands and the glass into the other.

I didn't know Mr. Sanderson from a hole in the

wall, and from everything I'd heard, he wasn't a very nice person, but even he deserved more respect than this. I shoved my hand toward the young man and said, "Hi, I'm Calli Barnow."

I'd caught him off guard, perhaps only because it was out of the ordinary for visitors to communicate with staff. He scowled and ignored my hand.

"And you are?" I tried to sound pleasant.

"Uh. Jerome," was all he said.

I gave him a sugary smile.

Mr. Sanderson had managed to deposit the pill in his mouth and was now dribbling the water down his chin.

"Yo, Mr. S., lemme help ya with that," said Jerome, steadying the glass.

When the pill ordeal was finally over, and Jerome had swaggered his way out of the room, Mr. Sanderson realized he had another visitor. He opened his still damp mouth to speak, but only "Aaah," came out.

Once more I extended my hand in greeting. Once more I gave my name.

Mr. Sanderson finally managed to force his hand in the general direction of mine, so I made the final move. His skin was cool and dry, and did little to disguise the bony structure underneath. I scaled back the strength of my own hand for fear of damaging his. With each passing minute, the cloud that had formed over my head upon entering the parking lot grew darker and more oppressive. It was quickly becoming clear that I would learn nothing useful from this poor man, who was a prisoner not only in his own body, but also in this shameful excuse for a care facility.

Nevertheless, since I was there, I might as well say my piece. "Mr. Sanderson, I'm here to see if you can give me any information on Mr. Ravi Mehta, or his wife, Indira."

I thought I saw a flicker of recognition on his face.

"I've been told that you were in business with Mr. Mehta at the time Mrs. Mehta was attacked."

This time Mr. Sanderson shifted his gaze out the window.

I waited, unsure what his movement meant, if indeed it meant anything. I had no experience in trying to communicate with someone who had this level of impairment, and there didn't seem to be anyone around who could help me.

"Mr. Sanderson?" I tried again.

"That won't do you any good." A voice stopped me, before I could say anymore.

A dark-eyed, fair-skinned man in an expensive summer suit stood in the doorway. As soon as I looked up at him, he strode into the room. "I'm Wayne Sanderson. That's my father you're trying to talk to."

"Oh, I see." Before I could explain my presence, he continued.

"Jerome said he had a visitor. You're lucky it happens to be my day to see Dad. Obviously he can't communicate. Is there something I can help you with?"

Based on his lack of enthusiasm for his job, I

found it hard to believe that Jerome would put in the effort to even talk to this man; on the other hand, everything about Wayne Sanderson commanded attention. Except for being a little out of shape, he was perfect: fine features, charming smile, and a recent manicure. But there was something about his eyes that disturbed me. Something about the way he looked not at, but through me. For the first time since I'd arrived, I felt as if I was trespassing. I had come here to ask some questions. Now it looked as if I was the one who would be giving the answers.

"I'm Calli Barnow, a private investigator. I was hoping to talk to your father about his former partner, Ravi Mehta, and his wife, Indira. Are you aware of what happened to Mrs. Mehta a number of years ago?"

Sanderson wrinkled his brow in concentration. He was about to deny knowledge, when his eyes suddenly widened. "Ah, yes, I remember. Tragic."

"Did you know she died recently?"

"No, I can't say I was aware of that. In fact, I didn't know she was still alive. Wasn't she in a coma after the attack?"

"Yes, that's right. She never came out of it."

Sanderson drew back in disbelief. "Really? I had no idea. Well, I guess it's probably a blessing that she finally passed on then."

I bit my tongue. "Her daughter has hired me to have another look at the attack."

"No offence, Ms....Barnow, but that seems like a

waste of money. Surely the police would have found someone at the time, if it was possible."

"I guess it depends on how you look at it. Some people are willing to pay for peace of mind."

"Yes, of course." He placed a patronizing smile on me, but instantly replaced it with a look of concern. "So why are you here? As you can see, my father is of no use to you."

"I'm sorry. I mean I'm sorry that he's not well."

"Thank you. He had a stroke last year. It left him like this." He looked down with sadness and resignation at his father.

"Maybe you could help me."

"I doubt it. But what do you want to know?"

"I understand your father got out of the importing business a couple of years after Ravi Mehta's death"

"That's right. It was getting too much for him, especially all the travel. He didn't need to keep working, so he decided to retire. I wasn't interested in carrying on any of his ventures; my law practice kept me busy, so I advised him to liquidate."

"Were you aware of any problems Mr. Mehta was having while they were still partners? Did your father ever talk about anything?"

"No. I had nothing to do with my father's business life. I think I only met Mr. Mehta a couple of times in all the years they worked together."

"Do you have any idea about how your father got along with Mr. Mehta?"

His smile signalled that he was about to give me

something other than a negative response.

At last! I brightened at the prospect of this trip providing me with more than a feeling of gloom.

"They were very good friends. I never heard my father say a bad word about Mr. Mehta."

"Really?"

"You seem surprised, Ms. Barnow."

"Well…" I couldn't let on what I'd been told by Mrs. Kumar. "I just find it unusual that you only met him a couple of times. I'm surprised that your families didn't socialize, seeing that the men were such good friends."

"Not at all, Ms. Barnow. People can be best of friends on the job but live quite separate lives outside of work. The store was the only interest they shared."

"Of course, you're right," I had to admit. At least he seemed satisfied that I was just a little slow when it came to the world of socializing. "Well, thanks for your help."

"Sorry I couldn't have helped more," he smiled and extended his hand. "Nice to meet you, Ms. Barnow."

I didn't think he was the least bit sorry, or the least bit pleased to meet me, and his limp handshake backed me up.

"And good luck with your case."

"Thanks. I'm going to need it."

Wayne Sanderson sat down and stared at the profile of his father.

His father examined the bricks.

CHAPTER EIGHT

Dewey and I had agreed to meet the following morning at my office. By the time I'd picked up my coffee and strolled down Baldwin and around the corner onto Augusta the heavy sky was beginning to spit. I chose to see this as confirmation of my decision to have a "get it all together" day. Although Dewey and I had been in constant contact about the case, we hadn't yet taken the time to review everything in detail and really take stock of how we were progressing. It was also about time I bit the bullet and caught up on my paperwork.

Svetlana is my fellow tenant on the second floor. She was busy in her computer repair shop, but she looked up from a disassembled laptop when I reached the landing. "Good morning, ducky," she trilled.

I poked my head in her door. "Morning, Svetlana. You're here early."

"I was about to say the same about you. Either you're in the midst of a big case, or you have no case at all, and you're here hoping the phone will give a dingle." Her eyes twinkled.

"I have a case. I wouldn't call it big though. It's kind of a dead end."

"Well, you know where Svetlana is should you need to ask for her assistance." She bent her hennaed curls over the bits of metal and plastic and continued to work her magic.

Svetlana had helped me with cases on more than one occasion. This morning her biggest help was just being there in the building. Although I loved my office, it still gave me the creeps after an incident last winter. A fresh coat of paint, new flooring, and a few other aesthetic touches had made the place quite attractive, but the spectre of what had happened there was still scorched in my memory. I feared it always would be.

"Calli!" Dewey's exuberance roused me from my note making. "I hate the rain sooooooooooo much." He shook himself like a dog, before coming through the door.

"Maybe it would help if you bought an umbrella. At least your expensive clothes wouldn't get wet."

"You are soooooooo right, babe. But umbrellas are soooooo ugly."

"Suit yourself, Dew. But it does sometimes rain in this country."

"The queen of understatement." He curtsied to me. "Well, now that I'm here, let's get down to work." He planted himself in the new chair on the other side of my old oak desk and withdrew his phone from his messenger bag.

"Can that wait?" I asked.

"It's my notes," he bristled. "Some of us are living in the twenty-first century."

Duly chastened, I flipped open my spiral notebook, which contained my rough case notes.

"By the way, how's the baby thing going with Jess?" he asked.

"Funny you should ask. Your performance at Studs didn't help my case for staying childless. The song was beautiful, but now there's a soundtrack to the ongoing debate."

"I'm sorry, Calli. But I think it would be so great."

"I know you do. I just wish I could be that certain." I looked at my notebook, intending to begin a discussion about the case; instead, I said, "I just found out I have a brother."

"You what?" Dewey's voice landed in his upper register.

"You heard me right. I didn't mean to tell you, Dewey. I haven't even told Jess yet, but...I guess I must need to talk about it. I have a half-brother. My mother gave birth to him and put him up for adoption before she married my dad."

Dewey took a breath before asking, "So your mom just told you all this?"

"Uh huh."

"And how do you feel about it, Calli?"

"I really don't know. I was shocked of course. And

I feel sad that my mother had to go through that experience."

"And, or should I say but?" Dewey tilted his head and reinforced his question with his face.

"I don't like the idea that I was kept in the dark all these years."

"So you're saying that just because your mother is your mother, she doesn't deserve any privacy? That there's nothing about her life you don't have a right to know?"

"Well…"

"Does it go both ways, Calli? Have you told her everything about your life?"

"No. But this is big, Dewey. He's my brother."

"Give your mother a break, Calli. She loves you. Just be glad of that."

Dewey was right, of course. He could see things from a different perspective, and sometimes I needed him to remind me about my good fortune. "I am glad, Dew. It'll just take some time to get used to the idea of this new brother. I met him and he seems like a nice man."

"That's wonderful, babe!"

"Yeah, sometime I'll tell you all about it." I made an attempt to share Dewey's enthusiasm, but he saw through it.

"You're right, Calli. It will be different for you suddenly not being the only one. But try to keep an open mind and an open heart. Having a sibling can be a very special relationship. You might have to work at it, but it'll probably be worth it." Once again Dewey got that faraway look on his face.

"You know, don't you, Dew?"

He gave a little nod. "I know."

It was time to move on. I drew an emphatic line under the first word on the page of my notebook. "Okay, what do we have? You want to start?"

Dewey gave me a quick smile, then scrolled and poked at his screen a few times before answering me. "I went to see the man who lived near where Mrs. Mehta was attacked. He'd moved, but he wasn't that hard to find. Has a place in the Annex now. Anyway, he's a bit of a bore, but at least he had a good memory. I guess it's not every day someone gets attacked in front of your house."

"You'll need to give me the address and the particulars of your interview with him." With every other case, Dewey had just scribbled information on pieces of paper and handed them over to me.

"Of course, babe. I'll send you the document." He gave me a smug look.

"Great. I'll make a file." If you can't beat them, join them. "For now just tell me what you found out."

"Well, it was a cold winter night."

"I don't need a weather report."

"Listen, I'm telling you what the man said. It all ties in."

"Sorry." I leaned back and got comfortable.

"So, it was a cold winter night. He had been watching TV, but he had the sound down low, because he'd let Tinker out."

"Tinker?"

"His cat. Anyway, he wanted to be able to hear her meow. She'd already frozen her ear tips once that winter, and he was worried in case it happened again."

"I see." I started to fiddle with a paper clip in hopes of being able to control my desire to hurry Dewey along.

"So he was watching TV, when he thought he heard Tinker. He went to the window to check. It was a bay window, so he was able to see the front step, when he looked out at the correct angle. There was no point in letting cold air in through the door, if he didn't have to."

I had unfolded one side of the paperclip and resisted the desire to scratch my initials on the top of my desk.

"When he looked out the window, Tinker wasn't there. In fact, Tinker never came back again. He thinks that's why he remembers the evening so well."

"That's sad. What did he see, Dewey?" I couldn't help urging him along.

"He saw a figure crouched over on the sidewalk. He could only see the guy's back, and he couldn't tell exactly what he was doing, but there was something in front of him, and it could have been a person. He thought there must have been some sort of accident, so he went to his door to see if he could help."

"This doesn't match what Lucas Anasetti said."

"No, it does not. Anasetti said that he knocked at

the door."

"What else did the man say?" Now I was on the edge of my seat.

"Well, he called out to Anasetti, and asked what was wrong. This is where the two stories come together. Anasetti stood up, and the man could see Mrs. Mehta. Anasetti told the man that he didn't know what had happened, that he'd just come along and found her like that."

"What's the man's name?" I finally asked.

"Simon Black. Anyway, so Black ran into his place and snatched a blanket off his sofa, threw it out the door at Anasetti and then went to phone nine-one-one. The rest you know."

"Well done, Dew!" I gave him a thumbs-up. "Hey, didn't Anasetti say *he* was the person who phoned nine-one-one?"

"Yes he did."

"Why would anyone lie about that? Unless one of them isn't remembering correctly."

"Didn't I tell you I liked Anasetti for the attack?"

"Yes, you did. His story's starting to resemble Swiss cheese. So far the only thing he's said that hasn't been contradicted is the fact that he was walking down that street. We know he wasn't on the way to Straun's house."

"So what was he doing there?"

"Exactly. And according to Black, he didn't go and knock on the door for help."

"So maybe he didn't really want help. Maybe he

was actually interrupted in the process of mugging Mrs. Mehta!" Dewey was practically bouncing off his seat.

"It doesn't prove he did it, however."

"Oh, I'm sure he did. He gives me the willies," said Dewey.

"Unfortunately, willies don't hold up in court."

We sat searching each other's face for inspiration. "Wait a minute," I said. "What did you say was the reason Simon Black went to look out the window?"

"He was looking for Tinker."

"No, there was something else."

Dewey checked his notes. "He thought he heard a sound."

"Right. Did he say what kind of sound?"

"No."

"What kind of sound would he mistake for his cat?"

"Maybe a scratching at the door," Dewey offered.

"Dogs scratch at doors. Cats prefer furniture." I remembered the condition of our old sofa after Sherlock had used it as a claw-sharpening post. "It wouldn't be a car driving by, or a siren, or a man's voice," I tried to clarify.

"But it might be a woman," Dewey added.

"A woman making a frightened sound, or crying out when she's attacked."

"How long do you think it would have taken for Black to get from in front of the TV to his window?" Dewey asked.

"Probably no longer than a few seconds. He was close enough to hear a cat," I reasoned.

"Which means that if it was Mrs. Mehta he heard, there wouldn't have been time for her attacker to open her purse and run away." Dewey stopped to make sure I was with him. "And for Anasetti to happen along and find her before Black got to the window. You saw how far from the corner the attack took place."

"And don't forget that Anasetti told us and the police that other than Mrs. Mehta, he saw no one on the street," I added.

"If he's been lying about everything else, he really should have added a mysterious person to his story—someone he saw fleeing down the dark street." Dewey looked like the cat that had stolen the cream.

"I have to admit, Dew, it's starting to look as if you might be right about Anasetti. But what about motive?"

"He obviously likes money, and her money wasn't in her purse. And don't forget, at some point between then and now, Anasetti went from being a hairdresser at Waves to being the owner."

"Yeah, but there's one big problem," I explained. "Mrs. Mehta wouldn't be carrying enough cash around in her purse to enable Lucas Anasetti to put a down payment on the salon. If she had something valuable with her, you'd think her husband would have mentioned it to the police. Let's just put Anasetti on hold for a while, and see what else we've got."

Dewey reined in his enthusiasm. "You're right,

babe. Tell me what you've found."

"I already mentioned that Belic is a dead end."

"Yeah. That's too bad."

"Sanderson's no better. He's in a nursing home and he can't communicate. Just sits in a chair, the results of a stroke. I feel sorry for him. It's a horrible place, and I'm going to report it." I thought again of my mother, and was washed with guilt for not having contacted her and gratitude that she didn't have to spend her final days in a hellhole.

Dewey made a face. "Good for you."

"I did meet Sanderson's son though. Unfortunately, he was no help. He had his law practice and he wasn't interested in his father's work. If the old man had a problem with Ravi Mehta that somehow affected Mrs. Mehta, we won't find out from the Sandersons."

"It was worth a try."

"I guess so. I find it odd, though, that Wayne Sanderson had a different perception of his father's relationship with Mr. Mehta than Mrs. Kumar had. Of course, Wayne Sanderson could only go on what his father told him, whereas Mrs. Kumar would have seen the men interact. I guess it would be hard to work with a friend and always have things run smoothly."

"We seem to manage," Dewey reminded me.

"We're special," I teased him, but we both knew it was true.

"Speaking of partnerships, please remind your number one partner why you took this case in the first place. I mean we're dealing with people who are dead, or can't talk to us. And everything happened so long ago. This is crazy, Calli."

"Thanks, Dew." I faked a smile. "I know it seems crazy. Just remember that new wardrobe you're going to buy when we're finished."

"At the rate we're going, it'll only be a new pair of shoes. How long before we give up altogether? I know we have our suspicions about Anasetti, but how can we prove anything?"

"I don't know, Dew. In the meantime, let's write up what we do have."

The ringing phone took us both by surprise. It was Sashi, so I put her on speaker.

"Calli, I don't know if this has anything to do with your investigation, but I thought I should tell you."

"What is it, Sashi?"

"When I came out of work yesterday, the tires on my car were slashed."

"Where do you park?"

"Right next to the building."

"Has this ever happened before, either to you or anyone else around there?"

"No. Never. Not to me anyway. And I've never heard of anyone else having problems. It's a very safe neighbourhood. Nothing ever happens."

"It's probably just a coincidence, Sashi, but thanks for telling me. And let me know if anything else unusual happens."

I clicked off, sensing that Dewey was looking at

me with his look. I was right.

"Coincidence?" he asked.

"What else could it be?"

"Maybe we're not finished after all," Dewey said, excitement growing in his voice. "It's possible we're getting too close to something."

We looked at each other while the possibility sank in.

"I don't think so, Dew."

"Of course it would mean that the person who is involved with that *something* knows Sashi hired someone. And the person might also know that the someone she hired is you."

"Dewey, you're getting carried away. It's probably just some bored kids looking for excitement at the end of a long summer."

"But what if it isn't?" Dewey leaned over my desk for added effect. "What if it's a criminal with a dark, deadly secret? If he used a knife on Sashi's tires, what's next?"

We both jumped when the phone rang again. This time it was June.

"Calli, I thought you might want to know about this."

Dewey and I held our breath. Maybe if we sat in the office long enough, all the answers would come to us.

"It was a total fluke; I was just in the right place at the right time. Anyway, that vagrant I told you about, Belic, they brought him in yesterday. I checked into it, and he'd been arrested again for assaulting and robbing a woman. When they searched his place, they found articles that linked him to a couple more attacks going back as far as his prison release."

"Thanks, June. He had me convinced he'd turned over a new leaf."

"And Calli, this is off the record for now. It'll be public by tomorrow."

"Absolutely, June. You're a doll. I owe you another one." I clicked off the speaker.

"Does that mean Belic's a suspect again?" Dewey asked.

"We can't rule him out. Especially since we can't verify his alibi. At least not legally."

"Would Belic be smart enough to use a hospital stay, knowing we couldn't check it?" Dewey asked.

"Maybe. Initially I wouldn't have thought so, but he certainly had me fooled with his victim of circumstance, reformed offender act."

"So now we're back to two possible suspects, but no bright ideas about how to investigate them further."

"Exactly."

We didn't jump when the phone rang a third time; instead, we shared a "what now?" look.

I identified myself to the caller.

"My name is Sham Kumar," the man replied. "You were in my store the other day, and you talked to my mother and my daughter."

The name Kumar rang a bell and the only place that fit that description was the clothing shop on

Gerrard. "Yes, I did." I had given them my card, never expecting to be contacted. "How may I help you?"

"My mother was very upset by your visit."

"I'm sorry. I certainly never meant to upset her. I was just trying to find out anything I could about the Mehtas."

"I understand that, but all the talk of Sanderson agitated her. It brought up bad memories, for her and now for me."

"For you?"

"Yes, for me. You are meddling in our family. You have no right." His voice was hot with warning.

How could my innocent enquiries have elicited such an extreme reaction from him? "I'm confused, Mr. Kumar."

Dewey's face was a grimace that reflected how my stomach was feeling.

Rather than apologizing again and getting off the phone, I attempted to gain clarity. "I know that your mother was employed by Mr. Mehta and Mr. Sanderson, but how is all this related to your family?"

There was dead air and then, "You have no right to know this, but if it will stop your meddling, I will tell you. My daughter came to us through Mr. Sanderson's adoption agency. There, I've said it. She doesn't know and never will. Sanderson is an evil man. I love my daughter, but we got her from that evil man with his evil ways."

Dewey and I both looked as if we'd just been introduced to a Martian.

"Mr. Kumar, are we talking about the same Mr. Sanderson? I was asking your mother about Prabhakar Sanderson, Ravi Mehta's partner in the import business."

"Of course we're talking about the same Mr. Sanderson. Importing wasn't the only thing he did." Kumar was practically shouting at me.

"Okay. So he ran an adoption agency?" I was struggling to get up to speed.

"Yes, he ran an adoption agency!"

"And are you telling me that there was something wrong with the way Sanderson was running his agency?"

"I'm saying no more. No more! You leave my family alone!" He hung up.

Dewey had to spend the afternoon covering for a colleague at Mauve, but before he left my office, we'd managed to track down the name of Sanderson's former international adoption agency and from there do an Internet search that turned up two sources of information. I was delighted, since Sham Kumar had made it clear he wanted nothing more to do with me.

One of our finds was an old blog entry by someone ranting about allegations Sanderson's receptionist had made, but the tone of the writing ruined any credibility it might have held. The other was an article about a lawsuit that had been brought against the agency, which had subsequently been settled out of court. The family named in the article was easy to locate, and the wife was cooperative when I spoke to her on the phone.

I'd arranged to meet Leena Chaudhari in a Mississauga coffee shop down the road from the school where she would later pick up her youngest child. She was waiting for me at a small table by the window.

"Thanks for meeting me, Mrs. Chaudhari."

"You're welcome," she said, but it was clear she wasn't completely comfortable with what she had agreed to do. "I only have about half an hour before school lets out. Maybe we should get started."

"Of course. As I told you on the phone, I'm hoping you can give me some information about the Bachana Adoption Agency."

"I'd be glad to tell you anything I can, but it may not be very helpful."

"Anything at all would be wonderful. I'm starting from zero."

"Well, you know about the court case. My husband chose to settle, rather that pursue a long drawn-out civil trial. We just couldn't afford that. Not after what it had cost us to adopt our first child."

"So you adopted through Sanderson's agency, but then you were dissatisfied? The article didn't give many details."

"We were delighted with our daughter. She was everything we could have hoped for. But there were several problems along the way. Costs changed. When we went to India to pick her up, Sanderson's associates there had trouble getting her papers. Everything should have been done before we ever left Canada. I didn't trust them. And my husband and I both became suspicious of Sanderson. Once we were home and the adoption had gone through the courts here and everything was finalized, we approached Sanderson. We wanted an explanation at the very least. He just laughed at us."

"So you sued him."

"Yes. We wanted him to honour our original contract. Reimburse the additional charges. My husband threatened to expose his agency. Of course we had no proof of anything illegal, only the change in price and all the problems."

"But he gave you a settlement?"

"Yes, he made us an offer we couldn't refuse. I didn't want to accept. I thought he should be accountable. But as I said, we had no proof of anything. We had our daughter and we didn't want to take a chance on losing her. My husband said yes to the deal, and that was that. In fact, he wouldn't be very happy if he knew I was talking to you now about it."

"I really appreciate that you are." I wished I could somehow put her more at ease, but since I couldn't I continued. "Something must have been going on for Sanderson to offer payment rather than proving his innocence."

"That's the way I've always felt about it. Things really became apparent when we adopted our second child through a different agency. It was like night and day. Over the years I've felt guilty—by not continuing the lawsuit we might have caused grief for other families."

"I don't think you need to worry about that. The agency shut down not long after your settlement."

Relief brought a smile to her face, and then the words, "What else can I do to help?"

The Family Law Offices of Birk, Mankowsky, and Martin were unpretentious, nestled in a sprawling one-story industrial estate in Willowdale. The Chaudharis' lawyer was one of the partners, and I'd made an appointment to see him later in the day. Bill Birk didn't keep me waiting long before he invited me to join him in his office.

"Yes, I remember the Chaudharis. Nice young couple." He smoothed down the sides of his thick greying mustache. "After Mrs. Chaudhari called and gave me permission to cooperate with you, I had a quick look at their file just to refresh my memory."

"It was two thousand, wasn't it?" I asked.

"That's when it ended, but we actually filed late in nineteen ninety-nine. I only met with them a few times before the settlement."

"I gather Mr. Chaudhari was more inclined to accept a deal than his wife."

"Yes, I recall that, and between the two of them it appeared he had the final word. I was quite disappointed myself, because I felt we had the makings for class action."

I was trying to formulate a question that didn't

make me sound like an idiot when Birk continued, "Neither individuals nor companies tend to do something illegal just once. The problems the Chaudharis had were glaring enough that I would bet my career there was a whole list of similar families who hadn't come forward either from ignorance or fear. Sometimes all it takes is one person to stand up, and that gives others the courage to join in."

"So you felt that the Bachana Agency was breaking the law?" My scalp was beginning to tingle at the thought of having something definite to associate with Sanderson. Although even once I did have something definite, I had no idea how it related, or if it related, to Indira Mehta. It was highly unlikely that it did.

"Oh yes. It was doing something illegal. I remember from the first day I talked to the Chaudharis, my elbow started to ache." Birk gave me a sheepish grin, which turned him into a boy. "Whenever I have a case that has more to it than meets the eye, my crime elbow, as I call it, acts up like the dickens."

Apparently my body wasn't the only one that had a mind of its own, or a sixth sense, or whatever you want to call it.

"Sanderson and his agency colleagues both in Toronto and abroad were in it up to here." He raised his hand underneath his chin to indicate where here was.

"What sort of things are you talking about?" Although I was probably wasting my professional time finding out all of this, because of my new brother and

Jess's desire for a child, I wanted to learn whatever I could about the subject of adoption.

"Back when the Chaudhari's received their daughter and I subsequently represented them, international adoption was in the process of becoming more strictly controlled and regulated. Although the International Adoption Act had been passed in 'ninety-eight, it wasn't until two thousand that Ontario started to license agencies in accordance with it."

"So at that time, and before, I gather it was a lot easier for agencies to take advantage of parents."

"Definitely. They could basically charge as much as they could get away with. Bribes were common practice in some countries. Prospective parents often weren't vetted properly. And there was no guarantee that the origin or background of the child had been truthfully represented. There have been cases of children being kidnapped abroad and then literally sold to the highest bidder in North America. I heard of one case where a newborn was taken from the hospital and the birth parents were told it had died and been cremated."

Any desire for adoption I might have been fostering was starting to dwindle. "So agencies like Sanderson's would have had to shape up or get out of the business."

"That was the idea. And certainly the changes did make a huge difference. But like anything else, it wasn't an overnight fix."

"No wonder Sanderson packed up shop not many

years later."

"It was only a matter of time before he got caught and everything he was doing made public. He would eventually have been prosecuted, if he'd carried on in the same manner."

"Thanks for your time, Mr. Birk."

"You're welcome. But I'm curious: how and why did you get involved in this?"

"Well, I don't really think I am involved. All of the problems with the adoption agency happened several years before the incident I'm investigating." I explained the long, convoluted path that had led me to his office.

We shook hands at the door. He smiled at me again from underneath his mustache and said, "You never know, Ms. Barnow. Maybe Mrs. Mehta knew something about Sanderson that would have incriminated him. It can't hurt to poke around."

"I think you've been watching too much TV, Mr. Birk," I joked, "but thanks for the encouragement."

He gave a little shrug. "Maybe I just need to get out of my office more."

I was about to push open the door to leave, when I thought to ask, "By the way, who was Sanderson's lawyer? Do you remember?"

"You bet. I'll never forget that s.o.b. Wayne Sanderson."

CHAPTER NINE

I was on my way home, when I got a call from Jess telling me to meet her at my mother's place. She assured me there was nothing wrong, but I still had a sinking feeling in my gut. This had never happened before.

I almost collided with a Swiss Chalet deliveryman as I charged down the hallway to my mother's suite. I didn't knock, but flung the door open, expecting the worst. Instead of disaster I was greeted first by the smell of roast chicken, then by a calm domestic scene. Jess was trying to squeeze three place settings onto my mother's tiny kitchen table, while my mother unpacked the three quarter-chicken dinners.

I took a deep breath and tried to slow my heart rate, before I embraced each of them and waited for the instructions I knew would follow.

"Can you get out some ice and fill the water glasses, dear?" came the message from Mom.

I did as I was asked. Of course.

My mouth started to water at the thought of the special dipping sauce. I wouldn't dare tell Dewey about this, but I for one don't mind a bit of Swiss Chalet from time to time. At least you know what to expect, and that counts for something in this uncertain world.

Once we were sitting around the table and attacking our food I got up the courage to ask, "So, what's the occasion?"

Jess and Mom shot each other a quick glance. It must have been long enough for an agreement to be reached, for Mom answered me. "Well, Calli, it was my idea. I've wanted to see you ever since we met Ken. When I didn't hear from you, I called Jess. I thought that between the two of us, we could get you over here and pin you down."

This was the one thing I hadn't anticipated. Unlike my father, my mother had never shunned me, or been antagonistic to me about my sexuality. She had tried to be understanding, and I certainly never doubted her love for me. It hadn't, however, been easy for her, and one of the most difficult things had been establishing a comfortable relationship with my girlfriends. She and Jess had eventually grown close, but it still astonished me that Mom would open up to her like this about her past—especially when it had taken a lifetime for her to open up to me.

I knew I should be glad at this proof of their growing bond, but it was overshadowed by the feeling that once more I was the last to know something. Why couldn't my mother have just called me? Why this elaborate scheme to get me here for a chat? Of course I had been avoiding just such a conversation. Instead of answering my mother I filled my mouth with chicken breast and chewed in guilt-riddled silence. I needed sustenance for whatever was about to take place.

Jess took over, as I knew she would. "Calli, why didn't you tell me about your brother? How could you keep something like that from me?"

Her wounded face took away my appetite. "I'm sorry, Jess. I was going to. I wanted to sort out a few things in my own head first. I probably should have realized that if I told you, you'd be able to help me." I knew I should have told her. After all, I had told Dewey. But every time I thought about sharing the information with her, I had found a reason not to.

The damage I'd done hadn't been repaired by my apology, and the disappointment was clear in Jess's voice when she said, "I can't guarantee that I would have been any help in sorting out your head, but at least you wouldn't have been alone with your thoughts. I could have given you moral support if nothing else."

"You're right." There was really nothing more I could say in my defence.

"Now young lady, it's my turn." My mother tried to sound jovial, but the hurt she felt at my silence seeped through the cracks in her voice.

"I know, Mom, I should have been in touch. I'm

sure you really needed to talk to me about Ken. I was being selfish and insensitive."

Both women looked at me, silent in their agreement over my shortcomings.

It was my mother who finally spoke. "Well, now that you are here, I'd really like to discuss it." She proceeded to meticulously cut her chicken into bite-sized portions. This unaccustomed action made it clear that I would have to do some serious making-up.

Jess watched. Despite the rocky start to their relationship, the growing admiration Jess felt for my mother was clear.

"How are you feeling about everything, Mom?" I figured I'd already been selfish enough, and I really did want to hear how she felt about it. About him.

"Well." She finished slicing the last piece of chicken and looked up at me. "I have now accomplished the one thing I have always wanted to accomplish before I died. I've met my son. And from what I was able to tell during the short time we were together, he's a fine man. Not only do I feel more complete now, but I also feel as if I did the right thing by giving him up. I've been carrying guilt around for fifty years, and the weight of it has worn me down. Now I can almost stand up straight again."

Her words were logical and sincere, almost rehearsed in their delivery. But when I looked into her eyes I could see the devastation that had been left behind by her actions of so long ago.

"I could never have provided for him, or given

him the opportunities he received from his adoptive parents," she continued. "And I'm sure as a single mother I wouldn't have ended up marrying your father, Calli. And then there'd be no you." She gave me a wistful smile. "I guess the best way of describing it is to say that I'm finally...at peace."

She wiped her nose, and I could feel mine starting to run. I knew it was time for me speak, to be a good daughter, maybe give her a hug. But, although we were now closer than we had ever been, we still weren't demonstrative in our relationship.

Jess has tried to educate me in how to be emotionally supportive. Although I might be making headway where my wife is concerned, I was quickly discovering that with my mother, I still had a lot to learn. I sniffed, swallowed, and made an attempt, however, by saying, "That's great, Mom. I'm very happy for you. Happy that it turned out so well. Do you know how Ken felt about everything?" I hoped it wasn't too obvious that I was avoiding my own feelings.

"He called the day after we met. He was feeling very positive about the whole thing. He was also glad that he'd met you."

"So you'll be staying in contact with him then."

"We'll all be staying in contact," she corrected.

"That's good," I said. The time had come. "I really liked him too. I could tell he was your son just by looking at him."

My mother smiled the smile that only mothers can.

"I have to admit, it all feels a bit strange for me," I added. "Just finding out about him, and then walking into the room and...I hadn't mentally prepared myself."

"I'm sorry about that, Calli, but I didn't know he would be visiting that day until about an hour before he arrived. Yes, I could have warned you, probably should have warned you, but I was afraid you'd find an excuse for not coming over. I know how you like to avoid anything that's emotionally difficult."

My mother was right, of course. She knows me better than anyone else. There was no point in denying it. Instead, I pushed myself a step closer to where I knew she wanted me to be. "I'm glad I met him. I would like to get to know him better. I think...I could get used to the idea of having a big brother."

My mother gave me a satisfied grin. "How's your chicken?"

I was down to my last chip. The conversation had been light and cheerful, since the subject of Ken was off the table.

My mother scooped some of her leftover fries onto my plate and said, "There's another reason why I asked you both here."

Jess set her jaw and gave me a worried look. Neither of us dared ask what my mother had up her sleeve.

"I want to talk to you both about this idea you

have of becoming parents." Her gaze rested on Jess and then on me. When neither of us responded, she continued. "When I talked to you before, Calli, I didn't think it was a good idea. And from what I could tell neither did you, but not for the same reason."

I could feel Jess's eyes boring into me, but I didn't dare look at her. I wanted to tell my mother to stop. I needed to do damage control before things got out of hand and Jess became upset, but before I could think of what to say, my mother forged ahead.

"I was worried about the child growing up in a… a non-traditional family."

"Mom, lots of non-traditional families have children, and the kids turn out fine. Being in a traditional family doesn't guarantee a child's happiness." I'd managed to stop my mother from saying anything more that might be damaging, but in the process, I might have gone too far. There I was, casting a shadow on my own upbringing and at the same time defending once again our decision to be parents. Decision? Had we actually decided? Had *I* decided? No, and no. What I was defending was our right to be parents.

"I'm aware of that, dear."

I should have left it at that, but I didn't; I opened my mouth and wedged both feet firmly inside. "At least our type of non-traditional family has a child because we really want one. We don't get pregnant by accident."

Jess gasped.

My mother just looked at me, her thoughts hidden

behind her tired eyes.

I had never before spoken to her like that. Our distance over the years had not only precluded overt demonstrations of affection, but also harsh words or disagreements. For the first time in my life I said, "I'm sorry, Mom. That was uncalled for. I…"

"No, dear, you're right," my mother said. "I wish you had let me finish though, before getting on your high horse."

"Please, what were you going to say?" Whatever she was going to tell us couldn't be as bad as what had just come out of my mouth.

"Well." She smoothed the unwrinkled tablecloth. "I was going to tell you that since meeting Ken, I've been thinking. Not just about him, but also about the two of you and the possibility of a child."

Jess and I exchanged a glance.

"I think I was wrong before. A child would be lucky to have you both as parents. Jess has every right to give birth, if that's what she chooses. But should you prefer to adopt, you would be giving a child a good home. A child who might not otherwise have one." She sat back in her chair, finished not only with her dinner, but also with her announcement.

"Thank you," I said. "But I still don't know…*we* still don't know…"

"Thank you," Jess added.

Mrs. Kumar was waiting for me when I arrived at the shop. She invited me through the beaded door into the back room where we made ourselves comfortable in a couple of worn armchairs.

"We could talk in the front," I said.

"Piff," she said, and waved her hand. "The bell will ring, if someone comes."

"Thank you for calling me. I'm sorry I distressed you with my last visit. I didn't expect to hear from you."

"I'm an old woman. My life has been full of ups and downs. It's not the end of the world. My son is always trying to spare me, but he doesn't know how strong I am. I can stand on my own feet."

"You said you had remembered something you wanted to tell me."

"Yes. Sometimes it takes a long time for a memory to return. Only when my son became upset at your visit did I start to remember. You were asking about dear Ravi Mehta. So that is where my memories were coming from. When my son grew angry, his memories were coming from Mr. Sanderson. Not because of the store, but because of my granddaughter. I had not remembered the connection. I don't think of her as being born to someone else. I only think of her as ours."

"I understand," I said. "So because of your son you remembered something about Mr. Sanderson that you want to tell me?"

"Yes. Since you were asking about how Mr. Sanderson and Ravi were together, I thought you might want to know." She looked pleased with herself.

"Yes, I would."

"One day I was in the front of the store, and Ravi was in the back, working with stock. Then I heard voices. I was surprised, because I thought we were the only two people here. Someone must have come in through the back door. As the talking continued it became louder, and I knew the other man was Mr. Sanderson."

"So that was unusual?"

"Oh yes," she assured me.

"You said before that you didn't see much of Mr. Sanderson, but he visited the store sometimes."

"Every few months. He came to see the things he had ordered. Make sure everything was as it should be."

"Was this not a normal visit then?"

"No. He usually came through the front. Looked at the displays, the shelves, then went to the back. That day he never came to see the shelves. He stayed in the back with Ravi."

It was beginning to look as if my return to the shop was in vain. So far Mrs. Kumar was just elaborating on what she had already told me about the uneasy relationship that had existed between her two employers. Maybe she would be willing to tell me what her son so adamantly refused to discuss. "Is there anything else? Something about Mr. Sanderson and your granddaughter?"

"Of course there is. But my granddaughter has

nothing to do with it." Her head wobbled to reinforce her indignation. "As I told you, they were in the back. I would have ignored them, but their voices grew louder, until they were shouting. Mr. Sanderson was telling dear Ravi to mind his own business, and Ravi was telling him that he'd gone too far. That he'd broken his promise. This time the police were going to know."

"Know about what?"

"They didn't say. But Ravi told the other one he had proof. He still had proof from before and now he had new proof. Some words like that." She stopped talking and took a deep breath through her nose. "Ravi was keeping it safe. Just like before. Locked away somewhere Mr. Sanderson couldn't get to. This time Ravi was going to the police, unless Mr. Sanderson turned himself in. Ravi was only giving him the opportunity to do the right thing because they were business partners and their mothers were cousins, and Ravi was showing him that respect."

"Do you remember what else they said?" If I'd had a crime elbow, it would have been aching.

"Only that Mr. Sanderson told Ravi not to interfere, or he would be sorry. Ravi told him not to make threats. They wouldn't work. Mr. Sanderson had a week to prove he was putting things to rights, or Ravi would do it for him."

I'd been jotting down a few notes as she spoke. What I wanted to add to the bottom of the page were some specific details. "Did you get any indication at all about what was upsetting Mr. Mehta?"

"Only something about Mr. Sanderson's trips to India. The next words I heard Ravi say were about home—closer to home—maybe something like that. There was much mumbling as well as shouting."

"Do you by any chance remember when this happened?"

I was about to put away my pencil, when Mrs. Kumar spoke. "Of course I remember. It was just before Ravi became really ill. He hadn't been himself for years, but this is when the sickness took over. Almost the same day. And then Mrs. Mehta was attacked not long after. My memory doesn't have the dates, but it knows the events. Nothing was ever the same."

I wrote a final line in my notebook, thanked Mrs. Kumar, and almost skipped back to my Forester.

I ran up the stairs to my office, anxious to talk to Sashi about her father. Svetlana's door was closed, so she wasn't at work. My door, however, was open.

It shouldn't have been.

I am the only person with a key.

I froze on the top step, poised to make a hasty retreat. All was quiet. I leaned forward and peeked around the doorjamb. From where I was I could see most of the room, and there was no one visible. What was visible made me want to vomit. The place had been tossed.

I know better than to barge into the middle of a crime scene, especially if the perpetrator could be hiding behind the door. I didn't dare rely on my rusty boxing moves, so I carefully turned around then raced down the stairs and outside.

By the time the police arrived I had convinced myself that my office is jinxed and I should start looking for a new place. The two constables had a quick look around before letting me back in to see if anything was missing. It was hard to tell. File folders and their contents were strewn over most of the floor space. Even the door to my mini-fridge was open.

My nausea returned when I looked under my desk and saw the space where my computer tower used to be.

The constables confirmed my fear that this was probably not a random burglary. I had been targetted. Someone had been looking for something specific. Otherwise the files wouldn't have been searched and my ancient Pentium wouldn't have been lugged away. If someone really wanted a computer, Svetlana's treasure trove was just across the hall. The mess was either a diversion, or the result of a sloppy search. If it was the latter, and the desired information hadn't been found in the paper files, the thief had hoped it would be on my hard drive.

While one constable made arrangements for the forensic team to make an undoubtedly futile visit, I gave a statement to the other constable. He took the description of my computer, although we both knew it wouldn't turn up and it wasn't worth the effort of even filling out a report. Fortunately I use online backup for my files, so I wouldn't be missing anything important. What was more disturbing than the loss of my tower was the idea that someone now had access to my case notes, which unfortunately were up to date for a change.

"When were you last in your office?" the constable asked.

"Yesterday afternoon," I said, realizing he had to establish a timeframe.

"Are you working on anything at the moment which might result in this?" His pencil was poised over an almost blank page in his notebook.

"I only have one case right now. It's possible that someone might be getting worried, but so far there isn't just one person I could point a finger at." I gave a brief overview of what I'd been doing.

"We'll let you know when you can get in to clean up."

Although the mess, inconvenience, and feeling of personal invasion gave me sickening flashbacks and a heavy sense of foreboding, there was a picture forming in the back of my mind that included a beautiful new Mac sitting on my desk.

I was on the sofa nursing a beer when Dewey phoned. Although he'd been called to work at Mauve again that morning, thanks to his new smartphone, he'd been able do some sleuthing and had managed to track down Borisav Belic's sister. If Dew continued this way, I'd soon be changing the name on my door to Barnow and Brande Investigations.

We met in front of a diner on Richmond, not far from Parliament. Without speaking, Dewey pulled me to him in a big hug. "You okay, babe?"

"Yeah. Why?" I said to his collarbone.

"Your office."

I shrugged to hide what I was really feeling, and more to convince myself than to mislead Dewey, I said, "I must be getting used to having my private spaces violated. At least I wasn't there this time. What really pisses me off is having to clean up the mess." I gave him a sickly sweet smile.

"Okay, babe, I'll help you—again. On one condition."

"Name it."

"You get some fancy lock and a security system."

"Done. Shall we?" I stood aside and Dewey pushed open the grimy glass door.

The diner had seen better days, but still appeared to have a loyal clientele. The beer hadn't been a good substitute for lunch, and since Miss Belic said she wouldn't be able to talk with us for about twenty minutes, I gave her one more job by ordering a home-style breakfast with eggs sunny side up. Maybe a little comfort food would return my mind to work mode.

Dewey ordered a bottle of water and examined our surroundings without trying to hide his distaste. Each time he was about to make a comment on the peeling paint or worn counter top or yellowed landscapes in unpainted frames, I gave him a narrow-eyed warning. When my meal arrived I allowed him the freedom to chastise me about my heart attack on a plate, while I enjoyed every mouthful.

Even if we hadn't confirmed the identity of Belic's sister when we arrived, and even if she weren't the only person working in the diner, given the context of my visit there, I think I would have recognized her. She was of a similar age to her brother. Her mousy hair sprouted from beneath her hairnet and formed a fringe around her sallow face. Unlike her wisp of a brother, however, she was solidly round, and her stained white uniform gaped at the front. The only thing about the woman that wasn't drab was a hint of gold that hung on a chain around her neck and occasionally peeked out through the space between her top two buttons.

I wondered whether it was coincidence that both siblings had found work cooking, or whether it ran in the family. Whichever was the case, it was impossible to tell from the woman's face whether she enjoyed what she was doing.

As I finished my meal, I complimented Dewey on finding Miss Belic.

"Why thank you." He soaked up the praise.

"It's lucky for us she still has her family name," I added.

He leaned toward me and in a monotone only I could hear said, "Calli, no one would want to marry that woman."

"Dewey!"

"I know." He rolled his eyes. "I have to learn to

look beyond the surface." He turned his attention to his water bottle and began to peel off the paper label.

We had purposely chosen to sit on stools at the counter, so that it would be easy to converse with Miss Belic when she had the time. As the twenty minutes turned into half an hour it looked as if she might never find a few minutes between cooking, cleaning up, and attending the till. The opportune moment presented itself after she had handed a baggily clad teenaged boy his change.

She scowled, planted herself in front of us, spread her arms, and grasped the edge of the counter with her rough hands. "What you want with me?"

I had just wiped up the last bit of yolk with my last bit of toast and was about to devour it with gusto. When it was clear that Dewey was still smarting from my rebuke, I put down my food and said, "We're wondering if you could answer some questions about your brother?"

Fury swallowed her scowl. "If I weren't standing in kitchen, I would spit on floor. Good for nothing layabout."

"So you wouldn't mind giving us information that could get your brother in trouble?"

Her huge smile came out of nowhere. "You ask me. I tell you. Borisav been a problem from moment he born. He kill our mother."

"He killed your mother?" I had to ask.

"Spend her money. Break her heart." She patted her bosom for emphasis.

"I believe he used to live with your mother, before her death?"

Miss Belic's smile had long since disappeared. "Mother was only thing that keep roof over his head. Only thing that keep him from finding more trouble."

"I'm interested in the time just after your mother's death, so maybe you would be able to remember some details about what was happening to your brother then."

"I have a good memory." She knocked on her head. "What you want to know?"

"Borisav spent time in jail for attacking and robbing some women."

"I remember." She clenched her teeth before continuing. "I cheer when they arrest him. He call me for help. I tell him he can rot there for all I care."

"Do you remember if just before the time of the arrest he was in hospital for a while?"

"Of course I remember. Borisav never in hospital. Not a day in his miserable life."

"You're sure?"

"As sure as my name Anastasia Belic!" She pulled in her chin and glowered at me. "I try to keep him out of my life, but every time something wrong he come crying to me. More since our sainted mother pass on. 'Ana, help me. Ana, I need money. Ana, I need place to live.' You think I not know if he sick in hospital? I would get call. I would get many calls to beg me to take care for him, to visit him, to take him food or money. No, he never in hospital. I would know."

CHAPTER TEN

Rather than talk to Sashi on the phone, we arranged to meet in a coffee shop next door to her dental practice. I bought us each a cup of gourmet coffee and we hunkered down at a table near the back, as far away as possible from the bustle on the street and other patrons. When a man in a hoodie sat down at the next table I considered taking our meeting elsewhere, but it soon became apparent he was too interested in texting to bother with us.

"Any more incidents like the tires?" I asked.

"Not so far. I'm sure it had nothing to do with your investigation." Sashi looked hopeful.

"I'm sure it didn't either." I gave her a reassuring smile and watched as the worry lines around her eyes disappeared. "I just want to bring you up to date on what's been happening."

"So you're making headway?"

"Good question. I wish I knew the answer. We're following three lines of investigation. All of them present problems as far as finding proof. I'm hoping you might remember something more that relates to your mother or father, something that could help."

"I'll try, but I'm sure I've told you all I know."

"Let me tell you about our suspects. It's possible that some detail about one of them will jog your memory."

Sashi strangled her thick ceramic mug and waited.

"One person we're checking out is Lucas Anasetti, the man who found your mother. He worked in the neighbourhood and was apparently walking down the street on his way to a friend's house."

"Why is he on your list? Surely he was questioned by the police."

"Yes, he was, but I'm not completely satisfied that he's innocent. Not everything he's told us checks out. And at some point after your mother was attacked he managed to buy the salon where he had worked. I don't know yet where the money came from."

"It couldn't have come from my mother. She carried around cash, but certainly not that much." Sashi pulled a face at the thought of her mother's purse full of thousand-dollar bills. "No more than a few hundred dollars at most. Just what she needed for the day."

"I know it sounds unlikely, but he's the one person who was definitely there."

Sashi considered my point then said, "Well, you can't argue with that."

"By the way, do you know where your mother had her hair done?"

Sashi thought for a moment. "I don't know the

name of the salon, but I think it was in Yorkville."

"Did she always go to the same place?"

"We never discussed it, but I'm sure she would have. She hated change. Once she found something she liked, she stayed with it."

"Was she a friendly person?"

"Oh yes. She loved people. She could strike up a conversation with a complete stranger, just standing at a crosswalk waiting for the green light."

I was beginning to form a picture of what Mrs. Mehta's last normal day might have been like. I was also getting to know the woman, and that could be just as important.

"Where else did your mother go that day besides the salon and the theatre? Any idea?"

"She probably went out to dinner with Mrs. Nassar. I guess I knew at the time."

"Yes she did. Mrs. Nassar told me. She also said your mother was doing something for your father, because he was ill."

"It's possible. Other than that, maybe she did some shopping. I don't know." Sashi looked past me at nothing, as the memory of her mother alive and well threatened to take over.

"Okay, so the second person I'm investigating is a man who was robbing women around the time your mother was attacked." I once more had her attention. "He usually wasn't very violent, more of a purse snatcher. He was arrested later that year, but was never connected to your mother. When I talked to him, of course he denied any involvement. But his alibi doesn't check out. Borisav Belic. Ring any bells?"

"Never heard of him. But that's the sort of thing the police thought happened. That's why they feared the case would never be solved."

"It still might never be, Sashi. You know it's a real long shot."

"I know, Calli, and I appreciate your trying."

Her reassurance was what I needed in order to tell her about the longest shot of all. "The only other lead I have is more related to your father than your mother. If it had been your father who was attacked, this is where I'd point a finger, but I don't see any connection to your mother. Unless it was some act of retaliation against your dad, but that seems very unlikely. And the location of the attack makes it look even more implausible."

"Who is it?"

"Do you remember your father's old business partner, Prabhakar Sanderson?"

"Of course. What connection could he have to my mother's attack?"

"Probably none. But let me ask you something, before I tell you why I'm even mentioning him. I've had contradictory reports regarding the nature of his friendship with your father. In fact, I'm not sure whether they were friends at all. What was your take on it?"

"I never really thought about it." She gave me a

bewildered look.

"If Sanderson had been a good friend as well as a business partner, would you have known?"

"I'm sure I would have. I only met the man once or twice in all the years they worked together, and I wasn't aware of any great warmth between them. In fact, he didn't even attend my father's funeral."

"I see. Well, apparently your father was very upset with him about something just before the time of your mother's attack."

"Oh?"

"You didn't know?"

"My dad talked very little about his work. He liked to keep it separate from his family life. He never mentioned it to me, and if he'd told my mother, she didn't pass it on."

"That's too bad, but understandable."

"Do you know what the disagreement was about?" she asked.

"Apparently your father discovered something Sanderson was doing. He told Sanderson that if he didn't take responsibility for it, he would report him. He said he had the proof. Whatever Sanderson was up to, it must have been illegal."

"That sounds right. My father was an incredibly honest man. He wouldn't have stood for anything that was against the law."

"Was it possible Sanderson was doing something he shouldn't have at the import company, something that your father found out about?"

"Maybe, but I doubt it. Dad was very astute in his business dealings. He would have picked up on it at the first hint and dealt with it immediately, before the police would need to be involved. A warning doesn't sound like his style, but of course it would depend on what Sanderson was doing, I guess."

I thought about the possibilities. "The information I received made it sound like an ongoing problem. Something your father thought was over and done with. Then he discovered it wasn't"

"I do know that Sanderson was an opportunist, always ready to get involved in one venture or another," Sashi said. "I didn't hear this directly from my dad, but my mother once mentioned that Dad wished Sanderson would just concentrate on the importing and leave everything else to others, or else get out of the import business altogether. I'm sure I only remember the occasion because it was so unusual to hear anything about his work."

"Yes, that fits. The only dirt I've been able to dig up on Sanderson had to do with an adoption agency he used to run."

"But that would have had nothing to do with my father."

"I know. As I said, Sanderson is not looking like a real possibility. I'm just throwing things out there in case I get lucky."

"I understand," Sashi said.

"Just out of curiosity, if your father were to have put something away in a safe place, somewhere that no one could get to, where would that have been? Did he have a safe in the house? Anything like that?"

"No. There was no safe." Sashi gazed into her coffee for help. "There was a safe deposit box at the bank. That's where they kept important papers, my mother's good jewellery, that sort of thing. I cleaned it out after he died. There wasn't anything unusual nothing like what you're talking about."

"Which bank?"

"The Royal Bank at Yonge and Bloor. I had my first account at that branch. I think my dad did his business banking there as well."

"So if your mother were doing some banking on the day she was attacked, it would likely have been there."

"That would be my guess."

A phone rang at the next table and the man answered it and began to mumble.

Sashi lowered her voice. "Come to think of it, my mother had the safe deposit key with her the day she was attacked. I remember seeing it in the plastic bag of her possessions that the police returned to us."

"Did she always carry the key around with her?"

"I doubt it. There'd be no reason."

"So she might have made a trip to the bank on that day. Maybe she put something into or took something out of the box."

"Possibly."

"Did your father say anything about it? Did he mention anything about the bank, or that your mother should have had something with her that was missing?"

"No. I don't think so. Why?"

"It's probably nothing. I was just remembering what Mrs. Nassar said about your mother doing something for your father that day. I thought maybe it was to do with the bank."

"I guess we'll never know." Sashi looked disheartened for the first time.

"Maybe not. But we'll get all the answers we can. You won't be able to say you didn't try."

Neither of us spoke.

The silence was becoming uncomfortable, so I said the first thing that came to mind. "Was your mother missing anything at all that you haven't mentioned before?"

Sashi shook her head.

"Since she was a woman of habit, is there anything she always wore or had with her that was missing after the attack?" I'd finished my coffee, and I really wanted to bring the meeting to an end. I didn't, however, want to end on a negative note, which is why I was blindly casting around for a glimmer of hope. It also occurred to me that I should have asked Sashi this before.

"Nothing. She always wore a watch. She still had it on. And her wedding ring and bangles."

I watched as Sashi visualized her mother alive and well; the journey back was a painful one.

Suddenly her eyes locked with mine. "The little

yellow god."

I didn't have a chance to ask her what she was talking about.

"The little yellow god was a small gold figure—actually it was a goddess, the goddess of love and devotion, Parvati. My father had it made for my mother on one of their anniversaries, and she always wore it on a chain around her neck. They affectionately called it the little yellow god, because of some poem they had studied at school."

"And she wasn't wearing it when she was found?"

"No. She mustn't have been. The police didn't give it to us, and now that I think of it, she didn't have it in the hospital. I was so used to her wearing it that I never thought anything about it. My father was ill and so distraught after what happened to her that he barely knew his own name. I'm positive I haven't seen it since."

"That's too bad, since it was so important to her. I'm sure you would have wanted it."

"Yes. Of course I would want it. How could I not have noticed?" The fresh loss threatened to release the tears that always waited just under Sashi's calm exterior.

"Why don't you describe it for me?" I didn't know if my question would help her, or just make things worse.

She gave me a grateful smile. "It was about this big." Holding her thumb and forefinger in the air, she measured off a space of about two centimetres. "Her legs were crossed Buddha style, she was wearing a headdress, and she was holding one of her four hands up in front of her like this." Sashi held up her own hand, as if she were telling someone to stop.

"It sounds beautiful...but I don't know that the missing necklace will lead me to her attacker."

"It's okay, Calli. I'm not expecting a miracle."

All the way home I felt as if someone were following me. I tried to ignore it at first, but the farther I walked, the stronger the feeling grew. Eventually I stopped and pretended to look at the displays in a store window, but I could see nothing unusual in the reflections on the glass or in my peripheral vision. I entered a building, but stopped just inside the door and waited. No one followed me, and I couldn't see anyone hanging around outside when I exited a few minutes later. When I boarded a streetcar, no one suspicious climbed on with me. My worry stone was growing hot in the palm of my hand, and I had to acknowledge that the break-in at my office had affected me more than I wanted to let on.

No sooner was I in the door of my apartment than my cell rang. It was Mrs. Nassar. She hadn't exactly jumped on the memory train with everyone else, but she'd had what she referred to as a stroke of luck by connecting with a friend Mrs. Mehta might have run into at the salon on the day of her attack. Mrs. Nassar had seen the woman at a fundraiser the day before and was telling her about poor Mrs. Mehta's death, when the information surfaced. Mrs. Nassar was sure I would be interested.

I didn't feel like hanging around home and making supper, and Mrs. Nassar had been helpful enough to get the woman's phone number and address for me, so I set up a four-thirty meeting.

Because of my paranoia on the journey back from seeing Sashi, I decided to drive. By the time I'd made my way through the market bustle on Baldwin and reached my Forester in the parking garage I was feeling more secure. So much more secure in fact, that just as I was about to put my key in the car door, I changed my mind. After all, it was rush hour. On top of that I would have to find a parking spot. It would be far more sensible just to hop on the TTC.

It was only a short walk from the bus stop down the tree-lined street to where Miss Violet Pritchard lived. The three-story apartment building was old, but immaculately maintained. Manicured landscaping set off the stately brown bricks and the pristine white trim. The picture was made complete by the backdrop of Casa Loma, which loomed protectively above its diminutive neighbours.

Miss Pritchard buzzed me in and we were soon sharing tea in her over-stuffed living room. She was a woman about the same age as Mrs. Nassar, but instead of exuding warmth and motherly comfort, she was studied and brittle. It's not that she was unpleasant by any means, but she wore her conservative clothes and recently styled hair like a kind of armour.

I didn't feel like an intruder so much as a visitor from another time and place.

"I didn't know Indira Mehta very well," she said. "We lived very different lives. Obviously. But she was always friendly to me. We would occasionally run into each other at events. The library. The symphony. The art gallery. That sort of thing. And we'd get to talking. I always thought she was a bit too forthcoming with information, if you know what I mean."

I nodded and drank my tea.

"Normally I would just let her talk and not pay much attention. She would be going on about her children, or her husband. Things in which I had no interest."

I nodded again.

"It wasn't the first time I'd seen her at the salon, and the only reason I remember the occasion at all is because I was getting my hair done before leaving the next day on an extended holiday. I didn't hear about the attack until months later, after my return. Yesterday when Mrs. Nassar mentioned that you are looking into the attack again it reminded me that I must have seen Mrs. Mehta on the same day she met with her misfortune. It also brought to mind something rather unusual about my conversation with Mrs. Mehta on that day."

"Are you sure it was the day of Mrs. Mehta's attack?"

"Oh yes. I checked. You see, I keep a diary. Have done ever since I was a girl. When I was talking to Mrs. Nassar yesterday and she said that you might want to talk to me, I thought I should have my facts straight, so I looked it up." Miss Pritchard picked up a leather-bound journal from the table next to her and opened it. "That was the day. Page two hundred and one." She closed the book without offering to show me, but there was no reason to doubt her accuracy.

"You say there was something unusual about your talk with Mrs. Mehta on that day. Unusual in what way?" The tea was so weak I knew I couldn't blame it for the sprint my heart was running.

"As I said, I was going away. I used to travel a lot, with friends. I happened to mention this to Mrs. Mehta, and she became very excited. She told me about what she was planning as a surprise for her husband. Now normally that is where I would have stopped listening, but it had to do with travel, and it all sounded rather bizarre to me. So I paid attention.

"Apparently he'd been working too hard and he wasn't well. He needed to take it easy for a while, so Mrs. Mehta got it into her head that she would arrange for them to go on a long trip to many of the places they had never been, but always talked about visiting."

"So she was planning the trip as a surprise for her husband," I said.

"That's right."

"And that was bizarre?"

"It was the way she was going about it that was highly questionable. Most people decide where they want to go, they contact a travel agent, particularly for the sort of thing she was planning, and they pay for it with a credit card."

"I've heard that Mrs. Mehta preferred cash."

"Fair enough. But I'm not talking about cash and I'm not talking about a few hundred, or even a few thousand dollars here. This trip she was planning would have cost her...well, I dread to think."

"I see. And she told you how she was going to pay for it?"

"Oh yes. That's one of the things she was very excited about. She had figured out a way to pay for the trip and keep it secret from her husband until she was ready to tell him about it. I think she was afraid he'd put an end to the idea if he knew about it in time, and I'm sure he would have."

"So what was she doing?"

"She was planning to pay for it by selling some antique jewellery that had been in her family, for generations I believe. She'd been to the bank to pick it up and she was going to take it to a dealer the following day. She even showed me—an ornate necklace and earrings, gold and gemstones. I could tell the moment I saw the pieces that they were worth a lot of money. I asked her if she was sure she wanted to part with family heirlooms and she assured me she did. They meant very little to her compared to the health of her husband, and she still had pieces tucked away that were of more sentimental value.

"I also asked her if she was sure she should be walking around downtown with them, and suggested that maybe she should go directly to the dealer after getting her hair done. She just laughed at me—told me that no one in this day and age would be interested in such old fashioned pieces. I reminded her that she was planning to sell them for a great deal of money. She laughed again and said that most people would think they were worthless."

"So she didn't take your advice."

"Well, I don't know, but I gather she didn't. I don't think she would have had time. You see, she told me what her plans for the rest of the day and the evening were: dinner and a movie. It was already late afternoon. The last thing I said to her was a warning to be careful. I assume the jewellery was stolen." She looked at me for an answer.

"It's beginning to look that way," I said. "Just one more thing, Miss Pritchard: where did you and Mrs. Mehta get your hair done?"

"The best salon in Yorkville," she said. "Waves."

Jess had made one of my favourite summer dishes, chicken Caesar salad. It was just what the doctor ordered after a day filled with more downs than ups. Although I hadn't seen or talked to Jess since that morning, and therefore hadn't told her about what had happened to my office until I arrived home, she'd had a feeling I would need a little taking care of—hence the nice dinner.

"Don't you think it's time to look for a new office space?" she asked before popping the first piece of crisp romaine into her beautiful mouth.

"Maybe," I sulked. "But I like my office."

"I know you do, Calli, but come on, look at what's happened there. How much blood and destruction do you want to put up with inside those four walls? I know it's handy, but we won't be living here forever. And I know you like things that are familiar to you, but you need somewhere more secure. It's not as if you have a bakery or a toy store. This won't be the last time someone has a reason to break into your office. You know that."

"I know." I fiddled with a crouton.

"Promise me you'll at least think about it."

"I promise." I didn't tell her that I'd already been thinking about it. Jess would have taken that as meaning it was a done deal. I wanted time to look at the options. At the moment, I preferred Dewey's solution of a new lock and a security system. I had enough common sense, however, to realize that was just a band-aid. Eventually, for one reason or another, I would be looking for new premises. I just didn't want it to be now.

"Besides," she added, "I don't want anything to happen to my child's other mama." She ran her bare foot up the inside of my leg.

Jess now had my full attention, for two reasons: one was in my lap; the other had come out of her mouth. I was glad to get off the topic of my office, but would rather it had been a different subject that took its place. I tried to make the best of it by keeping things light. "What's happening in baby land?"

"Well." She wiggled her strategically placed toe. "I've been giving a lot of thought to what your mother said. And I've been giving a lot of thought to our situation. Babies are cute, but I don't have any experience, and neither do you. Also, I really want the child to be as much yours as mine."

"It sounds as if you're leaning toward adoption," I said, sounding as noncommittal as possible.

"Yes, I am. What do you think?"

I took a moment to process what Jess had said. This was getting too close for comfort, and I didn't want to say anything I would later regret.

Jess had enough sense to wait. She pretended to be absorbed in her salad.

At last I spoke. "If we were to have a child—and in my mind it's still a big 'if'—I agree that adopting would be the best option. But we'd have to be very sure about the integrity of the agency. And I agree that it wouldn't have to be an infant. Considering our nontraditional family, as my mother calls it, the child probably shouldn't be too old though. You know, so it could grow up with two moms, rather than suddenly be landed in that situation."

The smile I received from across the table made my careful statement worth the trouble. "That's that, then," she said. "We've made the first big decision."

"Yes, that's that." I speared my last piece of chicken with my fork. I could swear I heard it scream in terror.

"There's one more thing, though," she said.

The serious tone of Jess's statement drew me from my self-absorption. "What thing?"

Her face was like a frozen field, as she left her end of the table and headed toward mine.

My heart started to stampede in apprehension of whatever terrible thing she was about to share.

When she reached my side, she looked down at me, still showing no hint of her intentions. Then she took my head in her hands, held it steady, and gave me a long, seductive kiss.

When I finally opened my eyes Jess was still there, but her face had transformed. Now she was smiling and giving me a definite come hither look.

So *that* was the one more thing.

CHAPTER ELEVEN

It had been far too long since my last visit to the boxing club. If anything could get rid of the tension that had been building in my neck and shoulders and get my scattered mind to focus, it would be an hour in the gloves.

"Hey, Killer," came a familiar voice from the middle of the boxing ring. It was Pat, the owner of the club and the person who had trained me and given me the name, Killer.

"Hey, Pat. I'm just here for the bag." I waved on my way to the lockers.

"Sure thing. If you want to talk later, find me." She returned to her demonstration of correct uppercut technique.

By the time I'd finished taping my hands, I was already starting to feel better. The first time my glove hit the heavy bag I knew I'd made the right decision. What I didn't understand was why I'd stayed away from the club for so long, when I knew it was like a magic potion for me.

I started slow and easy, paying attention to my stance and left hook. My neglected muscles were singing with joy, and my mind was moving toward a wide plateau where it could roam free of the worries that had been eating away at it. Each time my glove connected with the leather of the bag I felt a release. Right, left, right, right, breathe. Left, left, right.

I started to dance in relation to the swaying of my silent but sturdy opponent. My heart pumped like a well-oiled engine, as sweat began to run down my bare arms and legs.

After about half an hour I gave my arms a break and did a few brisk laps around the perimeter of the gym. By the time I returned to the bag, fragments of my case had started to filter back into my mind. I mentally placed them one at a time on the smooth surface of the leather in front of me. Borisav Belic's darting eyes. Bam! Lucas Anasetti's supercilious arrogance. Bam! Bam! Prabhakar Sanderson's vacant stare. I dropped my hands to my sides. How could I hit a sick old man?

"Lost your inner fight, Killer?"

I turned to see Pat standing behind me, hands on hips. "You could say that." I made a face, a combination of resignation and disinterest.

"Why don't you get cleaned up and join me in my office? I'll spot you a bottle of water."

Pat's office, if you can call it that, is small. It's really just an enclosure formed by the outside walls and a couple of banks of lockers. The beat-up metal desk and old laptop make it qualify as an office, according to Pat, and I've never heard anyone challenge her on that point.

I was already sitting in the one guest chair when Pat joined me. Her muscles glistened with sweat and I envied her the body she'd sculpted for herself.

"So, what's up, Killer? Why the long face?" She handed me a chilled bottle from her stash in the refreshment area.

I felt supported just at the sound of my boxing name. Pat didn't know anything about investigating, but I didn't care. I felt my problems building up behind the dam of my denial. I knew as soon as I opened my mouth, everything would come spilling out. I postponed the inevitable by unscrewing the cap on the water bottle and taking a long drink.

"You couldn't possibly have worked up that much of a thirst," she laughed, her smile verging on a tease. "You must have a doozy of a problem." She swung her feet onto her desk and leaned back in her chair.

I tried to keep myself from looking up the length of her legs to where they disappeared into her shorts. "Did anyone ever tell you that you should have been a psychiatrist?" I asked, actually believing it would have been a solid idea.

"As a matter of fact yes. It's a good thing for you I'm not. You get my expert advice without the big bill." Her smile gave me the last little push I needed.

"It's the case I'm working on."

"I figured it was either that, or you aren't getting enough between the sheets." She winked.

"No, it's work," I assured her, battling the blush that was taking over my cheeks.

"Care to give me a hint then? What's causing you the frustration I was watching out there?" She cocked her thumb in the direction of the gym.

"The biggest problem is the fact that the event happened over four years ago."

"Yikes!"

"Yikes doesn't even come close. At first I didn't have any suspects. Now I have three."

"And that's a problem how?" she asked.

"It's a problem because although there are things that suggest each of the three people could be responsible, there isn't anything that *proves* one of them is responsible."

"And how have you been going about trying to find this proof?"

I thought for a moment. "In a very haphazard manner."

Pat raised her dark eyebrows, but her smirk stifled whatever it was she wanted to say.

"I've just been blundering along, going on intuition, following whatever lead presented itself."

"And how would you describe the state of your investigation at the moment?" She slid off the elastic that had been holding her long hair in a ponytail, and shook her head so that brown waves framed her face.

My cheeks were heating up again, so I said the first thing that popped into my head. "It's like a big pile of...string. Each time I move a strand...I see what's under it, but I...I can't find either end." As I spoke, my analogy began to make sense to me. "Until I find an end, I can't start untangling the heap and making it into a nice neat ball."

"I see." Pat looked at me for a moment then grinned. "It sounds like you need to simplify your approach. Make a plan. Think of it in boxing terms. If you were going into the ring with a really tough opponent, someone whom other, more experienced fighters hadn't been able to beat—what would you do?"

"I'd run in the other direction," I laughed.

"Good choice, but supposing you'd agreed to it." She swung her feet off the desk and leaned toward me. "Say that for some reason I'd asked you to take the match and you'd told me you would and then didn't want to let me down."

"Okay," I said, locking eyes with her. I was starting to see where Pat was going with this. "Well, I'd find out as much as I could about the other fighter. I'd talk to you about her."

"Another good choice." Pat smiled, and her eyes twinkled. "What else?"

"I'd do some research. See if there were any articles on her, or videos of her fights. I'd want to know her strengths, and if she had any weaknesses."

"Everyone has weaknesses." Pat winked again. "And then?"

"I'd train based on what I'd learned. I'd try to be as prepared as I could be to counteract her strong moves, and to take advantage of any moment she showed vulnerability."

"What about *your* strengths?" Pat asked.

"I'd make a plan based on them. I'd visualize myself following through with my plan, using what I am really good at to protect myself and land my punches."

"And then you'd get in the ring and do it." Pat gave me a playful punch on the shoulder.

The physical contact sent an electric shock through my body and momentarily erased any thought of work. I managed to say, "Right," but my momentary loss of reason meant I didn't sound as confident as Pat was hoping.

"Let me ask you this: are you even sure that any of the three people is involved at all in whatever you're trying to solve?" She was determined to help me.

I didn't have an immediate answer, but by the time I spoke I had managed to retrieve my thoughts from roaming over Pat's body and place them where they should have been the whole time. "Yes. My office was broken into and my computer stolen. Believe me, unless someone was looking for something specific, that wouldn't have happened. And I'm only working on the one case right now."

"Okay, so you're not just whistling Dixie. If you had to rank your three suspects, would you be able to?"

"Yes." In my mind I made a list. Anasetti was at the top, Sanderson at the bottom.

"Now instead of thinking of those three people as one opponent, think of them as three. Would you ever get in a ring with three other boxers and expect to be able to win?"

"Of course not," I said without thinking. Then I made the connection. "So I need to fight them one at a time. I get it. Simplify and make a plan."

"If I were you, I'd stop throwing punches in all directions, and concentrate on whoever is at the top of your list. If that fight doesn't give you what you need, move on."

The punching bag had done me a lot of good, but despite my inner battle with my wandering eye, nowhere near as much good as my chat with Pat. I burst into the sunshine ready to take action.

Dewey's apartment building on Isabella is dated, and the white brick and glass balconies make no attempt at any sort of style. Its proximity to Church Street, where Dewey works and socializes, however, makes it the perfect spot for him to call home. His tastefully decorated apartment also became the perfect spot for us to call a temporary office, after the break-in and theft of my computer.

I'd brought a pad of poster-sized paper and some coloured markers with me. I felt more like a primary school teacher than a P.I. as I carefully attached four pieces to a bare wall with masking tape. Dewey was doing what he did best: he hummed some opera song in the kitchen while he made a pitcher of iced tea from scratch. Just as I finished the bold, blue heading on the fourth piece of paper Dewey arrived with two frosted glasses.

The expanse of unsullied white paper hung before us, while we sat on the sofa and sipped in silence. Finally Dewey spoke. "Don't get me wrong, Calli, I do understand what we're trying to do."

"But?"

"Well." He bunched up his face.

"Well?"

"Okay, I'm just going to try and flow with this." He rested his head on the high leather back of his chair and gazed at the ceiling.

"Okay, so I'm going to get this started." I chose a marker from the coffee table and headed toward the paper entitled *Indira Mehta*. I wrote down the date, time, and location of the attack, and after telling Dewey about my visit with Miss Pritchard, added a point about the jewellery.

He stared at the paper before asking, "How did she get the head trauma?"

"She was hit with something. They never found whatever it was."

"So let me get this straight: someone attacked her

with something big enough and heavy enough to do that much damage, then took it away with him."

"Maybe. Or, the police just didn't find it."

We finished listing details on Mrs. Mehta's sheet and that of Borisav Belic. His included not only what we knew about him, but also notes on his sister and his relationship with her. I put an arrow next to the lines detailing his proven crimes and his lack of alibi.

Sanderson's sheet wasn't hard to complete, but I didn't write down anything worthy of an arrow. There was no direct motive. His conflict was with Mr. Mehta, not his wife. Since he couldn't communicate, we would never be able to establish an alibi, but there was no evidence that he was anywhere near Yorkville on that night. Just because he was probably involved in illegal adoption activities prior to the time of the attack and his son had lied about being involved in his father's business, it didn't mean he had anything to do with what happened to Mrs. Mehta.

I was about to remove Sanderson's sheet from the wall altogether when Dewey stopped me. "You may as well leave it there for now. At least it makes it look like we've been doing some work."

The last sheet was easy. All the information we had about Lucas Anasetti galloped onto the paper, one incriminating fact after another. He knew the victim. He had seen her earlier that day. He may have known she was carrying valuables and he had possibly overheard her plans for the rest of the day and evening. He was actually with Mrs. Mehta at the place she was attacked.

He had lied about his friend on Davenport and about the events with the man in the house. And last but not least, he had suddenly acquired enough money to purchase the salon in which he was employed.

It looked as if we had at least isolated our real opponent. Now we had to plan our moves.

Dewey had made the ultimate sacrifice for the case: he'd gone back to Waves and allowed a stylist armed with scissors and razor to attack his cherished cornrows. He wasn't sure how he felt about his new style, which was called a close shave. I thought it looked fantastic. It's impossible for Dewey to look bad, and his new hairstyle gave him a macho sophistication he hadn't had before.

Stick Woman had agreed to pair Dewey with the senior stylist, once Dewey made sure he had been employed at the salon when Anasetti took over. Dewey being Dewey, he'd sweet-talked enough information from the stylist for us to be able to move forward with our investigation.

Harry Lebow, the former owner of the salon, had agreed without hesitation to a visit from me. I gave Dewey the afternoon off to adjust to his new hair, or lack thereof, and maybe buy some clothes to complete the look. The day was gorgeous; I needed some alone time, and I didn't mind the drive to Oakville. The traffic on the expressway even cooperated.

Lebow had retired to a tree-lined street that ends

at the shore of Lake Ontario. His house was grand, but conservative compared to some of his neighbours' places. I found a shady spot by the curb to park my Forester, rather than pulling into the circular driveway.

"Ms.Barnow, I presume," said the distinguished looking man who opened the carved wooden door.

"Mr. Lebow?" I was certain he was the person I'd spoken to on the phone, but you never know.

"One and the same. Come in. Come in."

I followed him through the house to a solarium overlooking the pool and garden.

He motioned to a wicker chair. "Would you like anything to drink?"

"No thanks. I won't be staying long," I said.

"That's too bad." He sat in a matching chair, the varnished weave squeaking under his weight. "I don't get many visitors these days. We used to live downtown. When we moved out here, we hadn't realized that many of our social ties would start to fray."

I'd have to remember that if Jess suddenly decided she wanted to move out of the city. "You don't go into Toronto much?" I asked, willing to spend a few minutes on idle chat with the lonely man.

"Only a couple of times a month now. I used to go more often, but…"

I let the silence take over then I changed the subject. "You have a lovely house."

"Thank you. It's far too big, of course. When my wife was alive, she seemed to fill the rooms with her presence. Now it's just a waste of space. I should really consider downsizing but…"

"I'm sorry about your wife. Did she pass away recently?" I forced myself to ask.

He smiled a sad smile. "Thank you, Ms. Barnow. A couple of years ago, but sometimes it still feels like yesterday…"

Once again I stayed silent. Sometimes there's just nothing to be said. And although I really couldn't know what he was going through with his loss, I thought I could see why Harry Lebow was finding it hard to move. He had a gorgeous home in a wonderful location, and sad as it made him, it held memories he couldn't replicate.

"So, Mr. Lebow," I finally began.

"Please, call me Harry," he interrupted.

"If you'll call me Calli."

"Calli it is." He slapped his knees with the palms of his hands to seal the deal.

After my meeting with Lucas Anasetti, I'd been rather apprehensive about meeting Harry Lebow. I had expected them to be curled with the same tongs, but I couldn't have been more mistaken. The people who worked at Waves at the time it changed hands must have had quite a shock.

It was Harry who finally introduced the reason for my visit. "So Calli, what did you want to talk to me about? You mentioned Lucas Anasetti."

I almost hated to spoil things by discussing Anasetti. "I'm looking into an incident that involved him back in the winter of two thousand and eight. He came upon a woman who had been attacked a few blocks from the salon."

"I see. I don't have any recollection of it. How do I figure into this?"

"You were the owner of Waves at the time."

"Yes, on paper. I didn't spend much time there though. I had other business interests. My wife really ran the place."

"I understand. But you did know Anasetti?"

"Oh yes, I knew him, and he wasn't the sort of person you'd forget if you'd met him once." His kind face struggled to banish an expression of distaste.

"He hasn't changed much," I assured him.

"I don't know how my wife put up with him, to tell you the truth. Apparently he was a gifted stylist though, so he was good for business."

"Were you surprised when he wanted to buy the salon from you?"

"No, no, I wasn't. He was an ambitious young man. It actually made a lot of sense. He already had a loyal clientele. I knew it wouldn't be hard for him to use that as a basis to grow the business, put his own brand on things, so to speak."

"Were you aware if he was saving money for such a transaction?"

"I didn't know anything about Anasetti's financial situation. He may have had savings, but it was obvious he liked to spend. He certainly didn't scrimp on his appearance—clothes and the like. I never had the feeling that he *came* from money. He just tried too hard, if you know what I mean."

"Yes, I do."

"When he approached me about buying the salon I was glad. To be honest, the timing was a godsend."

Although when or why Harry Lebow and his wife wanted to get rid of the salon was none of my business, my face must have asked the question.

"We'd been having some trouble at the shop over the previous year. Break-ins, things going missing when there had been no obvious break-in. Nothing big, but annoying enough that at our age we just didn't want to be bothered with it."

"Did you or the police find out who was responsible?"

"Unfortunately no, but we had our suspicions that at least some of the incidents were connected to the cleaning company we employed. There were other businesses in the area experiencing similar problems. We switched to another company and things settled down. We notified our old company that we thought they were employing crooks, and they begged us not to get the police involved, that they'd deal with it. Well, I didn't have the energy to pursue it anyway, and that's the last I heard."

"So much for bonding employees," I said. There was a little light flashing in the back of my brain, but I ignored it.

"Just because someone has no record, doesn't mean they'll never have one," Harry added.

"You have *that* right. There's a first time for everything."

My digression reached its natural conclusion, so I returned to my original line of questioning. "When did Anasetti first approach you about buying the salon?"

"Let's see, it would have been late winter or early spring of ... two thousand eight." He looked at me with suspicion. "Is this going where I think it's going?"

"And where do you think it's going?" I asked. I was eager to see if someone other than me was connecting the dots.

"A woman was attacked. Anasetti found her. Then he suddenly had enough money to buy a business. Sounds pretty fishy. But the woman must have been carrying quite a roll of bills, if that was the case."

"Yes, that's why I came to see you, Harry. Could you tell me about the financial transaction for the salon? Did Lucas say anything, or do anything that would indicate the source of his money? Anything... I don't know...strange?" Although Harry could see the possibility of a connection, I knew it was tenuous at best, but even tenuous is better than nothing.

Harry leaned back and stroked his chin, then he gave a harrumph. "Now that you mention it, yes. You're not going to believe this, Calli. I'd forgotten all about it, until you asked."

I held my breath, quite prepared to not believe.

"I was at the salon one day when Anasetti cornered

me in the back room. He told me he wanted to buy the salon. Said his mother had died. Then he reached into his pocket and brought out a handful of old jewellery. Waved it in my face. I know nothing about jewellery, but it looked as if it might have some value for the gold in it. Still, I didn't take the offer seriously. I told him if he turned it into enough money for a down payment, the salon was his."

From the moment Harry had mentioned jewellery I hadn't been able to breathe. Now I forced myself to inhale, just enough to ask, "And he did?"

"Damn right. About a week later I dropped in to see my wife and what did Anasetti do but show me the balance in his savings account and ask if we could now do business. Well, I was shocked, I can tell you, but I just put it down to my not knowing anything about jewellery, as I told you. Or maybe his mother had investments or something, and left him that as well."

My heart was still pounding, but I was able to talk more easily. "So you went ahead with the sale."

"I had no reason not to. As I said, the timing was perfect. My lawyer drew up all the paperwork and the deal went through. I guess you could say you're sitting in what that jewellery, or whatever he had, helped pay for." His brow constricted to a landscape of knolls and valleys. "I'm getting the feeling that the jewellery didn't come from Anasetti's mother."

"Very unlikely," I said.

"The woman who was attacked?" Harry asked.

"It looks that way."

Harry glanced at his surroundings and shook his head.

Despite the glee I felt at discovering the information, I didn't envy Harry the burden of his new knowledge. "I'm so sorry," I said.

"Well." He forced the return of his customary sunny expression. "Maybe that's the push I need to get rid of this mausoleum."

Our visit soon came to a close, but before I got down the front steps, that little flashing light in my head stopped me.

Harry was still standing at the doorway when I turned around. "There's probably nothing to this, but do you happen to remember the name of the cleaning company?"

Harry's face split to a grin. "Sure do. Hard to forget a name like that. Especially under the circumstances. Secure Scouring."

CHAPTER TWELVE

As soon as I arrived home I did a search for the obituary of Anasetti's mother. Based on the timing of Lucas's purchase, she must have died early in 2008. There were no such records. When I widened my search, I found what I was looking for. Sophia Anasetti had died in 1995 in Cornwall, Ontario. She was survived not only by her husband, but by a son, Lucas, who lived in Toronto, four other sons, and three daughters. If this was my Lucas Anasetti, I now had one more incriminating fact to add to his list.

I called June, but while I waited for her to pick up, my elation over Harry's information and the obituary began to fade. What if my discoveries from the last few hours turned out to be no more than tantalizing pieces to a puzzle I couldn't complete?

I needed some assurance, but when I heard June's response to what I told her, I knew she wasn't about to provide it.

"Barnow, I don't deal with robberies anymore.

What do you expect me to do?"

I must have caught June at a bad time. She's always very businesslike about police work, but I hadn't heard such an edge to her voice in ages. It had to be more than just my interruption.

"Sorry, June. I know. I shouldn't have bothered you."

"No, it's okay. I'm the one who should be sorry. I didn't mean to bite your head off. I'm just kind of overwhelmed at the moment."

"I'll let you get back to work. We'll talk again soon," I said, not wanting to make things worse.

"I'm serious, Barnow. Give me a break. Let me at least explain about what you're trying to do. Even if I had the time to follow up on your robbery theory, it wouldn't get us anywhere. First of all, let me remind you how long ago this allegedly happened. But that's not the real issue. That jewellery Mrs. Mehta supposedly had in her possession, and which Lucas Anasetti supposedly sold for a down payment on the salon is virtually untraceable. Was it ever reported missing? Was it even insured?"

"I have no idea about insurance. All I do know is that my client wasn't aware that her mother was carrying it around, and neither was my client's father."

"Uh huh…so here's what would have happened, Calli, if the jewellery had been stolen from Mrs. Mehta: The guy who took it would have had no way of knowing if it was going to be reported missing-"

"Not necessarily," I interrupted. "If Anasetti is the

guy, he might have had a pretty good idea. He worked at the salon where Mrs. Mehta had her hair done that day, and I've spoken to another woman who had a conversation with her at the salon about the jewellery. Mrs. Mehta told the other woman that she was planning to sell it without telling her family. Anasetti could have overheard the conversation."

"Okay." June was trying to be patient with me. "But, even if that were true, he would have played it very safe. Keep in mind, since she told this woman about it, she might have told all sorts of people. Besides, Mrs. Mehta didn't die from the attack, and it only became apparent later that her coma would continue. Whoever was involved on that night couldn't be certain of anything."

I had to agree.

"So he probably got it valued at a couple of less than reputable dealers, the kind who give you a fraction of what something's worth, but in return don't keep records. He may have even gone to another city to get rid of the stuff. I can almost guarantee that before he put the money from the sale into his bank account, that jewellery had been melted down, and any stones had been used or sold. You get the picture?"

"Unfortunately I do. It would be as if it never existed."

"Precisely."

"But there were two people who saw the jewellery. One when Mrs. Mehta had it and one when Anasetti had it. And it looks as if Anasetti lied about where he got it. Isn't that some kind of proof?" I knew the answer before June replied.

"People lie all the time, Calli. It's rarely important enough to be considered proof, unless it can be linked to something much stronger. And as far as your two witnesses go, if they were experts in antique Indian jewellery and they'd both seen it for long enough to give detailed and accurate descriptions, it might cast some valid suspicion on Anasetti, but I'm guessing that isn't the case."

All I could say to that was, "No."

"Right, and don't forget, Calli, you also have no proof that it was Anasetti who attacked the woman."

"So basically I have nothing," I said.

"I'm afraid so."

"And Anasetti is going to get away with it."

"It happens, Calli. More often than we would like to admit."

I wanted to rail against the injustice of it all, but there was no point.

"Listen, Barnow, I've got to go, but let's meet for dinner or a drink or something. This week sometime. Just the two of us."

"That would be really nice, June. Thanks."

When June put the phone down, I was filled with a loneliness I hadn't felt in a long time. I was pretty much back to square one with the case. Actually, it was worse than square one. I was sure I'd found the culprit, but I could do nothing about it. Maybe Sashi would be satisfied with knowledge, since litigation seemed out of the question. Even if she wasn't, though, it didn't explain my emptiness. I'd had unsuccessful cases before, and it didn't feel like this.

My personal life couldn't be blamed either. Everything was chugging along beautifully—well almost. I had a gorgeous wife, wonderful friends, and a bright future. I tried to focus on each positive in turn, but finally gave up the struggle. It was becoming clear that contemplation wasn't the answer to my problem; it just made me feel worse.

I took several deep, measured breaths. That didn't help. I patted Sherlock's warm purring bulk. That didn't help either. I attacked my worry stone. Nothing. I couldn't remember if I had any Xanax left. It had been so long since I'd needed them. Even if I did have some, they were probably expired. I didn't care.

I was in the midst of a frantic rummage through the medicine cabinet, when the apartment door creaked.

"Honey, are you home?" Jess's voice reached me like a balm. My shoulders relaxed and I closed the door of the medicine cabinet.

Jess was filling the kettle by the time I entered the kitchen. "I was hoping you'd be here," she said.

"Why are *you* here?" I asked, and gave her a kiss before collapsing onto the closest chair. "Are you feeling okay?"

She blessed me with a smile. "I'm better than okay." She sat on my lap and put her arms around my neck. "You'll never guess what I did today."

"In that case, maybe you should tell me." I snuggled against her body which was still hot from being outside. She smelled of...Jess.

"I made some phone calls."

"Isn't that part of your job?" I teased and examined the fine contours of her face.

"About adoptions." She beamed at me.

"Ah." I tried to fill the sound with excitement, but I might have failed.

Jess was excited enough for the two of us. "I phoned the Adoption Council and asked some questions. They said we'd have to become what they call 'Adopt Ready' by having a home study and doing some training."

"What?"

"You know, Calli. Not everyone would make good adoptive parents. It just makes sense. Anyway, they referred me to their great website, and said to call back if I have any more questions. Then I phoned that place that your friend recommended, and they're going to send us out an information package. Oh, Calli, I'm so happy." She hugged me close.

As I watched Jess, so full of life and hope for the years ahead, and as I listened to her plans for our family, I waited for my old gut-wrenching anxiety to arrive. It didn't. Instead, a seed of possibility was taking root inside me. Maybe I really did want to be a parent. Maybe it was just what I needed to move beyond my occasional relapses into darkness. "So you've definitely decided you would rather adopt?" I asked.

"Yes. I *definitely* want to adopt." Her eyes made love to me.

"Well, I guess it wouldn't hurt to look at the information—no promises."

"It wouldn't hurt at all." She nuzzled my neck.

"I know one thing I can promise." I reached under her blouse and traced the line of her backbone with my finger.

"Why Calli, are you inviting me to the bedroom in the middle of the day?" she teased.

"I *am* inviting you. But not to the bedroom. If we have a kid, we won't be able to make love all over the apartment whenever we feel like it." I undid the top button on her blouse.

"We'd better make the most of it then." She took my hand and led me to the living room where she pushed me down on the sofa.

Sherlock had been fast asleep at one end and leapt as high into the air as a thirteen-pound cat can leap before landing on the floor, whiskers quivering in fright.

Standing in front of me, Jess continued to disrobe. She could have put most of the strippers in the city to shame with her moves. Although I remained still, every cell in my body was alive and pulsing, just waiting to see what gift she would give me next. Once she was down to her black lace bra and panties, she started to undress *me* using her hands and her teeth.

All this talk of parenthood must have ramped up Jess's hormones, and I for one was not complaining. Maybe there was something to this after all.

Jess and I had spent what was left of the evening looking at the website she'd told me about and discussing some of the pros and cons about various kinds of adoption. We even broached the subject of having to move somewhere more suitable for kids. Although I felt my sense of control slipping away, much to my surprise, I felt happier than I had in a long, long time. I'd slept better than I had in recent memory as well.

"You're in a good mood, babe," said Dewey, when he joined me at my office the next day.

I hadn't been back since the break-in, and it was time to get things in order. "I am in a good mood."

"Jess must have been very nice to you last night, because I know it's not due to the clean-up job." He looked at the pathetic scene before him.

I was sitting cross-legged in the middle of the floor surrounded by what had been the contents of my filing cabinet, but now looked more like the aftermath of an explosion in a paper factory.

Dewey somehow managed to join me, despite the restrictions imposed by his skin-tight jeans. "So was Jess nice to Calli, or do you have some good news about the case?" He opened the closest file folder and began searching the floor for what should be inside it.

"Some of the former, none of the latter."

"None? Didn't you go and see Lebow after I did this?" He pointed to his sleek head as if it were a blight on humanity, rather than a stunning addition to his image.

"Oh yes, I went."

"And?"

"And I found out that Anasetti is our man—at least I'm ninety-nine per cent sure he is."

"Didn't I tell you? That's wonderful!" He tossed the papers he was holding into the air. As they fluttered down like giant pieces of confetti, he saw my face. "It's not wonderful?"

"We can't prove it." I told him what Lebow had told me, what I'd discovered about Anasetti's mother, and how June had burst my bubble. Just to make myself feel better I added that I would have figured it out myself, had I not been so hopeful.

"So there's nothing we can do?"

"Not unless you have some form of torture in mind by which you could get a signed confession from Anasetti," I said.

Dewey doesn't often look downcast, but that's exactly how he looked as the realization sank in. "So what do we do now?"

"We clean up this mess, get a new lock and security system as you suggested, and then we go and buy me that new computer."

"And when you get paid for the case, I go and buy me some new threads. All the clothes I have went with 'da rows.' I need a new fashion statement to go with 'da shave.'" He ran his hand over his head and grinned.

The last file folder had just been returned to its proper spot, when Sashi appeared in the doorway. She'd phoned to say she was on her way over. Just as well. Dewey and I could have sat on the floor forever, daydreaming about what we were going to purchase once this frustrating case had been put to rest.

"You're timing is perfect," I said, "in more ways than one." I waited until we were all comfortably seated on chairs before I related the news regarding Anasetti.

Sashi confirmed that neither she nor her father knew anything about the missing pieces of jewellery. There was an insurance policy that covered all her mother's valuables, but since her mother's death, she hadn't had time to look at it. Because she was the sole beneficiary, Sashi had moved whatever was in her mother's safety deposit box to her own without sorting through it.

"You should check what you took from the box against whatever is listed on the insurance policy. The jewellery might be itemized. There may even be photos," I said.

"I will, but even if there's something missing, which seems likely, nothing can be done about it."

"Still, it's worth checking. And if it is missing, inform the insurance company."

"Sure. I'll do that, when I have some time." Sashi didn't sound as if she were promising anything.

"I thought you'd be more upset," I said to her.

"I don't care about the jewellery," she said. "And

as for Anasetti, well sure I'd like to see him pay for what he did. Of course I would. But even if *I* don't get to see it, he *will* pay. Karma may not be swift, but it's sure."

Although I don't share Sashi's belief in destiny, I was relieved. Not just because Sashi wasn't upset, but also because I would now be free to get on with other work. I'd had a few enquiries over the last couple of days, and I was anxious to get back to the sort of case where I felt competent and could look forward to some degree of success.

"So I'll do up the paperwork for you, and we can finalize things," I said, as delicately as possible.

"You're not finished yet, Calli," she replied.

"I'm not?"

"That's why I came to see you. Anasetti might get off scot-free under law for his attack on my mother and the theft of the jewellery, but something's still going on with Sanderson."

"Sashi, he's a sick old man. Sure he did some things in the past and he upset your father, but there's no connection to your mother. And he's incapable of causing any more trouble for anyone. Whatever it is that's bothering you, I'd suggest you just drop it, forget about it."

"I would like to drop it, just walk away from everything. In fact, I wish I'd never decided to start this wild goose chase in the first place. Yes, I got an answer in the end, but the only really good thing that's come from all of this is reconnecting with you, Calli."

I felt more or less the same way, although I was going to be handsomely reimbursed for my troubles. "So why *don't* you just walk away from it?"

"Because I've received a threat from Sanderson."

I wasn't sure I'd heard her correctly. "Sanderson? But he can't speak."

"From his son. He said that if I didn't stop you from poking around in his father's life, he would have you and me charged with harassment. Did you tell him I'd hired you?"

"I didn't name you. I only said I was looking into the attack on your mother on behalf of her daughter. I'm sorry, Sashi. I never anticipated something like this."

"It's not your fault, Calli, but can he really do that?"

I shook my head no. "I've only gone to see his father once. And that was useless. Yes, I've talked to some other people, but he doesn't know that."

Silence landed in the space between the three of us. We all knew without agreeing, that it should stay there.

Then the memory of feeling followed struck me like a stun gun, and my heart rate shot up. There were also Sashi's slashed tires. And someone had broken into my office and now had access to any notes that were on my computer. Anasetti had never struck me as the sort of man who would bother with any of that. He was far too secure; he considered himself not only superior but invincible. Besides, he didn't know that

I had made any connection, improbable as it might be, between himself and Mrs. Mehta's jewellery.

What we were dealing with in these instances was more the work of a bully, someone who was aware of his vulnerability but would never admit it. Someone who felt threatened by me and my investigation.

My stomach began to churn. It was possible that the person who broke in and stole my computer had also bugged the place. It wouldn't have done any good, however, until today, since I hadn't been back since the break-in. It also wasn't very smart of whoever it was to make the intrusion so obvious, if subsequent verbal information was a goal. On the other hand, until that moment I hadn't considered the possibility of any sort of surveillance equipment lurking in the room. Perhaps I was the one who wasn't very smart.

I held my finger to my lips to keep the others silent then I said, "As far as I'm concerned, Sanderson is of no interest to us. I found nothing that would tie him to your mother's attack. Any disagreement he might have had with your dad isn't worth bothering about. You should just do what he says, Sashi. That's what I'm going to do. My investigation is over." While I'd been talking I had written a message to Sashi and Dewey. I held up the paper: *play along*.

"I agree, Calli," said Dewey. "We've done what we set out to do, and I want to get back to my life."

"You've got a point," said Sashi. "The whole Sanderson thing was a waste of time. I just couldn't stand the thought of my father being put in that position. But it's all water under the bridge. It's over. My husband will be glad. He's always thought I was wasting my time and money."

"Great. We can finalize everything before the end of the week. I'll give you a detailed report along with the invoice."

"I appreciate it, Calli," said Sashi.

Keep talking. I'm going to look around.

I didn't know what Sashi's improvisational skills were like, but I was confident Dewey could hold up his end of the charade.

"I'm just going to put together a few things for you now, Sashi," I said, as I began to check my desk for any sign of a listening device.

"She can't do anything for you on the computer until she buys a new one," Dewey said.

"Why's that?" asked Sashi.

Having no luck with the desk, I used my mini-Swiss Army knife keychain to remove the covering on the phone jack.

"It was stolen. Can you believe it?" Dewey said. "It was just an old piece of junk."

Bingo! Nestled inside was a phone tap device.

"So it's no big loss," added Sashi.

I gave the others thumbs up before reattaching the cover, tap still in place.

"It's sooooooooooo not a big loss!" Dewey exclaimed.

I was guessing there was more than one device,

so I began to methodically examine every nook and cranny in my office. There were only so many places someone could hide a bug in the sparsely appointed room. "I'm looking forward to getting a new laptop," I said over my shoulder.

"I'm such a computer illiterate. My husband calls me *computersaur*."

Dewey laughed uproariously, and I continued to scour the room.

"You know, Calli, you and Dewey should come over for dinner some time."

I was beginning to think I was wrong about another bug.

"I'm not a bad cook."

Then I saw it.

Dewey had been keeping an eye on me and knew I'd found something. He fuelled the conversation. "That would be great, Sashi. I love to eat. If you tell me what you're serving ahead of time, I'll bring a special wine to go with it."

While Dewey gushed about culinary topics, I silently retrieved a stool and placed it in front of the open door. Once on top of it, I could get a clear view of what had caught my eye. Just above the doorjamb was a small white bump. It closely resembled a tiny golf ball that had been cut in half and stuck to the wall. At the bottom of each dimple was a pinhole. I managed to turn around without falling off the stool and pumped the air in victory.

Dewey realized he still had to keep things sounding normal, so he began to describe a chicken recipe he had recently tried. Sashi made all the appropriate responses. Between the two of them they provided me with enough time to climb down from the stool, put it back in its place, and return to my desk. I'd made a snap decision to leave the bug in place, just as I'd done with the phone tap. If we were going to continue investigating Sanderson, both of them might come in very useful.

Let's wrap it up and go outside to talk, I wrote.

"Here's all I have at the moment, Sashi." I rustled some papers, as if I were handing her something. "As I said, as soon as I get a new computer, I'll give you the rest."

"That's fine," she said. "I should get going. Thanks for everything, Calli. You too, Dewey."

"You're welcome," Dewey and I said almost on top of each other.

"I just wish we could have given you what you wanted," I added.

"Well, I did get some answers, even if justice can't be done in the courts. I feel better just knowing what I know." Sashi stood and made to go.

"We'll walk out with you, Sashi. We're finished here for today." I pushed back my chair and pointed to the door.

Outside on the street the real conversation took over, volume down. "There's no way I'm going to stop investigating Sanderson now." I'd been holding my anger in check during our performance upstairs.

"Anyone who breaks into my office and plants bugs is not going to get away with it."

"You go, girl," said Dewey.

Still not trusting our environment, we continued to talk as we walked toward College Street. "Dewey and I will get started on Sanderson, as soon as we can. We already have some preliminary information. Maybe now that we aren't trying to tie him to your mother, we'll be able to make more headway. We'll be in touch as soon as we know anything, Sashi. In the meantime, just carry on with your life. Don't do anything that might give the impression you haven't taken Sanderson's warning seriously. In fact, it would be a good idea to get in touch with him and tell him you're done with the whole thing."

"I'll do that, Calli. And you be careful."

I'd just put my feet up in front of the TV for a few minutes when the apartment landline rang. The phone is so old that there's no place for call display, and since most people now contact me on my cell, I assumed it was my mother.

"Calli?" A man's voice surprised me at the other end of the line.

"Yes."

"Oh good. You're at home. This is Ken."

It took me a moment, but I responded, "Hi, Ken."

"I hope this isn't a bad time, and I hope it's okay that I phoned. Your mom gave me your number."

"No, it's not a bad time. Is everything okay?" I jumped to the conclusion that for some reason my mother had given him bad news about herself and now as my older brother it was his job to break it to me.

He picked up on my distress. "Yes, of course. Everything's fine."

I shelved my irrational fear and managed to say, "Oh, good."

"I'm back to Toronto on business for the day, and I...well, I thought it would be nice if we could spend some time together, you know. Even half an hour. My meeting wasn't that far from where you live, so maybe if it's not inconvenient, we could meet."

"Uh, sure." I ran through possibilities in my mind before settling on what was easiest. "If you're close to here, why don't you just come over? I have to go out in a bit, but I've time for a short visit."

"Terrific!" His relief was audible.

Once I'd explained to Ken exactly where I lived in relation to where he was phoning from, I did a quick tidy of any room he might see or have need to visit. I'd just satisfied myself that I wouldn't be embarrassed, when the bell on the downstairs door rang.

Climbing the narrow set of stairs to reach the apartment didn't seem to bother him in the least, and we were soon seated in the little living room—Ken on the sofa and me on the easy chair.

"So, this is great. I'm really glad you called." My voice sounded unnatural. "Can I get you anything?"

"Oh, no thanks. I'm fine." He smiled and shifted

his position.

I was just about to make an inane comment of some sort, when he spoke. "I know this is awkward, Calli. It's bound to be. But avoiding each other won't make it any easier."

"I know," I agreed. His voice and even the way he looked at me helped the knots in my shoulders loosen. "But it's not like the last time we met."

"That's right. Your…our mother being there made a big difference. She was the reason we were together, kind of like two spokes only connected by the hub."

I gave him a look that commented on his appropriate but rather unusual simile.

"Sorry. I cycle in my spare time, and it sometimes creeps into my conversation." He blushed.

That made me smile. So I had a brother who, like me, turned red in the face at the drop of a hat.

"I'd really like to get to know you," he continued. "Have a relationship that doesn't always need her presence."

"I'd like that too." I'd said it before I realized it was true.

"I just want you to know, Calli, that she's *your* mother. I will never horn in on that. I have my own mother in Ottawa, a wonderful woman who raised me, and I love her beyond words. I don't know if I can explain how it feels to be in my position, but I'd like to try."

"It's okay, Ken. You don't have to explain anything to me."

"It's not for my benefit, Calli. I have been worried

about how you might feel, now after all these years suddenly having me land on your doorstep. And I want you to be honest with me, and tell me if there's anything in the situation, or anything in my actions that bothers you. Now or in the future. Okay?"

"Okay," I said.

"Well?"

Despite everything I liked Ken, so I decided to take him at his word. "I was upset to begin with. About the big secret Mom had kept from me. But I understand her position. What's still kind of unsettling is that after never having to share my mother with a sibling, suddenly there's you. And I know it's different and to you the woman who raised you is your mother, but when it comes right down to it both of us started out with the same relationship to my mom." I thought for a moment. "But I think it's going to be… fine. It's not like I'm twelve." I gave a nervous laugh.

"Maybe we can help each other get used to the whole thing," he said.

"Maybe," I agreed, and for the first time I acknowledged that what Ken was going through was far more profound than my discomfort.

"There's another reason I wanted to talk to you, Calli. Your mom told me that you and your wife are thinking about adopting. She also told me that you are having reservations about being a parent."

"That's true, but—"

"Don't be upset, Calli. Please. I know it's probably none of my business, but I figured it wouldn't hurt for you to hear what it's like to be on the other end of the adoption. It might just help you make up your mind one way or the other."

"I gather what you want to tell me is all positive." I thought this not only presumptuous on Ken's part, but also a waste of time.

"No. There are some negatives, of course. A lot depends on how and when the adoptive parents tell the child about the adoption. I was lucky; I've known as long as I can remember. And my adoptive parents not only told me how much they wanted me, but also showed me that through their love every single day. I was really lucky. Luckier than lots of kids raised by their birth parents."

My own father came to mind, but I pushed him out and asked, "And the negatives?"

"Well," a wistful look, similar to the one I'd seen on my mother's face, arranged Ken's features. "I always wondered why I'd been given away, why I wasn't wanted. That's a big thing to deal with when you're growing up. That's why I did the search. Of course I knew I was tempting fate, but it was worth it. I feel a lot better now after meeting your mother and hearing what happened. And, it's amazing to finally find people who look like me. To finally have the sort of reference points other people do: my mother's eyes, my father's chin. And now, seeing you and your—our mother, I have. Also, I wanted to know if I had any brothers or sisters." Ken had been deadly serious throughout his explanation, but now he smiled at me as if he'd never stop.

I couldn't help smiling back.

"And a few times when I was a kid I got teased, you know, if some other kid somehow found out I was adopted and wanted to give me a hard time. But I had such a stable and loving home that I could handle it."

"That's good."

"So for what it's worth, Calli, I'm happy. I wouldn't have had it any other way."

"Really?"

"Yes. Really." He warmed me again with his smile. "And I know we've only just met, but I think you'd make a dynamite parent."

"Thank you. I wish I were that sure."

"I'm a pretty good judge of character."

By the time we had to end our visit, I didn't want Ken to leave, so to stretch it out by a few more minutes I drove him to the foot of Bathurst Street. There he could catch the ferry to Billy Bishop Airport on the island.

"Come back soon, Ken. And thanks."

"Just try to keep me away." He gave me a quick hug and jumped out of the car.

We waved and he headed off, but I watched his back and the bounce in his step before I slipped back into the stream of traffic and headed north.

It's funny how life can throw you a curve ball and then provide you with a catcher's mitt, just at the moment you need it.

I'd decided to postpone my Sanderson enquiries until the next day by which time my anger at him would have had a chance to settle. Since I was in my Forester and still felt like doing a bit of work, however, following up on something Harry Lebow had said seemed like a good alternative.

Secure Scouring was nestled in a maze of streets that form an industrial park in Downsview not far from the old airport. A chain-link fence enclosed the lot full of company vans at the back of a one-story cinder block box of a building. Other than the logos on the vans, a small sign over the door was the only thing that announced the nature or name of the company.

The door was locked, so I rang the bell. If it hadn't been for the Chevy parked in front, I would have assumed the premises were empty. I was about to ring again when the door buzzed open. A man in a blue shirt with the company name embroidered on one pocket and *Alf* embroidered on the other was standing behind the front desk.

"Hi, Alf." I extended my hand.

He gave me the once over before reaching his hairy arm across the counter to engulf my hand in his. "You here from Eurogeniks?"

"No. I'm Calli Barnow, a private investigator."

He dropped my hand and took a step back. I began to fume. He might not like P.I.s, but he had no way of knowing why I was there. If I had been in the market for a cleaning company, as some day I might be, I would have already crossed Secure Scouring off my list.

I retrieved my hand from where it had landed on the counter and gave him an insincere smile.

His chinless face remained passive. "What do you want?"

His continued hostility fuelled a growing desire inside me for retaliation, so I decided on a course of action that I would normally avoid. It would take up more of my time, but it would also waste some of Alf's. "Well, Alf," I said, "I'm considering a move to a larger office space; my business is growing." This wasn't a complete lie, and although I wouldn't do business with Alf or his company, knowing his rates would certainly give me a basis for comparison down the road.

A flicker of embarrassment ran through his body before he became professional. "I see." He reached under the counter and produced an information sheet. "What size?"

Now I was on the spot. I said the first number that occurred to me. "Five hundred square feet. Approximately. I'm looking at a couple of different places."

He circled an area on the sheet with a red pen that had been in his *Alf* pocket. "That's your basic price for that size, for a once a week thorough cleaning. It goes up from there depending on type of floor covering, location, number of cleaners on the team, and special requirements."

I was actually starting to develop an interest in the possibility of such a service, but since that wasn't why I was there, I folded up the paper and slid it into my back pocket.

Alf had placed his palms on the counter and was waiting for me to leave when I got to the point of my visit. "I'm wondering if you could help me with something else?"

Alf curled his fingers into fists, making a scraping sound on the Formica. "Are you investigating me?" He glared at me from under his puffy eyelids. "Did my bitch wife hire you?"

So *that's* where he was coming from. "No. No. Nothing like that. I'm making enquiries about a former employee of yours."

Relief made Alf look almost pleasant.

"Are you the owner or manager?"

For the first time since I'd been there, Alf smiled. "I'm one of the owners."

"Terrific! So you would have been here five years ago, right?"

"That's right. I've been around since the beginning."

"So I'm hoping you'll be able to give me some information about someone you employed around two thousand and seven or eight."

"Is he still with us?"

"No."

"Then we wouldn't have a file on him anymore. We only keep them two years. In case of a reference request. In a business like this we have a high employee turnover. If we kept the files any longer, we'd run out of room."

"Maybe you'd remember this person. There was

some trouble. A complaint from a salon and some other Yorkville businesses. Suspected thefts."

Alf tucked what there was of his chin into the loose skin on his neck as he scrolled through his memories. It didn't take long. "Yes, I remember." His eyes shot to mine. "It's the only time we've had a problem like that. We take pride in the honesty of our employees." He pointed to the company name on his pocket. "Turned out to be just the one man. We convinced our clients not to press charges and we dealt with the guy. Fired his ass and made sure he'd never get hired by another cleaning company in the city."

"Do you remember his name?"

Alf squinted into the distance, his eyes almost disappearing between his cheeks and his eyelids. "I can see him. Skinny guy. Looked like he could use a good meal."

My heart sped up and I tried not to smile.

Alf drummed his sausage fingers on the counter. "Bu...Bra...Blarick...Something like that."

"Belic?" I offered.

"Yes!"

"Borisav Belic?"

"That's him!" Alf looked victorious, even though I'd supplied him with the name. "What's he done now?"

"Well, he's been in and out of trouble since you let him go. His thievery didn't end with you."

"Glad he got what was coming to him." Alf nodded his substantial head.

"Thanks for your help. And thanks for the rates." I patted my pocket. "I might get back to you on that. I really am considering a new space."

"You do that," said Alf. "And if my wife does contact you, I'm innocent."

CHAPTER THIRTEEN

The Weather Channel had forecast a high of thirty-four degrees Celsius, and by the time I emerged from my apartment onto Baldwin it felt that hot and then some. I made a quick visit to my office and produced enough normal business-like sounds to convince any eavesdroppers I was getting on with my life, sans Sanderson. I was of course limited by not having a computer. The monitor and keypad looked forlorn without their brains, and I was tempted to rush out and buy the beautiful Mac. Until I was fairly sure it wouldn't be stolen, however, I wasn't willing to take a chance. I still hadn't contacted a locksmith, or a security company.

After an hour or so of mundane phone calls and pen scratching, I braved the heat and headed off for Dewey's place and what I was really going to do with my day. I bought a newspaper from the dispenser at the corner of Spadina and flagged a cab that had its windows up. A hefty tip would reward the cabbie; they aren't all willing to use extra gas for air conditioning.

Traffic was heavier than usual for early afternoon, so I settled into the cool comfort of the back seat and began my perusal of the paper. Jess would be proud of me, I thought, since I normally rely on her to keep me informed. I might even be able to participate in an exciting discussion of current events at the dinner table tonight. She would also be proud that I was making some effort and maybe even a little headway in coming to terms with the idea of being a parent. I'd told her about Ken's visit but hadn't gone into details. I still needed thinking time.

The front page of the *Star* was dominated by world news. Nothing new and nothing cheerful.

Traffic slowed even more as we neared Queen's Park. A protest of some sort was in progress. I was about to read an article on page three, but was distracted by the colourful crowd waving placards on the lawn in front of the pink stone legislative buildings. I could hear them chanting, but I couldn't make out the words through the closed windows. Unlike some cabbies, my lover of cool refrained from comment, and I appreciated his silence.

Although the action outside the cab was more interesting than anything I'd read so far in the paper, something drew me back to the small article near the top of the page. Despite the temperature inside the sedan, the words in those few inches of print made me sweat. An elderly woman had been pushed in front of the Dundas streetcar during rush hour yesterday. She had died from her injuries shortly thereafter. A search was under way for a male in his mid to late twenties who had fled the scene. Normally the event would have registered in my "Oh my god, how sad" file, and I would have moved on to something else. This, however, was not normal. There was a grainy picture of the woman next to the article. I knew her. Initially the name hadn't rung any bells, but I recognized the face at once.

It was Mrs. Kumar, the old woman from the clothing shop on Gerrard.

Dewey had seen Mrs. Kumar in the store, but hadn't spoken to her. Nevertheless, when I told him about her death, he was upset.

"Do you think this is related to Sanderson?" Dewey voiced what I had been trying without success to push to the back of my mind.

Once it was said, I couldn't ignore it. "As much as I would like to think it's a coincidence, something's telling me it isn't."

"According to a good friend of mine, coincidences do happen," Dewey said.

"Not this time, Dew. I phoned June from the cab. She's coming over. Mrs. Kumar's death involves the police obviously, but June had no idea there might be a connection to our case. She wants to learn what we've found out, and I'm sure she also wants to make sure we don't blunder into anything we need to stay out of."

"Good. I think we could use some help, even if it's June telling us what not to do," said Dewey.

"I swear to god, Barnow, you are like a trouble magnet. Don't you ever have a case that doesn't include one or two dead bodies?" June hadn't bothered with any socializing, but had marched into Dewey's apartment and collapsed in the chair closest to the fan. Her blond curls were plastered to her flushed forehead and cheeks, and her once crisp outfit had long since wilted.

"Dewey, I think June could use some of your iced tea." I was stalling. I remembered from our time together as lovers that June gets very grumpy when she's hot. Since it was obvious she was already none too happy to have me involved in yet another one of her cases, I needed to make every attempt to rid her of extraneous irritants.

Somehow I managed to make enough small talk to fill the time until Dewey returned with an icy jug and three glasses.

June downed her first glassful and started on her second, before she returned to the reason for her visit. "I can't believe you've landed in the middle of one of my cases again, Barnow."

"It would be more correct to say you landed in the middle of *my* case." I'd never gotten over my habit of contradicting her.

"Let's not split hairs," she growled. "So tell me, what possible connection can you have to Mrs. Kumar?"

"She gave me information about an argument between Ravi Mehta and Prabhakar Sanderson."

"What's the connection between Ravi Mehta and Indira Mehta?"

"Her husband. Now dead," I clarified.

"And Sanderson?"

"Mehta's former partner in an import business. Sanderson also ran an international adoption agency, and may have had other sidelines as well." I was wishing Dewey had allowed me to leave the chart paper on his pristine wall but it clashed with his other artworks. "Mrs. Kumar worked in the shop on Gerrard that sold the imports. And there's something else: her granddaughter was adopted through Sanderson's agency."

June's face was almost back to its normal colour, and her expression was less confrontational. "Okay, I see the connections, but what could any of this have to do with some sadistic thug pushing Mrs. Kumar in front of a moving streetcar?"

"Maybe nothing, but Sanderson's son warned my client to stop the investigation of his father. She'd already had her tires slashed, and my office has been broken into. I'd felt as if I was being followed and then discovered my office had been bugged."

"And you think Sanderson is responsible for all that, as well as Mrs. Kumar's death?" June had perked up, as she envisioned where the information might lead her.

"Not Sanderson. He's incapacitated and living in a nursing home. But I've met the son. Although he comes across like a graduate from charm school, everyone I've talked to about him thinks he's bad news."

June narrowed her eyes. "Back up. I'm getting confused. Weren't you hired to find the person who attacked Indira Mehta? And didn't you find circumstantial evidence that pointed at the hairdresser? But you couldn't prove it? All that unverifiable information about the jewellery?"

"That's right. But until we focussed on Anasetti, the hairdresser, we were also looking at Belic, the vagrant you told us about, and Sanderson, just in case the motive for the attack had somehow originated with Ravi Mehta."

"I see. At least I think I do." June put her empty glass on the coffee table and slid forward on her chair. "So why are you still interested in Sanderson? You seemed so convinced the other day that Anasetti was the person you were looking for."

Dewey had been nursing his iced tea and listening. Now he chose to speak. "Because she's pissed off."

June's face asked the question.

Dewey looked at me. "Do you want to explain, or shall I do the honours?'

I hate having to justify myself to June. You'd think it would get easier, but it doesn't. Nevertheless, there was no reason for Dewey to tell her just to spare me the chore. "I will," I said. "It's true. I was ready to call it quits. More than ready. As you know, we couldn't prove anything about Anasetti. And although our two other suspects were and are both dubious characters, they had nothing to do with our case. That's when my client told me about the threat and I discovered the listening devices. We were obviously getting close to something, something Sanderson Junior was willing to break the law to hide. My client doesn't like being threatened, and I don't like my office being targetted."

"So you're still on the case," June said.

"Well, to be more precise, I'm kind of on another case. Sanderson believes my client no longer employs me. That's what we want him to believe. But although I'm no longer looking for Indira Mehta's attacker, I am now investigating Sanderson to see what it was that Ravi Mehta was so upset about. With any luck I can keep the investigation under Sanderson's radar. It's beginning to look as if he will stop at nothing to keep whatever it is from being discovered."

June just shook her head.

"And I'm not ready to give up on Belic either. I've linked him to the salon that Anasetti bought."

"When did you turn into the new Superwoman, Barnow? If I didn't know better, I'd think you were chasing your tail with all these old, possible crimes just to avoid something else that's going on in your life."

Out of the corner of my eye I could see Dewey escaping to the kitchen before he said something he shouldn't.

"Well, you'd be wrong." As always, June had managed to see through me. "I'm fine, and I'll be even better once I'm finished with all of this."

"Whatever you say, Barnow. So there's nothing I can say to change your mind?" June had to ask, even though she knew me well enough to know the answer.

"Have some more iced tea," I said and smiled.

"I thought so." She went to the window. Dewey's apartment is on the tenth floor and overlooks Isabella Street. "Since you're going to continue being an idiot, Calli, keep an eye on the blue Honda. I noticed it when I came in. I think you might have a tail."

June left, after giving me her usual warnings. She knows I'll try to heed them, but will probably end up getting myself into trouble one way or another. It doesn't seem to matter that I'm not by nature a very brave person, or that my brain works pretty well most of the time. Somehow I manage to inadvertently home in on the situation or the person representing the biggest threat. That's why I have June on speed-dial.

Dewey and I began our online search for anything to do with Sanderson Junior, and anything I might have missed the first time I'd investigated Sanderson Senior. Periodically we'd check the street to see if the blue Honda was still in front of the building. It hadn't moved all morning, and if it hadn't been for the smoke coming from the window on a couple of occasions, I would have thought it was empty.

Dewey's laptop is almost as ancient as my stolen computer, but it did the job. We managed to find out that Wayne Sanderson had graduated from Osgoode Hall Law School in 1995. After being out of sight for a few years, he had established his own practice not far from the intersection of Yonge and Bloor, where he specialized in commercial and family law, including private adoptions. Bingo!

I continued my Internet search, while Dewey phoned an old flame who worked at the Law Society of Upper Canada. Current complaints and hearings appear on the society's website, but nothing was listed for Wayne Sanderson. We needed someone with access to the archives, which aren't online. The old flame was quick to give Dewey the information. Wayne Sanderson had managed to get himself into hot water a couple of times. One instance of misconduct with regards to a contract resulted in a regulatory meeting. The other charge had something to do with money. Sanderson was suspended for a year over that.

I was coming up empty, when I once again landed on the old blog entry that mentioned the adoption agency. This time I took a closer look. It had been written by a young aspiring journalist. He was blathering on in rather colourful prose about sexism in the workplace. One of his examples was a situation involving the elder Sanderson's receptionist at the adoption agency.

The blogger talked about several instances of sexual harassment and mentioned a report the receptionist had lodged with the authorities about unethical practices. Everything was apparently swept under the carpet and the case never went to court. The blogger claimed that had the employee been a man, the situation would have ended in a very different manner.

Perhaps there was something here worth looking into after all. Fortunately for us, the aspiring young journalist had been cocky enough not only to write the piece in the first place but also to use his full name. I did a quick search on Canada 411 for Jon M. Russario and gave the list of numbers to Dewey. While he tried to phone the five leads, I widened my search, found Google references to some of the names as well as some new possibilities and a Facebook page for one man. All of them appeared to live in Toronto. If the Russario we were looking for had left our fair city, then there seemed to be no trace of him.

By the time I had put together my new list, Dewey had finished his calls, but come up empty handed. None of the original five possibilities that he'd managed to contact had anything to do with journalism or writing of any kind. I gave Dewey half the names on my new list, and I settled down with the other four. It didn't really matter where I started, so I began to dial the number of J. Russario, the real estate agent. I tapped four-one-six on my touchscreen and was about to continue with two, when something stopped me. I clicked off my phone and returned to the Facebook page I'd been looking at for Jonathan Russario.

There it was—a long shot, but a shot none the less. Under "Interests" he had listed his membership in a writers' group called 9 Lines. I examined his profile and discovered that he was employed by an insurance company. A quick cross-reference with my list of names showed one insurance broker.

Dewey joined me on the sofa while I phoned the number for J. Russario at Insurance Brokers of Greater Toronto. Voice mail picked up, and I left a message for Russario to call me back a.s.a.p. Until he responded, we'd pretty much come to a standstill, and there was no guarantee that once we did hear from him we'd be any further ahead. He might not be the right man, and even if he were, the odds of his remembering anything about the details that gave rise to the blog entry were remote.

Dewey decided to call the remaining numbers just in case. I decided to pace. I returned several times to the window. The Honda hadn't moved. Other vehicles came and went, but the blue roof remained a constant patch on the grey pavement.

The few sentences that Dewey repeated into his phone became the rhythmical background to my fragmented thoughts as they zigzagged around inside my brain. What connection did Borisav Belic have with Indira Mehta? There must be something. He had previously worked at the salon she visited the afternoon of her attack, but he would have done the cleaning after the salon was closed. They had probably never been on the premises at the same time. If Harry Lebow or Alf had just reported the thefts to the police, perhaps a connection could have been made years ago. But of course that didn't make sense, because it was clear to me, even if it couldn't be proven in a court of law, that Lucas Anasetti was the culprit.

I looked down at the blue car once again, and my gut constricted. Now could be a really good time to take an extended holiday—phone Jess, book some plane tickets, and get the hell out of Dodge. Just because someone stole my crappy computer and put some second-rate listening devices in my office, it didn't mean I had to see this—whatever it was—through to the end. If our morning's work had proved anything, it was that there was no case for us to work on. I'd made a rash decision in the heat of the moment, when Sashi was in my office. It was now time to do the sensible thing, for once.

"Sorry to trouble you," Dewey said and clicked off. "Well, babe, that's it. No luck."

"I've been thinking, Dew. Maybe we're just wasting our time."

"You could be right." He crossed to where I was and held my hand as he looked down on the street. "I see our friend's still around."

"You know it could be some innocent person sitting there while his wife is shopping. Maybe he's just too cheap to pay for a parking lot," I said.

"Yeah, you're probably right." He kissed the top of my head and left my side.

"So what do you think, shall we pack it in? If the insurance guy doesn't give us anything, shall we just cut our losses?"

"Am I hearing you right, Calli? You never give

up. You might threaten to give up, but you never do. This time you sound as if you mean it."

"You're right, but there's no place to go with this."

Dewey shrugged and did nothing to hide his disappointment.

My phone rang.

"Calli Barnow," I said, not entirely sure what I was hoping for in response.

Dewey hovered, so I pushed past him and sat in the armchair.

The voice that reached me through the tiny speaker was male, business-like, and wanted to make a sale.

I was quick to dash his hopes. "Are you the Jon M. Russario who used to write a blog called *Wanna B. Journalist*?"

The silence at the other end was ominous, but eventually a tentative "Yes" came back to me. I could picture Russario, sitting at his desk, white shirt sleeves rolled up, intent on dealing with the insurance policies that surrounded him. Then one phone call throws him back to a life he'd maybe rather forget, or perhaps to an unfulfilled dream. "What's this about?" he asked.

"You once wrote an entry about sexism in the workplace."

"Ye…s, I remember that." He still formed his words with caution. "Who are you?"

"As I said in the message I left, my name is Calli Barnow. I'm conducting an investigation that might involve the adoption agency you mention in your blog. I'm wondering if you might be able to give me any details about the unethical practices you referred to: the complaint that a female employee had made against the agency."

"I thought all that was dead in the water years ago. That's why I was writing about it." His voice betrayed a hint of interest.

"It was, but I'd like to have a look at it from a different angle, so anything you can tell me would be very helpful."

"Unfortunately, I don't have my notes from back then. The wife insisted I get rid of what she called my junk boxes, when we bought a house a few years ago. But I do remember what that was all about, more so than most of the other things I wrote. Probably because I had a personal interest."

"You had a connection to the agency?" I asked.

"Indirectly. I was dating the receptionist who made the complaint."

"And besides the sexual harassment, what was the problem?"

"Well...she never did tell me all the details, and it wasn't because I didn't ask. She didn't want me to get involved. In fact she was furious that I wrote about it at all."

"So what did she tell you?"

"Only that she was sure the agency was doing something unethical and possibly illegal with their international adoptions," he said.

"But no details?"

"That's right."

"And I gather she withdrew her complaint."

"Right again. Money changed hands. That's all I know."

"And what happened to the receptionist? Are you still in touch with her?"

"No. She disappeared from my life just after that. As I said, she was furious with me. We never officially broke up, but we just stopped seeing each other." Russario tried unsuccessfully to cover the regret in his voice with macho indifference.

"Do you mind telling me her name?"

"Maria Pappas," came the quick reply.

"So you wouldn't know where she might be living or have a phone number, I guess?"

"No. When I knew her she still lived at home. One of those side streets off the Danforth. Eaton Avenue, I think."

"Thanks," I said. "You've been a great help."

The call ended and I turned to see Dewey stretched out on his sofa, waiting for a report.

Because the Honda was still out front and I was more than slightly paranoid thanks to the case, Dewey came up with a plan. He dug up a couple of old baseball caps, which he assured me were not his but had been left behind by visitors. He then talked his neighbour and friend, Basil, into lending us his car. With caps pulled down to meet our sunglasses we drove Basil's shiny Acura out of the underground parking garage and onto Isabella. By the time we reached the corner, we were confident we weren't being followed.

Although the online listings were full of people by the name of M. Pappas, none had an address on Eaton. There was, however, an O. Pappas on the street. A phone call had been fruitless, so we aimed our new set of wheels in that direction, sat back, and enjoyed the cool air and surround sound.

I had to wake up Dewey once I'd parked in front of the tidy semi-detached home on the tree-lined street in Danforth Village. There was no bell, so we entered the enclosed porch. It was empty, and looked as if someone had scrubbed every inch of the linoleum and clapboard. I knocked on the inside door.

Eventually the curtain in the big front window moved, and I caught the flash of a woman's face. A moment later the door cracked open to reveal more of the same person—work dress and greying hair caught back from a dispirited face.

"Mrs. Pappas?" I asked.

"Yes." Her voice was wary.

I handed her my card and introduced myself, then Dewey. We looked relatively respectable, since we'd left the caps behind in the car. "We're looking for your daughter, Maria," I said.

She stopped herself just short of slamming the door in our faces then she asked, "Why?"

I explained how we just wanted to talk to Maria

about the complaint she had made against her employer a number of years ago.

The door eased open a few more inches, just enough to show, even in the darkness of the hallway, the tears that glistened in the eyes of Mrs. Pappas. "Thank God someone is investigating that man. He and his evil son ruined my girl's life."

Although I'd heard bad reports already about both men, now the younger Sanderson had joined his father with a reputation for being evil. "I understand your daughter received some sort of a settlement," I said.

"Money. What good is money? It can be spent like water. It doesn't make a life." She dabbed her eyes with a tissue she'd been carrying in her apron pocket.

"We'd like to speak with your daughter. Does she still live here?" Dewey asked.

"No, she hasn't lived here in years," was the bitter reply.

"Would you be willing to give us her address?" I asked.

"I'll give it to you," said Mrs. Pappas, "but you might not find her. If you do, you'll see what he did to her. If you don't, come back here and I'll tell you."

Since there was no street parking on Bathurst, I pulled into the alleyway next to St. Volodymyr's church. A few houses south of the church we found the address Mrs. Pappas had given us. A young woman sat on the steps of the rundown row house nursing a cigarette.

Dewey took over, without so much as giving me a glance. "Hey, sista, what's up?"

The girl raised her head and gave us the once over. "Not much, man. Wha' chu wan'?"

"We're looking for Maria Pappas. I hear she lives here."

"That depends." The girl blew smoke in our direction.

"Her mama sent her some money." Dewey reached into his pocket and took out some bills.

The girl reached out her shaking hand. "I'll give it to her."

"Can't do that, sista. But tell you what, you point me in her direction, and I'll make it worth your while." He peeled off a ten-dollar bill and held it in front of the girl.

She ripped it out of Dewey's hand and stuffed it down her cleavage. "Over there." She pointed across the street. "Looking to score. Yellow shirt."

We dodged the traffic and made it safely across Bathurst in the direction the girl had indicated. Before us stretched Alexandra Park, the green space for the entire neighbourhood, which was named after it. The trees and lawns and outdoor recreational facilities are next to the community centre, and it's all an attempt to provide the local population with a safe and pleasant location for exercise and leisure. Unfortunately, the park is also home to the drug trade for the surrounding area.

Because of this, I watched my feet, as we crossed

the grass towards the middle of the park where picnic tables were dotted under towering maples and ash. I'd successfully avoided a couple of syringes and a broken crack pipe, when Dewey spotted a flash of yellow.

The woman's back was toward us. She was sitting at a picnic table, but even from behind we could see she was tense and fidgeting. We circled around, so as not to startle her. The last thing we wanted was to chase the poor woman through a park full of strollers and users just to ask her a few questions.

As Dewey and I slowly approached the picnic table, we talked to each other and made an attempt to look unthreatening. We must have succeeded, because the woman saw us, then she looked off in the other direction. When we were near enough, I took the lead.

"Excuse me, are you Maria Pappas?" I tried to sound friendly.

The woman's eyes snapped back to me and stayed on my face long enough to make sure it was I who had spoken. Then she looked at Dewey.

"Maria?" I asked again.

She returned her attention to me. Although she looked much older, she couldn't have been more than about thirty-five. What must have once been stunning dark eyes were now black centres in the hollows above her cheekbones. Her thick curly hair hung uncombed over her scrawny shoulders. She repeatedly opened and shut the empty cigarette packet she was holding, as if something might suddenly appear inside if she gave it one more try. "Yeah," she said at last, then she coughed until she had to rest her head on the rough wood of the tabletop.

Dewey and I waited. Neither of us spoke, nor did we look at each other.

When she finally lifted her head, I asked, "May we sit?"

She didn't say, "No," but eyed us with suspicion. "You got a smoke?" She held up her empty pack.

"Sorry," we both said.

"What do you want? Whatever it is, I didn't do it." She took the foil from the inside of the packet and smoothed it out. "And I don't have much time." She glanced around the park.

"You're not in trouble, Maria. We just have a few questions about a job."

She began a throaty chuckle, but had to stop when it brought on another coughing fit. "Do I look like I have a job?" she said at last.

"It's about a job you used to have, several years ago," I said, "at Bachana Adoption Agency, run by Prabhakar Sanderson."

Maria crumpled the cigarette foil into a tight ball and leaned toward us. "What the fuck do you want?"

Before I could answer, she continued. "You can tell that fucker Sanderson I'm doing what he wants. Still."

"Maria—"

"He fucked up my life. Look at me!" She began to wheeze from the exertion.

I reached over and placed my hand on top of her clenched fist.

Maria snatched her hand away from me, as if I'd burnt her. "Tell him to leave me the fuck alone!" she coughed and spat.

"We aren't working for Sanderson," I said. "We're actually trying to find out what he and his son were up to, and hopefully make them pay for it."

A rattle began low in her chest. As it grew louder it became a rasping laugh that shook her whole body. She threw her head back and let it roll out. When it had finally run its course, she panted and wiped her eyes with the back of her hand. "You're shitting me."

"No, we're not. I swear, Maria. We don't work for Sanderson. We're working against him. Because of a man he worked with in another business. Ravi Mehta." I took out my card and gave it to her. "Prabhakar Sanderson's old and sick and out of the picture now, but I know you reported him, tried to stop him doing whatever he was doing years ago. I talked to an old friend of yours, Jon Russario. And your mother."

"So that's how you found me."

"Yes, it is. Please, I need you to tell me what was going on, if you can remember. It might help us a lot."

Her bloodshot eyes had lost their suspicion and were now filled with guarded hope. "You're for real?"

"If by real you mean are we here to help, not hurt you—yes."

"You think you might be able to get him? Or at least his son?"

"We're sure going to try."

Maria fingered my card and looked at the mangled

cigarette pack in front of her.

"Dewey, maybe you could go and get Maria some cigarettes while we have a little chat."

Dewey headed off across the park in the direction of a corner store.

"Why don't you start at the beginning, Maria?"

She sized me up for a few more moments, then she reached into what was left of her memory. "It was maybe the second job I'd ever had, and I was really excited." She sniffed and rubbed her nose. "I'd been working there about eight months when I started to notice things that didn't seem quite right. I handled all the correspondence, so I had a good idea of what was happening, how the agency worked. At least I thought I did." Her eyes drifted into the foliage above us and she started to rock.

"Go on," I urged.

"What?" She studied my face.

"You were telling me about some things that didn't seem right at the agency."

"Oh. Okay." She searched the splintered tabletop and found the memories she was looking for. "There were some little things I noticed like padding bills, other stuff I can't remember. But what really bothered me were some of the adoptions."

"Was he using his son as the lawyer for those adoptions?"

"Yeah, that's right. I never heard of another lawyer. It took me a while to figure out their connection. Anyway, he was getting me to alter paperwork about the kids. That sort of thing. I can't remember the details now. My memory isn't what it used to be. I just know it fucking stank. Sometimes he'd make up stuff or tell me to use the same information I'd used before."

"And these were international adoptions?"

"Yeah. From India. Some papers were in another language—Hindi, I think. And some stuff had been translated. He was always going over there. Sometimes his son would go too."

"Do you remember ever hearing about the man I mentioned: Mr. Mehta? Ravi Mehta?"

Maria shifted, sniffed, coughed and asked, "An Indian guy?"

"Yes."

"There were a lot of Indian guys."

"Of course. This one would have been about the same age as the older Mr. Sanderson. A nice man, but maybe his bad relationship with your boss was evident."

The birds were challenging the street traffic, but Maria was silent.

I waited, unsure of how to help her.

She looked at me then her gaze drifted across the park to where Dewey had disappeared.

"Maria?"

"Yeah?" She refocussed.

"Do you remember such a man?"

She shrugged. "No. I don't think so. Do I still get the smokes?"

"Of course," I assured her and forced a smile past

my disappointment that she couldn't tell me anything about Ravi Mehta. "You did great, Maria."

The tension that had been growing in her jaw released enough for her to attempt a smile of her own.

"So you reported Sanderson, because of the paperwork."

"That's right," she said with more confidence. "That's when my life became hell. He threatened me and my family. Harassed me. Planted drugs and then called the cops on me. I finally had a breakdown. Ended up in hospital. And I took back everything I'd said about him."

"He paid you off, though. There was an official settlement."

"You could say that. I never saw most of the money. By that time the drugs had me good. Started with prescriptions from being sick. Then Sanderson made sure it carried on. Had one of his guys visit me on a regular basis, so I knew the threats were still for real. Always left me a little present to make me feel better." Her hollow chest rattled with the irony of her situation, and then she erupted into a fractured guffaw as a fresh memory appeared.

"You won't believe this." She checked me with her eyes to make sure I was prepared for the new revelation. "After all of that shit—the complaint, the drugs and all—the slimy son comes to me to see if I want to be his secretary. Tells me he'll help me have a decent life, since no one else will ever hire me. He says the agency is closed, but he and his old man are still doing some adoptions, only closer to home, more private-like, so there won't be problems. And since I know the ropes we can help each other out. That everything before was a big misunderstanding."

Ca-ching! So the Sandersons hadn't stopped; they'd just gone underground. If Ravi Mehta and Prabhakar Sanderson were in conflict over the adoptions issue, that would explain what Mrs. Kumar had overheard. Maria was waiting patiently for a response to her last bombshell, so I asked, "What did you do?"

"I told them to go to hell. I'd rather die on a street corner with a needle in my arm than work for them."

"But you're still threatened?"

"Once in a while someone finds me, reminds me to keep being a good girl. That's who I thought you were. The presents stopped after I said no to going back, but they know I'm totally fucked up and I'll do anything to get a fix myself."

Dewey arrived and handed Maria two packs of her brand.

"Thanks, dude," she said, attacking the cellophane on one of them.

"You've been a huge help, Maria. Thank you." I untangled myself from the attached bench of the picnic table. "You have my card. Please call me, if you remember anything else."

She was too concerned with the first drag on her cigarette to answer.

My phone vibrated with a text: "What's up?" No caller ID.

CHAPTER FOURTEEN

Dewey and I were pretty bummed out after our interview with Maria. We picked up a pizza, but by the time we'd returned the car keys to Basil and collapsed on the sofa in Dewey's apartment, neither of us had much of an appetite. Nor did we feel much like talking.

My phone rang. It was June.

"What the hell are you doing, Barnow?" she yelled.

"Nice to hear your voice, June. Did you call to make that dinner date?" My attempt at a joke fell flat.

"Why is there always a trail of dead bodies wherever you go?" She'd lowered her volume enough that I could put the phone back to my ear.

"June, we've already discussed Mrs. Kumar, and I wouldn't exactly call her a trail."

"It's not just Mrs. Kumar. Add Maria Pappas."

"Pardon?"

"You heard me, Calli."

"Maria's not dead. We just saw her this afternoon." Dewey caught my eye, but I could only shrug.

"I figured as much," said June. "Well, unless you've turned into a murderer, something went down after you saw her."

"What are you talking about?" My question was pointless, since I already knew the answer.

"Her body was just found in Alexandra Park. That's where I'm calling from. The scene's still being processed."

"Shit! What happened?" Nausea rolled through my empty stomach.

"It looks like an overdose."

I closed my eyes and breathed before replying, "That's too bad, but no surprise. She was a nice woman. But why is Homicide involved?"

"I said it looks like an overdose. I didn't say *accidental* overdose."

"Suicide?" I was grasping at straws. There was only one reason why the Homicide Squad would be there; I just didn't want to hear it.

"No," was all June said.

"Poor Maria." I still had a vivid image of the ravaged woman in the yellow shirt as she sat at the picnic table, alive. She'd had good reason to fear us. My next thought was more selfish. "Oh my god, June. What have I got myself into?"

"You tell me, Barnow. In fact, you'll have to come to headquarters and make a statement."

"Of course." I was about to hang up when something occurred to me. "How did you connect me to

Maria? I didn't tell you about her. I didn't even *know* about her until after you left us this morning."

"I could say it was a lucky guess, but there's a piece of evidence that suggests you and Maria were together at some point. Recently."

"Evidence?"

"Your business card."

"Yeah, I gave her one today, when I was talking to her. Just like I do with lots of people." Although I still felt sick about Maria's death and how it might relate to the case, finding my card in her possession was not a big deal.

June's response changed my mind. "I don't think you usually stuff your card in their mouths."

The pizza grew cold in the box.

My phone signalled a text: "U should order new cards."

I turned the screen towards Dewey.

"Calli, this is really bad."

"You can say that again."

"Calli, this is—"

I cut him off with a glare. "Thanks for trying to lighten the mood, Dew, but I don't think we can joke our way out of this."

"You're right." He put a comforting arm around me.

"It looks as if Sanderson knows we're still poking around in his past and his father's. He hasn't only been listening to us; he's definitely been watching us. It wasn't just my imagination. I guess June was right about the blue Honda."

"You think he's behind Maria's death?" he asked.

"Who else?"

"You have a point."

"It appears we have two choices." I was struggling to keep my voice even, but my insides were jelly and my hand had found the comfort of my worry stone amongst the fluff in my pocket.

"I would have thought we had no choice, Calli. It's clear we have to stop the investigation for real."

"That's one option, but there's no guarantee Sanderson would believe it since we tried to trick him before. If he went as far as killing Maria after all these years, I don't think I'll ever feel safe until he's behind bars."

Dewey chewed the inside of his cheek as he thought about what I'd just said. "What's the other option?"

"We step it up. Go on the offensive—stop pussyfooting around." The sound of my own voice was miraculously giving me confidence. I remembered my conversation with Pat at the gym. We had our opponent worried. He'd been on the offensive. So far I'd just been dancing around the ring, trying to avoid getting hit while I figured out his style. Maybe now was the time to attack. He wouldn't be expecting it.

"I don't like the sound of this, Calli. What exactly do you have in mind?" Dewey had begun to fiddle with the diamond stud in his left earlobe.

"We'll play by Sanderson's rules."

"I don't kill people, babe. Me no be yo man!" His attempt at levity did little to hide his real shock and apprehension.

"That's not what I meant." I pressed speed-dial on my phone and held it to my ear.

I had some time before my meeting with Sashi, so I arranged to drop by police headquarters and make my statement about Maria Pappas. June was busy when I arrived, but a young Detective Constable with a recent haircut and a new suit took care of the necessary paperwork. He'd just told me we were finished when June entered the interview room.

"Thanks, Doug," she said to the young man.

"My pleasure, June. Any time." He collected the file from the table and left us.

I pushed back my chair and was about to stand up when June closed the door. "Do you have a few minutes, Calli?"

Even if I'd been in a hurry to leave, June's manner would have been enough to make me stay. "Sure." I settled back into my seat.

"Good." She sat across from me and rested her elbows on the table. "It looks as if we're not going to get that dinner anytime soon, so I thought we could have a talk while you're here."

"Sure. Okay." I swallowed. I didn't particularly want another one of June's lectures. Not when I had planned what I had planned for the rest of the day.

"Is something wrong, Calli? You haven't seemed quite yourself lately." Her eyes held me.

I'd forgotten June's capacity to turn from a brash, tough-talking cop into a strong, nurturing woman. When she made that transformation, I was powerless to hold back anything. "I guess you were right the other day. I probably have been using work to take my mind off some personal issues. If I hadn't, I probably would have finished with the case when it proved to be unworkable."

"Uh huh. So what are the issues?" She tilted her head, and her blond curls bounced.

"Well, which one shall I start with?"

"That bad, eh?" Her dimples appeared.

"Okay. So Jess has decided that she wants a child." I made an attempt to sound positive.

"But, Calli, you've never wanted children."

I checked to see if she was serious. "You knew?"

"Of course I knew. I don't think we ever discussed it, but I knew."

I could contribute nothing in response, but I couldn't stop staring at the face across the table, a face almost as familiar to me as my own.

"So what are you and Jess going to do about it?" she asked.

"We're looking into adoption."

"You've changed your mind, then?" June was far from convinced.

"I'm still thinking about it," I said. "I haven't promised anything. But it's what Jess wants, so...." I shrugged.

"I see," she said and fell silent, but continued to look at me.

That's when I noticed for the first time a sadness behind her lovely eyes. If we'd been anywhere else but this barren room, doing anything other than sitting across this empty table staring at one another, I might have missed it. But I hadn't. Maybe it wasn't my problem she wanted to discuss, but I knew better than to pry. If she needed to talk about herself, she would—in her own good time.

I had to say something, so I did. "Anyway, that's one of the things that's been bothering me, I suppose. The other is that I discovered I have a brother."

June jumped on the change of topic. "No way! Do tell."

I tried to keep it light as I told her about Ken, and my mother, and our meetings.

"It must have been quite a shock to you, even though it seems to be working out," June stated.

"Of course."

"Especially since you and Jess are going through the adoption thing yourselves." A hint of sorrow returned.

"It'll all work out," I assured her.

"I'm sure it will. Things usually do for you." Her gaze rested on me and I had trouble thinking. "There's another reason I wanted to talk to you," she added.

I broke eye contact long enough to take a breath. "Yeah? What?"

"First I want to apologize to you. I know I've been short with you lately."

I gave her a smile. "You're always short with me."

"You know what I mean, Calli. I've been grouchy and preoccupied, and not a very good friend."

"Well, okay. I admit you have been a bit grouchier than usual. But June...." Now it was I who held her with my eyes. "You are *always* a good friend. I don't know what I'd do without you."

"Thanks, Calli. That means a lot to me. But as usual, you are full of shit."

We both smiled at that.

"So what do you want to tell me," I urged.

She laced her fingers and examined them before turning her attention back to me. "Nadia and I broke up."

I blinked at her in disbelief. "But...."

"I know. I thought it would never happen. The first six years were great. But this last year, I don't know, it was different. We were different. And I guess I just gradually fell out of love with her. We tried to resurrect things, but it didn't work. So in the end, we decided it would be better to just call it quits. That way both of us could get on with our lives."

"I'm so sorry, June."

"Thanks. But it's okay. I'm okay. It just takes some getting used to. Being single again." Her words were braver than her face.

"I'm glad you told me. You know I'm here for you."

"Yeah, Barnow. I know." After a moment she checked her watch. "Well, I gotta run." We both stood up, but neither moved to leave. Instead, we studied each other. My heart started to pick up speed, and I knew I had to get out, so I headed for the door. I was almost there when June caught me by the arm. I turned and she stepped toward me, her eyes never leaving mine. We were so close I could smell the subtle perfume she'd worn for as long as I'd known her. It would have been so easy to lean in to her and do what I so desperately wanted to do.

"Be careful, Barnow," were the words she said. Her eyes said something else.

Then she was gone.

Sashi had agreed to meet Dewey and me in the fast-food restaurant across the street from Sanderson's law office. She was keeping us waiting, and a couple of times I was tempted to tell Dewey about my meeting with June. But I didn't know quite what or how much to tell him. In the end I chose to concentrate on the words I was going to say to Sashi. I was counting on her to be a good sport; otherwise, my plan wouldn't get off the ground.

By the time she arrived, exhausted from her day, and I'd bought her a cup of coffee and brought her up to speed on the Sandersons, the expression on her face made it clear that being a good sport didn't come close to what I was about to request from her. And she was right. If she were to agree, she would have to be as desperate or as foolhardy as I. She was, however, very upset at the thought of Sanderson's actions affecting her father's health to the extent it had.

I'd never before asked for a client's help in this manner, and as I attacked my worry stone I hoped I would never have to again. "Sashi, I'm going to ask you to do something...well, it's possible that it could put you in danger." I paused to let that sink in.

She looked quizzical, but said nothing, so I continued. "Have you ever met Wayne Sanderson, either recently or when his father bought out your share of the business?"

"No. I just spoke to him on the phone. That one time I told you about."

"Good. And you've never been to his office."

"No. Never. I don't even know where it is."

"As far as you know, have you ever met anyone who works for Sanderson?"

"Not that I'm aware of. Calli—"

"Bear with me, Sashi." I tried to slow my breathing. If she saw my fear, there would be no way she'd involve herself, and I wouldn't blame her. "Since you told Sanderson you were finished with any investigation of his father...you did tell him, didn't you?"

"Yes, I called as soon as I left you that day. He was pleased to hear from me and it sounded as if he believed me."

"So, since then have you had any indication, anything at all that might suggest he's been keeping an eye on you?" I gripped the edge of my chair, remembering that I had probably been instrumental in the deaths of two women already. Since the text message about my cards, Dewey and I had taken every possible precaution with our movements, so I was as certain as I could be that Sanderson didn't know where we were at that moment. Precautions, of course, were no guarantee.

"No. Nothing." Sashi's worry lines were deepening with each successive question.

"Good." I took a deep breath and continued. "Have you ever done any acting?"

My strange question caught her off guard. "Uh... not since high school. Calli, what on earth—"

"Well, I hope you're willing to try."

Dewey knew what I was going to ask Sashi to do. He wasn't offering any verbal encouragement. In fact, he was shaking his head just enough that I could see it and remember the protests he'd made before she'd arrived.

"I'm a dentist, Calli. Even if I'm willing to try, I can't guarantee I'll be any good at it. Whatever it is."

"Please, Sashi. I'd do it myself, except that I've met Wayne Sanderson. This shouldn't involve him in person, but I don't want to gamble." I was stalling, laying my arguments on the table, hoping that she'd see I had no other options. It would be twice as hard to change her mind once she said no as it would be to get agreement from her in the first place.

"So that's why you were asking all those questions." She was starting to understand some of what I was getting at, and I could see the more she understood, the less she liked it.

I barrelled on, not wanting to hear her refusal. "I also wouldn't be the least bit convincing. Not for what I have in mind."

"Calli, stop!" Sashi held up her hand. "Maybe you should explain exactly what it is you have in mind."

Unable to beat around the bush any longer, I let the aroma of french fries and coffee take over while I looked at the pedestrians sweating their way along the sidewalk. If Sashi didn't agree to my plan, it wouldn't be the end of the world. I could still progress to step two. It would just be a lot easier to take that step if she was willing to help out now. In fact, depending on what she might find out, step two might not even be an option.

"Okay, Sashi, this is what I want you to do." I looked at Dewey for moral support, but he just shook his head once again.

Sashi's doubt-filled face didn't help. I thought of Mrs. Kumar and Maria Pappas. Then I said, "Across the street is Wayne Sanderson's law office."

Sashi's doubt grew to fear.

Undaunted, I continued. "Just before you arrived, Sanderson left. We watched him leave the building and walk away. I then phoned the office and pretended that

I wanted to speak with him. His receptionist told me he'd be gone for the rest of the day."

Even though Sashi still had no idea what I wanted her to do, she looked a little less frantic.

"I'd like you to go to his office. If you see anyone you recognize, or even *think* you recognize, tell them your real name and that you just dropped by to make sure that Mr. Sanderson knew you were still doing what you said you would be doing when you talked to him on the phone."

"I don't get it, Calli."

"That's just your safeguard...Plan B. Here's the real deal: if you're sure you don't know anyone, I want you to pretend you're an adoptive parent from his father's former agency. Don't use your own name, of course. Ask whoever is there whether Mr. Sanderson has the records of adoptions done through the Bachana Agency back in, I don't know, let's say two thousand and two thousand and one. It was still operating then."

"Why would I be doing this?" Sashi asked.

"Because the child you adopted has become ill, and you really need to get a family medical history if possible. You're desperate for his help. Make up any details you need to. It's better than if I tell you what to say."

"So you're hoping that Wayne Sanderson still has his records or the records from the adoption agency from all those years ago?"

"He should have. By law he's required to keep them. And if he has them from that far back, then he's bound to have the records from later on, after he and his father started to work without the agency."

"Aren't they all filed with the government? Couldn't I just enquire there, if I were an adoptive parent?" Sasha still doubted my sanity.

"Yes, of course, the main documents would have been, but for international adoptions in all likelihood the medical history would be minimal, if it existed at all. That's why you would need Sanderson's help. In theory, he might be able to get some additional information from their contacts in India. Besides, you're a distraught mother. Sanderson would have been the first person who came to mind. It makes sense that since the agency is gone, you'd contact the lawyer who handled the paperwork."

"Do you really think he'd still have something around that could implicate him in illegal practices?" Her skepticism still stood in the way.

"That's what I want to find out." I tried to hide the turmoil inside me with a veneer of calm control.

Dewey looked at the table.

"I don't know, Calli. I don't like the feel of this." She shook her head.

"There's another reason I need you to go, Sashi." I realized that what I was about to say might not further my cause, but it had to be said.

She waited, still incredulous at what I had already asked her.

"I need you to look around while you're there. Get a feel for the layout of the place. Where things are kept. How secure everything is." I tried to maintain an encouraging exterior, while still battling my own misgivings.

"Oh no. Calli, you can't be serious. You aren't planning to do what I think you are."

"I'm not planning anything," I lied. "I'm just interested in how lawyers manage their office space." I gave her a false grin. My attempt to keep Sashi from being implicated in anything I might do that would be breaking the law was pathetic, and we all knew it.

Sashi made movements to leave.

"Please, Sashi. All I'm *telling* you is that I'd be interested in knowing if Sanderson still has any records of those adoptions. All I'm *asking* you to do is to be observant, nothing more."

Sashi settled on the edge of her seat.

I didn't wait for her to deny my request. "If Sanderson is involved in the deaths of two women already, he's a dangerous man. It looks as if he's trying to cover up what he's done in the past by getting rid of anyone who might be able to incriminate him. I told you before that what I'm asking you to do could have risks, but the fact is you might already be in danger. I'm pretty sure that Sanderson is just waiting for me to get too close to the truth, or to make a false move. Maybe I've even reached that point already. I don't know. But what I do know is that because of your association with me, he might think you're a threat as well. He's already warned you once. And even if we were to walk away from this today, there's no guarantee that Sanderson would forget about us."

We all sat in silence, while Sashi chewed her lip and weighed the pros and cons. More than once I thought she was going to wash her hands of the whole thing, officially fire me, and try to get back to her former life.

Finally she spoke. "All right. I'll do it. I was the one who got you involved in this whole mess in the first place. Stirred everything up. I'm not comfortable with any of it, but I feel responsible and if I can help bring it to an end I will. I don't like feeling afraid. And I don't like breaking the law. But I'm going to put aside my fear and look at my reconnaissance mission as nothing more than getting you a piece of information about the adoption records. If I happen to notice my surroundings, so be it."

Sashi had been gone at least twenty minutes, and I was beginning to get worried, when she emerged from the doorway across the street. By the time she'd gone down to the lights, travelled the crosswalk, and returned to the restaurant, I'd bought her a fresh cup of coffee.

She took her time adding sugar and milk, stirring, and finally taking her first tentative sip.

"Well?" I couldn't wait any longer.

Dewey had been texting his boyfriend, Chris, but now put his phone away. From the expression on his face, I could tell he was waiting for my plan to fall flat on its face.

"Well," Sashi said and then paused for effect. "I believe an Oscar is in order." She grinned at us both.

"So?" I wasn't even sure what questions to ask.

"It wasn't nearly as bad as I had expected. His office is on the second floor, and he's the only lawyer."

I had figured out as much from the listing I'd looked at, but now that Sashi was on a bit of a roll, I didn't want to interrupt her.

"So I went into the outer office where his receptionist, or assistant, or whoever she is, sits. She's a very nice woman, but not too bright. At least that's how she comes across. There was no one else around. Anyway, I introduced myself and asked if Mr. Sanderson was in. Of course she told me he wasn't and wanted to know if she could help me. That was when my Oscar-winning performance began. I looked as if I might start to cry, and she grew very concerned. I could tell right away she would give me any information I asked for.

"I told her my sad story with only enough details to make it sound plausible. At that point she became very excited. She lifted up a whole pile of file folders from the floor next to her desk. Believe it or not, Sanderson had asked her to shred the contents about a week ago, but she'd forgotten all about it until that morning, when he'd checked to see if she'd done it. Of course she'd had to admit they were still in one piece. He'd become very angry that she hadn't followed his instructions right away."

"She told you all this?" I was developing a whole

new level of admiration for Sashi.

"Oh yes. Anyway, after his outburst, she'd started to shred them, but she'd only had time to do a few, because she'd been busy with other things he wanted immediately. She intends to have them all done by the time he comes back to the office tomorrow afternoon. She said that she's glad he isn't a morning person, because she'd never get it finished before she leaves work today."

"Please tell me those are the files about the adoptions," I begged.

"None other."

If there hadn't been a table between us, I would have hugged her.

Even Dewey was impressed.

Sashi was basking in her success and our surprise at it, so we didn't have to encourage her to continue. "Of course I acted all hopeful that the information I needed was in one of the files, but I was actually terrified that maybe there was a family with the name I'd chosen to use, and then I'd have to explain that it wasn't me, that it's a common name. And I'd have to act excited and then disappointed. I didn't know how much longer I could keep it up. You know what I mean. I just wanted to get out of there as quickly as I could."

"Then what happened?" Dewey had forgotten his misgivings at my scheme and was caught up in the adventure along with Sashi.

"So the poor woman checked every folder to see

if one of them had my name on it. She couldn't check the names on the empty files from the material she'd already shredded, because she'd destroyed them too. Apparently Mr. Sanderson has a habit of making notations on the folders themselves, so they can never be reused. While she was searching, I scanned the office for any details you might want to know."

"And?" I asked.

"Nothing of interest. At least I don't think so. The whole place isn't very big. Sanderson's private office looked to be behind where the woman's desk is located, but the door was shut, so I couldn't see inside. On one side there's a small counter with a sink and cupboard, a couple of filing cabinets, some chairs—you know, just regular office things."

"Did you see any security equipment?"

Sashi thought for a moment. "No, nothing obvious anyway."

"So continue your story," Dewey interrupted.

"Well, eventually she got to the bottom of the pile. She was very upset that she hadn't found what she was looking for, and that she was obviously responsible for destroying the information I so desperately needed. I asked her if anything might be on the computer and she assured me it wasn't. In the end, I had to console her, instead of the other way around. I told her that I'd call and make an appointment with Mr. Sanderson, and that she should just take it easy until it was time to go home. She thought that was a good idea, and as I was leaving I could hear her running water to make tea." Sashi sat back, satisfaction written all over her face.

"So those files should still be there tomorrow morning," I said.

"Should be."

"You're a doll, Sashi. I don't know how to thank you."

"Well, we are in this together," she said. "I wouldn't want to do it every day, but I have to admit, the experience gave me a real buzz."

"I'm glad it wasn't too bad," I said.

"So the information I got will be useful?"

"Absolutely."

"What's your next move?" Her eyes shone with anticipation of more to come.

"Sashi, I really appreciate what you've done, but I'm not going to get you involved any further. I don't want you to know what I might or might not do as a result of your information. Under the circumstances, I think the less you know the better. You need to go back to being a dentist. Forget about this afternoon. But keep your eyes open and do tell me if anything out of the ordinary happens either at home or at work."

Sashi was still smiling as she waved good-bye to us through the restaurant window.

Dewey and I waved, but we were far from being able to smile back.

A text message arrived: "Are you worried yet?"

CHAPTER FIFTEEN

The table was set with a centrepiece of fresh flowers. A bowl of gourmet pasta was ready to serve and a bottle of good Chianti had been decanted.

And I had no appetite.

"What's the occasion?" I asked.

"I'll tell you over dinner," said Jess, as she spooned a savoury pile of food onto my plate. "How was your day?"

I thought of Maria Pappas and Dewey and Sashi, and everything that had happened. I thought of what I had to do that night, and a chill ran through me. Then I thought of June. The scent of the flowers on the table reminded me of her perfume. "My day was okay," I lied. "I have to work after dinner."

"Oh no, Calli. Not tonight. Please." Jess poured just a bit too much wine into my glass.

"Sorry, sweetie. I have to. It won't take long."

"What is it?"

"Nothing much, but it can't wait. Thanks for the

nice meal. What are we celebrating?" I pushed the pasta around my plate and finally took a bite.

Jess grinned at me over the top of the white and yellow daisies. "The information package from that private adoption agency arrived today, so maybe before you leave we can have a look at it, you know, see what we think, and maybe think about getting started. I hear it can take a long time."

"Sure. Whatever you like." I was still only half listening. The food was delicious, but each mouthful was a struggle. I didn't dare take more than one or two sips of wine. I would have liked nothing better than to crawl into the bottom of the bottle, but I was going to need to be sharp for what I had planned with Dewey.

I tried to stay focussed on Jess and what she wanted to show me as we settled onto the sofa together. There was more adoption information than I'd expected. It took us through the whole process step by step including what types of documents would be generated by the time the adoption was finalized. I only skimmed most of it, leaving Jess to pore over the package in more detail while I was out.

Dewey was waiting for me in the restaurant just where I'd left him. He assured me he'd gone and come back, and knowing his dislike of most fast foods, I believed him.

"Did you bring it?" he asked.

"Yes," I answered.

"And you're sure we have to do this?"

"I'm sure."

Then silence.

Only our eyes continued the conversation, sharing the concern that boiled inside us. My hand found my pocket and checked—again. Still there.

When it was dark outside, we crossed the street.

We'd made a plan. The exterior door to Sanderson's office was recessed from the sidewalk. Dewey would stand in front of it facing the street. I would stand behind him and break in.

I put my hand on the knob and turned. It wasn't locked.

Our luck ran out with the office door upstairs.

"You really know how to do this, Calli?"

"Of course I do."

"Right," Dewey said under his breath.

"Thanks," I almost snarled at him. "Watch the front door, if you think you can manage that."

Normally he would have had a witty retort. Tonight he just turned his back to me and did as he was instructed.

My lock-picking kit was brand new. My first. I'd practised with it a few times, but never under pressure. My fingers were shaking, not just from inexperience, but also because a life of crime was new to me. If Dewey and I got ourselves arrested for breaking and entering, June would personally have my hide. A police record and the loss of my private investigator licence would pale in comparison to her wrath. Now more than ever I wanted to avoid that. If I hadn't believed this was the only option, I wouldn't have been taking the risk.

Fortunately for me, Sanderson spent his money on things other than good locks. Despite my faltering fingers and the wavering of the small flashlight I held in my teeth, I managed to turn the tumbler. It only took me a couple of minutes, but it felt like a couple of hours. Dewey's frequent orders to hurry up didn't help.

Because the office overlooked the street, we didn't dare turn on the lights. Although my flashlight wasn't very big, it was strong. Dewey had brought one about the same size, but his beam was weaker. Between the two of us we were able to illuminate only a small portion of the office space at a time. Just to be on the safe side, the first thing I did was close the Venetian blinds.

From what I could tell, Sanderson hadn't invested any more in decorating than he had in security. The outer office was minimally furnished and contained only what was absolutely necessary to carry on business. The computer on the secretary's desk was adequate, but not a recent model. Nothing in the office gave the impression that Sanderson was intending to go paperless anytime soon, so it was no surprise that the hard copies of the adoption files hadn't been computerized. Whatever Sanderson was up to in his professional life, he wasn't achieving it through high tech.

I told Dewey to do a quick but thorough search of the filing cabinets. I also warned him not to leave a trace they'd been disturbed. He didn't so much as blink an eye at my detailed instructions but quietly slipped open the first drawer.

On the other side of the room was the receptionist's desk, and on the floor beside it was the pile of file folders, exactly where Sashi said it would be. I placed the top file on the desk and shone my flashlight on the contents. As I examined the sheets of paper I began to realize that the time I'd just spent with Jess had been a big help. Although I'd only been half paying attention when she showed me the adoption packages, I now recognized some of the forms and references that lay before me.

The first Sanderson file didn't appear unusual, and if I had only looked at it, I would have thought Maria was mistaken. It wasn't until I read the information about the third adoption that problems started to surface. To make sure I wasn't seeing things, I skimmed through several other files, and the more I looked the more blatant the doctoring. There was repetition of information, primarily regarding the origin of some of the children—birthplace, parental details, and so on. The dates ranged from the 1990s up to 2008. The older documents listed the Bachana Adoption Agency and dealt with children brought from India, while the more recent ones only named Wayne Sanderson and children who originated in various parts of Canada.

Dewey helped me spread a few sample documents side by side on the desk, and I used my new phone to take some quick shots that I hoped would be good enough quality to be enlarged. My heart was pounding so hard I was afraid it might jump right out of my chest and land on the desk. For once I didn't care what my heart was doing: I just prayed that my trembling hands hadn't blurred the images.

What we had discovered was damning for both the Sanderson men. No wonder Wayne didn't want me poking around. No wonder he and his father had destroyed Maria's life and credibility. No wonder he wanted these files destroyed as well.

We put everything back beside the desk, opened the blinds, and did a quick double check to make sure the place was exactly as we'd found it. Dewey was heading for the stairs, when I stopped him.

"What?" he yelled at me under his breath.

"I have to lock the door," I said.

"Why? How?"

"I'm sure the receptionist would think she'd forgotten to lock it, but I'm not taking chances. Not with Sanderson the way he is."

"Fine, but how do you unpick a lock?"

"Watch and learn."

"I don't want to learn. I'm never doing this again." He meant what he said, and I didn't blame him.

"The faster I do this, the faster we can get out of here." I handed him my more efficient flashlight. "Aim the beam on the inside lock."

"I should never have agreed to any of this." He continued to mutter under his breath, but once more did as I asked. The beam shook in his hand, and I regretted having put him in this position, even though we'd struck gold.

I took a length of thick, waxed dental floss from my pocket. Dewey continued to mumble, but I ignored him as I tied the floss to the top of the deadbolt latch. "Okay, move onto the landing, but try to keep the light on the lock area."

I stepped onto the landing with Dewey. I held the end of the dental floss in one hand and pulled the door after me with the other. Once the door was shut, I tugged the floss tight and in a downward direction. I felt it catch, then stretch. I held my breath and pulled harder. Nothing happened. I kept increasing the tension and moved the floss farther down the doorjamb.

Dewey took a deep breath, and I was sure he was going to beg me to stop.

Then it gave. The floss grew limp as the bolt clicked into place.

Dewey pressed his lips together and began glancing at the street-level door.

I kept my focus on slipping the floss out of the doorjamb without it getting hung up on anything. It took some manoeuvring, but within a few seconds the loop appeared. Only then did my heart begin to slow down.

Dewey and I said nothing, but fled down the stairs and into the night.

"Barnow, why are you calling at this hour?" June growled. "Are you in trouble?"

"Not exactly." I wasn't sure how to tell June what

I had to tell her, but she needed to know.

"Just spit it out. I'm beat, and I want to hit the sack early." Her voice sagged under the weight of resignation and all the times she had come to my assistance in the past. There was no hint of anything else.

Maybe I'd misread what had happened in the interview room that afternoon. I didn't have time right then to worry about it; I was just glad to have the old June on the other end of the phone line when I needed her. "Well, I've been receiving messages. First texts on my cell, and then while I was out tonight, on my home phone. They aren't threats, but they give the impression that someone is still watching me."

"I suppose it's too much to hope that there was any caller ID."

"My land line doesn't show it. Jess answered, so there's no recorded message, just what she told me. And my cell just said Unknown Caller."

"Probably a throwaway cell. I'll get your phone records checked, just in case. So that's why you called, Barnow?"

"That's one reason, but not the big one."

There was silence then, "Is it work?"

So maybe I hadn't been mistaken about this afternoon. "Yes, it's work."

June's voice sounded lighter when she said, "So what is it? Something tells me I'm not going to sleep tonight."

I cleared my throat. I could hear June cursing under her breath, and I knew we were back on solid ground. "You know Maria Pappas?" I asked.

"Of course I do. I was the one who told you she was dead."

"Did you read the statement I gave at headquarters today?"

"No, not yet."

"Well, when I was talking to Maria, she told me about the reason she stopped working for Sanderson."

"Who?"

"Prabhakar Sanderson, Ravi Mehta's partner in the import business. I told you about him at Dewey's apartment."

"Right. And Maria Pappas worked for him?"

"Not at the import business, at his adoption agency," I explained.

"I see."

"Anyway, it was a big mess for her, and it resulted in Sanderson ruining her life. And I'm sure Sanderson is behind her death. I—"

"Get on with it, Barnow."

"I did some checking on the son, Wayne Sanderson. And I discovered that Maria was telling the truth."

"About what?"

"Illegal adoptions."

"Go on." Her voice betrayed interest.

"Well...I might have just come into possession of some proof." Even if my words hadn't started the warning bells ringing, the tone of my voice would have.

"Holy shit, Barnow! What in the name of god

have you been up to?" June's voice was an octave higher and a hundred decibels louder than usual.

I'd been standing in front of my kitchen window, looking down on an almost deserted Baldwin Avenue. Now I dragged myself into the living room and collapsed on the sofa. June's reaction had made real my evening's escapade. The lead in my stomach confirmed that I had probably made a huge mistake in lowering myself to Sanderson's level. "Let's just say I saw some paperwork that proves both of the Sandersons were doing something unethical and undoubtedly illegal with at least some international adoptions and that they later carried on the same sort of thing with more local children."

"And where did you happen to see this paperwork?" June struggled to keep her voice level.

"In Wayne Sanderson's office."

The technology connecting us was silent.

My sleek phone became heavy in my sweaty hand.

When June finally spoke, her voice had acquired an edge. "I'm assuming he didn't voluntarily show you this."

"Of course he didn't show me." I made a snap decision and blurted out everything before June could say more and maybe frighten me into silence. "Listen June, I don't need a lecture," I added, hoping to soften what I knew would come. "I'm a grown woman. I know sometimes it doesn't seem that way to you, but I am. I made a decision and I came across something important. I know I'm asking for trouble by telling you, by making this information available to the police, but so be it. I took photos of some of the papers. If you want, I can send them to you. Then you can decide for yourself if they're of any use. Think of me as an informant, like on TV."

There was silence again at the other end of the line. Finally June spoke. "Send them. I'll have a look."

I forwarded the shots to June and waited. After a very long five minutes she was back on the phone.

"I don't want to know how you got these, Barnow. But if the information is going to be of any use, we need the originals."

"Now wait a minute, June."

"Relax, Calli, I'm not asking you to get them. In fact, that would be the worst thing you could do."

"Well, if you intend to confiscate them, you'll have to move fast. They'll all be shredded by tomorrow afternoon." I was beginning to let go of the knots in my shoulders.

"I also don't want to know how you come by *that* information. I'll have to make out a strong enough connection to the Maria Pappas case to warrant a legal search and seizure."

I had no doubt June could figure out something. I also had no doubt that whatever she figured out would have no loopholes that could discredit the evidence. By the time we ended the phone call, I was ready for a good night's sleep. Finally. For the first time in ages, it looked like it might happen. My case was coming to an end.

I knew someone had been trying to phone while I was giving June my ill-gotten proof of Sanderson's adoption techniques. If I'd known it was Belic's sister, I might have braved more of June's displeasure by putting her on hold. As it was, Miss Belic had been forced to leave a stilted message informing me that she had information about her good-for-nothing brother. She made it clear I couldn't call her back because she was going to bed, but suggested I drop by the diner in the morning after the breakfast rush.

So there I was, standing outside the Sunnyside Up Diner in the pouring rain. I'd chosen not to bother Dewey with this unexpected visit, and much as I would have liked to enjoy another breakfast made by Miss Belic, I'd thought better of it and had eaten a bowl of Cheerios at home.

Inside the diner a few people, most of them older men, were finishing up their greasy meals and bottomless cups of coffee. Judging by the number of thick plates and heavy china mugs that cluttered many of the vacant tables, I had managed to miss the busiest time. I chose the same stool I'd occupied on my first visit and prepared to wait.

Miss Belic gave me a quick nod from the back where she was clearing a table but she made no move to join me, so I slid the laminated menu from its metal holder and began to read through the selections. Breakfast choices took up the front, while lunch and dinner shared the back. I'd made it down to liver and onions with mashed potatoes and vegetables when the clattering stopped and Miss Belic came to stand before me on the other side of the counter.

"You want coffee?" she asked, wiping her hands on her apron.

Although I was tempted, I declined. I wanted this to be quick.

"Why did you call me, Miss Belic?"

"My no good brother. I should have cut him off long time ago. I should have moved far away and not told him where, but no, here I stay. Family is family, and my sainted mother, she beg me. 'Ana,' she say, 'you can't leave me. Ana, be nice to Borisav. He your brother.' So I stay. And I try to be nice. And then my mother she die. And leave me with him. He get worse. Go from being blister on my foot to hole in my belly. By then it too late. Too old to leave. Too old to start again."

The poor woman was shaking, the tiny blood vessels on her cheeks bright and angry. Although she said nothing much I hadn't already heard and certainly nothing of any use, I let her vent. She seemed desperately in need of the outlet.

"I think—I pray his time in jail teach him," she continued, "but oh no. Off he go again, back to his old way, get himself in trouble."

"Yes, I'd heard that he was arrested again," I

squeezed in.

Not surprised that the news was common knowledge, Miss Belic proceeded. "So he call me from jail. He cry and act so innocent like it big mistake, and he want money for lawyer. He say our sainted mother she watch from heaven and would want me to help him. I laugh into phone and tell him our sainted mother she die of shame if she still alive. And if she watch from heaven, she know why I want nothing to do with him. I tell him I am done. This is it. I spend no more on him. I want to never hear from him again."

"I'm sorry," I said. "It must be very difficult for you. But I don't understand how I can help. Why did you want to tell me this?"

"Because of what he say next. He say people—the police and some woman—they look at his past. They try to blame him for things from before. Bad things. Things he not do. I laugh again. So he tell me." She paused and gave me a triumphant look.

"What did he tell you?" I asked.

She reached behind her neck and unfastened the clasp of her necklace. Then she dangled it in front of me. The light from the windows and the dirty overhead fixtures glinted off the little gold figurine that hung from the chain. I recognized it at once, and I was filled with awe. There, right in front of me in that rundown diner, suspended by Ana Belic's work-worn fingers, was Mrs. Mehta's little yellow god, the gift from her loving husband so long ago. It matched Sashi's description in every intricate detail.

"Where did you get this?"

"From Borisav. Only present to me in…I have no memory. He give it to me years ago. Four, maybe five. He say that since our sainted mother dead, I am all he has in whole world and he want to give me something. Like fool, I believe him. I wear it all these years. The one nice thing he ever do for me. And now he tell me to get rid of it. Tell me it could get him in big trouble. So I tell him he already in big trouble. And I will get rid of it. To someone who can make sure he get in bigger trouble. Then I hang up on him forever. And I call you."

She dropped the necklace into my hand. It was heavier than it looked, high quality gold. If Belic was aware of its value at the time it was taken from Indira Mehta, he must have been very tempted to sell it. Maybe he was afraid to take a risk with something so unusual, something that could tie him to a serious crime. Maybe he was planning to hang on to it for a rainy day and gave it to his sister for safe keeping, pretending it was a gift. Or, maybe he had a moment of genuine brotherly love and really did want to do something nice for Ana. Whatever the reason, I now had an important piece of evidence from the attack on Indira Mehta, and if I knew Sashi, as I thought I now did, she would want me back on that case.

"Thank you," I said. "I know who this belonged to; I'll make sure it's returned to the family. It'll mean a lot to the daughter of the woman who owned it. First, I'll let the police know."

Miss Belic gave me a look of satisfaction then took a damp cloth from beside the sink. "I wash my hands of Borisav and his…gift." She wiped her hands with the cloth and then pitched it into a large garbage can full of kitchen waste.

"June, I'm not sure where to go with this, but I've come into possession of stolen property." I held the phone away from my ear in anticipation of June's reaction. I wasn't disappointed. Everything seemed to be back to normal between us. At least for the time being.

"Barnow, what the hell have you gotten yourself into now?!"

Silence followed, during which I inched the phone closer to my head.

"I'm still dealing with the bombshell from last night," June announced. "Which, by the way, didn't turn out. When Sanderson's office was searched first thing this morning the files weren't there." Although the volume had been turned down, June didn't attempt to hide her exasperation with me.

"But they must have been. They were…" I thought better of incriminating myself any further.

"Well, they weren't." June was emphatic.

Sanderson or his guilt-riddled receptionist must have taken them or destroyed them between the time I was in his office and the time the police arrived the next morning.

"It was a waste of time and energy, and now Sanderson is furious and threatening retaliation," June continued, "so you'll have to excuse me if I don't seem too enthusiastic about whatever you've landed in now."

It was going to be an uphill battle getting June to cooperate. "I haven't landed in or gotten myself into anything. I went to see Borisav Belic's sister, at her request, and she presented me with a necklace her brother had given her several years ago. He wanted her to get rid of it now because he's afraid it could incriminate him in something from his past. I'm almost positive it's the necklace that Indira Mehta was wearing when she was attacked."

"I see...." Her voice had lost its bite. "I thought you were convinced that Anasetti had attacked Mrs. Mehta."

"I was, but Belic had possession of the necklace, so he must have had something to do with it. Maybe I've been wrong about Anasetti."

"Okay, Calli, here's what you're going to do: phone your client and ask her to meet you at headquarters to identify the necklace. Let's say...an hour from now. I'll be waiting for you in the lobby. It has to be documented as stolen property. And you'll have to make a statement about where you got it. After that you and I will go and see Borisav Belic. See what he has to say for himself."

I might not have been in June's good books at that moment, but she wasn't going to let it interfere with new evidence. At least this time I had the evidence in my hands.

The holding cells at 52 Division are used to temporarily detain people who have been arrested locally and are waiting to move on to the next stage in the legal process. Borisav Belic was one of those people. June had called ahead and made arrangements for us to meet with him.

Although Belic had tried to convince his sister to pay for a lawyer, he'd made no attempt to have legal aid present at our meeting, so there was no one with him in the barren interview room when we entered. He looked as anaemic as he had the first time I'd seen him, and far less pulled together. A slight puckering around his eyes was the only reaction he registered at seeing me again.

June had warned me to keep my mouth shut unless specifically called upon by her to speak. That was fine by me. We sat on the two stiff chairs across the metal table from Belic, and June placed a closed file folder in front of us.

"Mr. Belic," June said, "I'm Detective Sergeant Thompson from the Homicide Squad, Toronto Police Services. This interview is being videotaped. Do you understand?"

"Yes," he said, and looked up at the corner where the camera eye was located.

"Please identify yourself for the camera, Mr. Belic."

"Borisav Belic."

June then looked at me.

"Calli Barnow, Private Investigator," I said, louder than necessary.

"I believe you have met Ms. Barnow already," June said to Belic.

He chose not to respond.

"You have the right to legal counsel at this interview," June added.

"I need no lawyer. I did nothing." Belic stuck out his stubbly chin.

"So, Mr. Belic," June began, then looked at a sheet of paper on the table in front of her. "You were arrested at your home, two-oh-one A Franklin Avenue, Toronto, on August twenty-sixth of this year and later charged in the robberies of Helen Ferguson, Doreen McDonald, and Jeannette Laportaire, all of which had occurred during the previous two-week period. You had sold a necklace and ring you allegedly stole from Mrs. McDonald to Hank Brown, the owner of Number One Pawn Shop on Church Street in Toronto on August twenty-fifth of this year, and the police had been notified by Mr. Brown. Upon a search of your residence by police on August twenty-sixth of this year, items from the robberies of Mrs. Ferguson and Mrs. McDonald were recovered, and you were subsequently taken into police custody. Do you agree with the events as I have stated them?"

"Yes, but I already told cops I'm innocent."

"Just a moment, Mr. Belic. When you were

brought to 52 Division on August twenty-sixth you were questioned by Sergeant Schmitt and you made a statement to the effect that you were innocent of all charges. Is that correct?"

"Yes, I told you." Belic leaned forward and glared at June.

"Good. Now, what was it you wanted to say, Mr. Belic?"

"I'm innocent. A friend, he stay for a few days with me. He leave those things. I only try to sell jewellery to pay for what he owe me for food." Belic's explanation was almost cocky.

"And where is this friend?" June asked.

Belic's glare became more intense.

"Well, Mr. Belic, all of that is for the court to deal with. It's not why I'm here." June put her hand on top of the file she'd brought with her. "The last time you met Ms. Barnow, she was asking you about a woman who was attacked in Yorkville in two thousand and eight."

"I told her, I had nothing to do with that. I not lie."

"But you were subsequently arrested for several similar attacks, and you were convicted and served time."

"So why would I not tell truth?" He shrugged.

I nudged June with my toe under the table. She scowled at me, but got the message. She wasn't ready for me to speak, however, so she continued.

"Maybe because that specific attack, the attack on Mrs. Mehta in Yorkville in two thousand and eight, went farther than the others."

"I sick in hospital then. I tell her," Belic interrupted June, then looked at me.

I kept my mouth shut, but poked June once more with my foot.

"Would you like to respond to that, Ms. Barnow?" June invited.

"Yes. I've spoken with your sister, Mr. Belic. She assured me that you were not in the hospital. And both you and I know that if you were, you have the power to request your medical records as proof," I said.

"Would you like me to arrange for you to do that, Mr. Belic?" June asked.

Belic lowered his eyes to the table.

June awarded me a smile. I had just earned my place in the interview room. "So, Mr. Belic, it appears that you don't have an alibi for the time of Mrs. Mehta's attack," June said.

Belic raised his eyes to her. The cockiness had gone. "Not prove I do it."

"No, it doesn't," she said, "but this makes you look very much like the guilty party." June opened the folder and removed a plastic evidence bag. She placed it in front of Belic. The gold figure that had slid down to one corner was hard to miss.

Belic's body went rigid, but he said nothing.

June only glanced at me, but she clearly meant me to speak.

"Your sister gave it to me this morning, Mr. Belic, and explained to me where she got it. Maybe you didn't believe her when she told you what she was going to do, but here it is."

June took over. "Mrs. Mehta was wearing that when she was attacked. I suggest that you were the person who attacked her. You stole her money and this necklace, and then you gave the necklace to your sister."

Belic remained silent. I could see his options wrestling behind the stony expression he was attempting to maintain. Finally he spoke. "I tell truth. I not attack that woman. Even if I steal from her, it too long ago to count now." He looked smug.

I sensed that June shared my disappointment in his denial, but she wasn't finished. "Well, Mr. Belic, if all you or someone else had done was to steal the necklace from Mrs. Mehta, you would be correct about the timing. That sort of theft would be considered a summary conviction offence, and there is a time limit on that. But you see, what we're talking about went beyond simple theft. The woman was seriously hurt. She ended up in a coma. And now she's dead, quite possibly because of that attack." June waited.

Belic remained silent.

"That's why I'm here. I don't deal with theft."

June now had his undivided attention. You could see the throbbing of his pulse in the side of his neck.

"Of course, I think you already knew we could still investigate and indict you for attacking Mrs. Mehta. Otherwise you wouldn't have asked your sister to get rid of the evidence." June's final statement worked.

Belic swallowed. It looked as if his Adam's apple were pushing up what next came out of his mouth. "I not attack her, but I know who." He paused so the information could sink in with us. "I work in Yorkville back then. I clean. A few places."

I nodded at June to let her know he was telling the truth about that.

"At one place. A hair place. I get to know this man who work there. He give me that." Belic pointed to the evidence bag.

"Lucas Anasetti?" I asked.

Belic shrugged. "He tell me his name is Luke."

"Why would he give you that necklace?" June asked.

"We...we work together sometimes back then."

"I don't understand." June leaned forward in her push for information.

"Kind of partners. He know many rich women from doing hair. He tell me when one come to him worth stealing from. Then I follow her and sometimes rob her. Then we split what I get."

"But you say you didn't steal that necklace." June pointed at the bag. "You say that Luke gave it to you. Why?" June persisted.

"It was last time I saw him. He say it was final payoff. That he need me no more. But he warn me not to sell it. To wait. Since it could get us in trouble, if I sell too soon."

June and I looked at each other. That made some sense. It was along the lines of what I'd considered before. Although Anasetti had managed to sell the other jewellery he'd taken from Mrs. Mehta, if he'd heard her talking about the secrecy surrounding it, then he would have felt fairly secure that it wouldn't be reported missing right away, especially considering her condition after the attack. The pendant, however, was another matter. Even if a person didn't know it was one of a kind, it was unusual, and she wore it all the time. Someone was bound to notice its absence, so he wouldn't have wanted to hang onto the necklace, and he must have trusted Belic enough to rely on a warning.

It also made sense that since he was planning on buying the salon, Anasetti would no longer need or want to be involved with Belic in their snatch and grab operation. Once again we had answers, but nothing we could prove. The accusation came from a convicted thief. Besides that, Anasetti could say he had found the necklace in the salon.

Two steps forward—one back.

CHAPTER SIXTEEN

"Calli." Jess shook me awake.

"Hm?" I pried open one eye and shifted Sherlock off my sleeping arm. "What time is it?"

"It's after eight." She planted a wet kiss on my forehead. "Do you need the car today?"

I thought for a foggy moment. "No. You want it?"

"I have to drive up to Newmarket later, and all the company cars are being used. It'll save me the hassle of renting one. You'll get mileage paid. I meant to ask you last night, but I forgot. Sorry."

"Sure. Drive safe." I reached up and drew her down to me. She smelled like morning and sunshine, and I wished I could just kidnap her for the day.

"See you later." She blew me a kiss from the bedroom door.

My morning coffee was waiting in the kitchen. I smiled as I pictured Jess making it, her hair a tousled mess, her bare legs stretching from beneath an oversized t-shirt. If I'd dragged myself out of bed in time

I could have seen it first-hand instead of relying on my imagination. I really needed to pay more attention to her. Those moments with June just proved that for whatever reason, I had been starting to lose my bearings lately. It was time to get myself back on the straight and narrow, and put more effort into my relationship with Jess. In fact, I needed to put more effort into my life in general. I wasn't a kid anymore.

While I waited for the toaster, I filled my cup and turned on the TV news. The latest shooting, a labour strike, and a house fire in Mississauga were headlining. Not a good way to start the day. I was about to switch it off when a detail about the blaze caught my attention. In the background of the scene, fire trucks sprayed water on a flaming house. The TV camera focussed on the stunned family huddled in the street. The reporter thrust the microphone toward the homeowner who relayed their ordeal. His wife watched him in silence, but when she turned toward the camera her face screamed tears of misery.

It was Leena Chaudhari.

The camera panned to the reporter who spoke directly to her TV audience. "Investigations into the cause of the fire will begin when the structure is safe to enter. Although the Fire Marshall says it's still far too early to determine whether or not arson played a part in the Chaudhari family's tragedy, it is not being ruled out at this time."

The wall phone rang. A male voice spoke. "Do you like fires? Turn on your TV news. It's a good one."

Dewey met me at my office. Before I left home I'd phoned June and told her about the connection between the Chaudharis and Sanderson, and about the brazen phone call. There was no point in playing cat and mouse with Sanderson anymore. Somehow he knew I had not stopped investigating him. With any luck, the police would carry out a quick investigation, tie everything together, and get him off the street and out of my life, out of the lives of anyone from his past who might be in danger. I was now convinced he was behind the deaths of Mrs. Kumar and Maria Pappas as well as the Chaudharis' fire. I was also fairly certain that the texts and phone calls originated with him, even if he didn't make them.

I removed Sanderson's listening devices from their hiding places and Dewey and I said a few choice phrases into the bugs before exterminating them under the heels of our shoes. It may have been a juvenile thing to do, but it felt good.

Both of us felt a sense of deliverance in finally seeing the tail end of the case. Dewey had never looked so beat nor acted so on edge, and I felt as if I'd not only hit the wall, but crashed through. It would be a long time before either of us accepted a case that hinted at such a toll.

After the recent chain of events, I planned to make it very clear to whoever had been shadowing me that I was well and truly finished digging around in Sanderson's past. It was time to get out of town. I would have a talk with Jess over dinner; I knew she wouldn't take much convincing. Our honeymoon was long overdue. We could be packed and on a plane tomorrow morning.

Dewey decided to follow suit. He had a friend with a cottage in Muskoka, and although Dewey rarely sets foot outside the city, the thought of a peaceful and safe week or two sitting on a dock suddenly took on a whole new appeal.

I phoned Sashi and suggested she and her family disappear for a while as well. Although she had no personal connection to Sanderson, she was the one who had opened the can of worms, and she was the one he had told to close it. Sanderson had no way of knowing exactly what I had or hadn't told her, and there was no telling how far he would go in retaliation before he was arrested. Sashi said she'd think about it, but wouldn't promise. She appeared to have inherited some of her mother's sense of invincibility.

It was too bad we hadn't been able to bring Lucas Anasetti to justice for attacking Mrs. Mehta and stealing the jewellery, but at least Sashi knew the truth. Only time would tell whether that knowledge would give her peace, or make her more dissatisfied.

We had possibly succeeded in discovering what was causing the conflict between Ravi Mehta and Prabhakar Sanderson, but more important, we had uncovered the illegal adoption activities of Sanderson Junior and Senior. I now wondered if it would have been better to leave that untouched. Two innocent people had died, and a family had lost its home as a direct result of my enquiries. That was something I couldn't run away from.

Prabhakar Sanderson would never pay for what he did all those years ago, and neither would his son. But I hoped Wayne Sanderson would be brought to justice for his recent spate of violence. I knew that wouldn't rid me of the guilt, but it would ensure he couldn't add to it by continuing with more illegal activities. All that remained was for me to write up my final report for Sashi, collect my tainted paycheque, and get on with my life.

"So, Dew, do you want to help me buy my new computer when I get back to town?"

"Why don't we go this afternoon?" he asked.

"Jess is using my car. I guess we could go to a store downtown, but Philip Straun promised me a good deal, and I intend to take him up on it."

"So with the money you're going to save on your computer, how about you take me to a movie this afternoon? We deserve some fun before we leave the city."

"Sure. Why not? I need to take my mind off everything."

The outside door squeaked, and two pairs of heavy boots thumped up the stairs. By the time Dewey and I had removed our feet from my desk, two uniformed police officers were standing in the doorway. I knew neither the man nor the woman.

"Calli Barnow?" asked the man.

"Yes."

"I'm Constable Jakes and this is Constable Mead. May we come in?" the woman asked.

"Of course," I said, standing up to greet them. I wondered why June had sent them to my office. Did I need to sign something? Verify some facts? It was strange, however, that June hadn't just phoned, or come over herself.

Or perhaps they were there because of the fire, to take my formal statement about the connection between the Chaudhari family and Sanderson. That must be it.

"And you are?" Constable Jakes looked at Dewey, her voice serious.

"Dwight Brande. Miss Barnow's associate and friend." He had picked up on the tone of the police officer.

"Good," said Captain Jakes.

Something about her response struck me as strange and a chill ran down my spine. Before I had time to consider it, she continued. "Ms. Barnow, please sit down." Her sad eyes told me I'd need the support of my chair.

My heart began to pump ice. I hadn't talked to my mother in a couple of days. I should have phoned her. I should have gone to see her. Now it was too late. But why would the police bring me the news?

I didn't ask.

Dewey looked at me. He knew lightning was about to strike, but he was powerless to save me from it.

"Ms. Barnow…Ms. Barnow?" Constable Jakes insisted.

It was Dewey who finally looked at the officer.

Only then could I peel my eyes from his familiar features and allow her into my life.

"I have some bad news for you," she said.

"No," I said, and swivelled my chair toward the window.

Dewey came around the desk and slowly turned me back toward the room. He then crouched down and took one of my hands in both of his.

Taking advantage of the opportunity, Jakes was quick to speak. "Ms. Barnow, your wife has been involved in a motor vehicle accident."

I hadn't heard her properly, so I asked, "How is my mother?"

"Not your mother, Ms. Barnow, your wife. Jessica Chang." Jakes clenched her jaw.

"It's Jess, Calli, not your mother," Dewey echoed, fighting back his tears.

"No, Jess is at work," I said, but the truth was starting to seep into the cracks that were forming around my heart.

"She has the car," Dewey said. "Remember?"

I did remember, but I didn't believe what the officer had told me.

There had been a mistake.

We'd been sitting in the surgical waiting room at Southlake Hospital in Newmarket for four hours. The volunteer who'd spoken to us shortly after we arrived had suggested we might want to go to one of the on-site restaurants, since Jess would be in surgery for quite some time.

Food was the last thing I wanted, so I remained rooted in the waiting room.

Dewey still held my hand.

The police officers had left once we were settled. They had contacted June, who had picked up the Changs and brought them to the hospital. The five of us now sat in a row on the industrial-strength waiting room chairs.

We watched the clock on the wall.

No one spoke. Even Jess's mother had been stunned into silence.

Eventually June went somewhere, and without asking, brought back pressed paper trays containing cups of coffee and packets of sugar. Although all of us might have declined an offer, we accepted her gift. I found the simple act of drinking helped pass the time, but the caffeine and sugar reminded my numb body that this wasn't all some hideous nightmare from which I would awake to find Jess safe beside me in bed.

We weren't the only ones waiting. As the hours passed, there was an ebb and flow. Individuals, couples, and sometimes small groups found spots as far away from each other as possible. Occasionally, a doctor would appear to speak with someone. When it was clear that the update wasn't for you, you tried not to listen.

At about hour five I reached a state of stasis. The

hands on the clock didn't move. I didn't blink until my eyeballs hurt. The room and everything in it took on surreal qualities, as if Salvador Dali had begun a painting, but never finished.

It was then that the door opened and a man in new shoes and a white coat walked into the middle of the waiting area. Everyone looked at him, eyes torn between fear and hope.

He stood, his hands plunged deep in the pockets of his starched lab coat, while he turned his haggard face from one side of the room to the other, scanning the people for some hint. Finally he asked, "Chang? Is the Chang family here?"

The five of us each raised a hand and straightened our backs in preparation for the news. I gripped the arm of my chair with my free hand. If I hung on tight enough I'd survive the landing.

The man approached us. It was impossible to tell from his expression what kind of news he was about to share. "Jessica Chang's family?" he checked.

"Yes, I'm Dr. Chang, Jessica's father." He stood up and extended his hand.

"Of course." The man accepted the handshake. "I'm Dr. Monahan, the neurosurgeon who operated on your daughter."

Dr. Chang's face registered the distress this news gave him, and I squeezed Dewey's hand.

"Mrs. Chang?" Dr. Monahan said to Jess's mother.

She looked up at him and bit her lip to stop it from trembling.

"Would you please come with me." He turned toward the door.

"Excuse me," June stood and put her hand on Dr. Monahan's arm, causing him to stop and turn back to us. "This is Jessica's wife." She pointed me out. "Calli Barnow."

A wave of gratitude washed over my pathetic, inert body. I would have just let them walk away without me.

Dr. Monahan's face beat his mouth to the apology. "I'm so sorry. I didn't realize Jessica was married. Please, come with us."

Dr. Monahan guided us a few metres down the squeaky hall and into a little room. There was a small table in the corner that held a stack of unopened tissue boxes. Three walls were lined with chairs and the door took up most of the fourth. There was no window and the fluorescent lights hummed out a cold illumination.

A woman and another doctor were waiting for us. They stood as we filed in. Someone shut the door behind us. Then we all sat down.

I couldn't look at the Changs. I knew what I would see in their faces. I dared not look at the others, for fear of what I might see. I examined the doorknob.

Dr. Monahan introduced the other man as Dr. Yazdani, one of the surgeons involved with Jess. I dared a glance at him, but saw no glimmer of information.

The woman spoke for herself. "I'm Deborah

Mason, a social worker with the hospital." Her round face tried to smile but failed.

Despite the stack of tissue boxes and the presence of a social worker, the vise that had been gripping my chest since Dr. Monahan had summoned us had eased somewhat. If Jess were dead, someone would have told us by now. And it wouldn't take two doctors and this woman to deliver the news. They must be going to give us a report on her condition and tell us when she'd be getting out of the hospital. I let go of my worry stone and managed a deep, steady breath.

Dr. Monahan looked at Jess's parents and then at me, but instead of giving us any details, he asked a question. "What have you been told about Jessica so far?"

My mind was a blank. I must know something. I'd been at the hospital for almost six hours. Someone must have talked to me.

It was Dr. Chang who spoke. "We don't know much. We were told that Jessica was in a single vehicle accident and seriously hurt. She was brought here and taken almost immediately to surgery. I gather she suffered some sort of head injury, but that mustn't have been all." He looked at Dr. Yazdani for confirmation.

The vise once more squeezed my chest, and I struggled to breath.

"You're right, Dr. Chang," said Monahan. Although he was replying to what Jess's father had said, he was including her mother and me. "Jessica sustained injuries to her head, likely as a result of the vehicle rolling."

My empty stomach heaved. I pictured Jess behind the wheel of the Forester as it careened off the highway, landing again and again on its roof.

"Her brain was swelling very quickly, so I performed a craniotomy."

Dr. Chang took his wife's hand and explained, "A piece of skull bone is removed to relieve pressure on the brain." He then turned to me.

Somehow I let him know I understood. But I didn't understand. The doctor on the chair not a metre away from me had cut a hole in the head of my beautiful Jess. And he was just sitting there in his shiny new shoes, as if nothing had happened.

"And her other injuries?" Dr. Chang asked.

Dr. Yazdani took over. "Her pelvis was broken in two places, but the orthopaedic surgeon was able to realign the bones without surgery."

"Good. Good," Dr. Chang said, and patted his wife's hand.

She gave him a feeble smile and wiped her nose.

"Her spleen was ruptured and I was unable to control the bleeding, so I had to remove it," Yazdani continued.

Mrs. Chang's alarm at this news filled the tiny room.

"It's not a problem," said her husband. "People can live without a spleen."

This wasn't sounding too bad after all. Everything had been taken care of. Some of it didn't even sound too serious. I was able to swallow actual spit, and the feeling was returning to my tongue. I took a deep breath and spoke for the first time. "So she's going to be fine."

No one answered me.

I must have just thought I made a sound. I tried again, putting more breath into it just to make sure my vocal cords were working. "She's going to be fine. Right?"

Dr. Yazdani stopped looking at the floor and looked at me.

"It's too soon to tell, Ms. Barnow. She made it through the actual surgeries, but she's still in very serious condition. We've done everything we can for now. Jessica is young and strong, so we're hopeful."

"I'd like to see her." I began to stand.

"I'm sorry," said Dr. Yazdani, "that's not possible. They're just finishing up in the operating room. After that she'll be in recovery for several hours."

I was about to protest when Deborah Mason spoke. "What you should do is go home and try to get some sleep. You're going to need it. Come back in the morning when you'll be able to spend some time with her."

"She's right," said Dr. Chang.

We had just turned onto the exit ramp from the expressway when my phone rang. It was the hospital.

Jess was gone.

CHAPTER SEVENTEEN

The apartment held its breath.

Dewey and I huddled on the sofa.

June brewed tea that no one would drink and made tuna sandwiches that no one would eat.

Sherlock sat on the floor and looked at me. He ignored the sound of the can opener and the smell of the fish.

The profound silence of loss swallowed the scene.

The sun set.

No one moved.

When the dark became too much, June switched on a lamp.

Only then—when I saw what was carved on the faces of my best friends did the block of cement that had hardened inside me crack. Only then did I let myself acknowledge the possibility that it might be true. Only at that possibility did I allow two tears to escape. More than two would have been an admission. And I wasn't ready for that. It wasn't time.

I hadn't seen Jess. No one had.

I looked at my uneaten sandwich.

Dewey and June discussed tomorrow.

I didn't listen—but I heard.

They had taken charge. They would make sure things got done. They would take care of me.

"I'm going to bed." I walked toward the hallway.

Dewey stopped me with a hug. His chin was moist on my forehead. "I'll be back in the morning," he said.

"I'm staying the night," said June. "I'll be out here, if you need me."

I drifted into the darkness of the hall. I heard the murmur of voices. Then the sound of the door opening and closing.

The bedroom was untouched. I hadn't made the bed. Jess would be upset with me. I pulled up the sheet and straightened the duvet over it. I puffed up the pillows and put them in their proper places. All this I did by the spill of light coming through the window.

I still had on my shoes. I always leave them at the door. I slipped them off and placed them with care in front of the night table, tucking the laces inside. I climbed onto my side of the bed and lay on top of the duvet, fully clothed. I was careful not to sprawl onto Jess's side.

I lay facing the window. The rays from the streetlight fell on my face and on the empty space behind me.

I heard June's voice, small and far away, droning into the phone.

The end of the bed bounced and Sherlock picked

his way up the middle. Instead of taking his place near my head, he returned to his landing spot at the end and curled up.

I rolled over and put my hand on the empty pillow next to mine. It was smooth and cool. I drew it towards me and curled up around it.

The sun rose.

Sleep came.

June was making eggs when I finally managed to force my hollow body off the bed.

"Take a shower and put on some clean clothes," she said, before giving me a solid hug. "We'll be going out later."

I let the warm water run over my body, not bothering to use soap. I turned the hot water tap farther on. Steam filled the tiny bathroom. My skin grew red. I twisted the tap again. The fiery wet pinpricks scalded me into admitting I was awake and alive. I could still feel physical pain. But…oh god…it was nothing like the pain Jess must have felt.

Damn you, Jess. Damn. Damn. Damn.

Hot tears joined the hot water that ran down my cheeks and onto my heaving breasts. I planted my palms on the slippery tiles and leaned in, resting my forehead against the wall. The scalding spray continued to punish my back. I sobbed, hoping the sound of the fan would drown out my misery. I don't know how long I stayed like that, but the water turned cold and my tears ran dry.

I knew I should brush my teeth. So I did.

My Xanax teased me from the back of the medicine cabinet.

No. Not now.

June said I needed clean clothes, so I opened the bedroom closet. My white shirt was there. Clean. Beside it was Jess's favourite dress.

I couldn't swallow.

The lump in my throat threatened to gag me.

I slammed the closet door.

Still naked, I opened the door of the medicine cabinet and seized the Xanax. Without giving myself a chance to change my mind, I forced a pill past the rock that was strangling me.

June took the omelette from the oven where she'd been keeping it warm for me. "That's better," she said, looking at my blue shirt and pressed pants. My white shirt still hung in the closet hugging the dress. "Sit down and get this into you. It'll help."

As usual, June was right. The nourishment and the pill began to temper the raw edges of my new existence. Any acknowledgment of what had happened to Jess was becoming wrapped in a kind of cotton wool cocoon that kept it separated from my sweet denial. I guessed this wouldn't last, but somehow I was able to sit there with the sun streaming through the window and not weep.

"The funeral home called." June touched my arm to make sure I was with her. "You can see her later this afternoon." I didn't remember making any arrangements with a funeral home, but I must have. Someone must have.

I buttered another piece of toast and cut it into four triangles.

"Calli?"

"What?"

June looked at me, and in the depths of her eyes I saw the path of pain that stretched before me.

I put down my knife and fork and pushed my plate into the middle of the table.

June's cellphone interrupted any further interaction we might have had. "Thompson here…Uh huh…. Are you sure?… It couldn't have been because of the accident?…So there's no doubt…I see. Thanks John." Her face shouted imminent bad news.

I pushed my chair back and prepared to retreat.

"Calli, wait."

"I have to take care of something," I lied.

"Calli, you have to hear this."

I had suddenly gone deaf, so I stayed sitting. Words couldn't hurt me.

"That was John at motor vehicle forensics. He put a rush on the Forester for me. I thought you'd want to know any details that you could."

My hearing had returned.

"It wasn't an accident, Calli."

I started to stand up.

June's hand on my shoulder eased me back onto my chair. "You need to listen to this, Calli. The steering had been tampered with. Someone wanted the crash to happen."

I hadn't lost my hearing, but June had certainly lost her mind. "That's impossible," I said. "It's in perfect condition."

"No, Calli. Someone did something to the steering."

"Why would anyone want to hurt Jess?" I asked. "It's absurd."

"I don't think they wanted to hurt Jess."

The penny dropped.

I just made it to the bathroom in time to lose my breakfast.

A polished mahogany table filled the middle of the space. It looked like the conference room for a small corporation, not like a room at a funeral home where death decisions are made. But then, how should such a room look?

A thin man with a quiet voice and a face like an axe ushered us in and took a seat at the end of the table. He placed a large binder on the shiny surface in front of him. June and I were on his right. Dr. and Mrs. Chang were on his left.

The man's monotone explained the decisions we had to make. Only the occasional word struggled through the fog and reached my mind: service, casket, plot, urn. The binder was passed to me from time to time and I looked at the pictures and agreed with whatever someone else wanted. The only thing I was able to clearly grasp was the fact that my Jess was somewhere in the building, and before long I'd be with her. My heart hurt.

I longed to see her more than I have ever longed for anything. It was all I could do to stay seated and not rush through the rooms and hallways in search of her. But at the same time I was frozen with a dread so deep I might never move again.

I was aware of Mrs. Chang's controlled crying, and of Dr. Chang's sensible voice now shaky, asking questions or giving his opinion. June sat beside me, her support silently trying to buoy me up, keep me from shattering into a million pieces. I signed some papers. And it was done.

It was time.

Everyone stood and forced themselves toward the door.

Everyone except me.

I sat, a stone stuck between fear and mute frenzy.

June came back for me, took me by the hand, and pulled me from my chair. I let her lead me across the hall to where the others were standing in front of a closed accordion door.

"You know the extent of Jessica's injuries," the man said. "We've done nothing to hide them. If you would rather not see her—if you would rather remember her as she was…"

Mrs. Chang let out a guttural moan and collapsed against her husband. He helped her back into the room with the polished table.

"Calli?" June put her hand on my shoulder. "You don't have to. Jess wouldn't mind. She'd understand."

My eyes were drawn to the sunshine beyond the glassed entrance to the building. It would be so easy to walk into the warmth of the outside world. Let the breeze blow away the terror that had taken hold of my body and was squeezing it till I could hardly breathe. Not carry the memory of what I was about to see, the pain of what I was about to experience into every moment of the rest of my life.

I turned from the sun and looked at June.

She gave the man a quick nod.

He slid open the door. "Take as long as you like."

I forced myself across the threshold. It was a large space used for visitations. Now, it was devoid of furniture and in semi-darkness. One pot light near the far wall shone on the only object in the room—a body. It lay small and still on a gurney.

My breaths came too fast. I swayed. June put her arm around my shoulder.

I heard the slide, click, as the door was shut behind us. Then all was silent except for the pounding in my ears.

We took the first step. The carpet was so thick it sucked at my feet. Maybe it was warning me. It wasn't too late to go back. But I couldn't leave Jess alone in this empty room. If it *was* Jess.

With each move forward ice crystals grew around my heart.

I shrugged off June's arm, propelled forward by

something other than my free will.

I stopped beside the stretcher.

I looked.

It was Jess.

But it wasn't Jess.

Jess was gone.

A white sheet covered her body to mid-chest, revealing a light blue hospital gown with a geometric design. Her head was swaddled with a gauze bandage. There was a long cut on her forehead that had been stitched and there had been time for bruises to form around each eye. These were only the injuries I could see. No wonder she'd left me.

I peeled back the sheet. Her hands were folded across her body, left hand over right. Her wedding ring was missing.

June saw too. "They'll have it safe. Don't worry. They'll give it to you. We can ask on the way out."

I put my hand on hers. The cold ran through my fingers to my soul.

I replaced the sheet, and looked once more at her beautiful battered face. The light shone at such an angle that it made the skin of her nostril almost translucent. I could see the fine red line of a stagnant capillary. So that would be the punctuation mark for this memory.

I kissed her unresponsive lips.

Turned.

And walked into the too-hot sun.

CHAPTER EIGHTEEN

I bought a package of razor blades at the drug store and headed for my office. I didn't pick up coffee at Joe's. I didn't stop at the produce store for a piece of fruit. I didn't pop my head into the boutique below my office to say hello to Keesha. I prayed Svetlana wouldn't be in her workshop.

I didn't want to see or talk to anyone.

I had other plans.

For the first time, the sight of my name on my office door didn't give me pleasure. Instead, it filled me with revulsion.

Who had I been trying to fool when I set myself up as a private investigator? How could I not have learned my lesson long ago, when I had put Jess and myself in danger? How had I not realized that it could happen again? Only this time it was worse. Much, much worse. It was unspeakable.

I took the metal razor blade dispenser from my pocket and slipped one out. Even in the dim light of the landing the sharp edges glistened an invitation. I ran my finger lightly down the length of the cool blade just beside one dangerous edge. A jolt of electricity shot through my finger and up the nerve in my arm.

Grasping the blade between my thumb and the knuckle of my forefinger, I positioned it, ready for the first stroke.

I took a deep breath, firm in my resolve, almost giddy from the knowledge that I was finally doing something about my hopeless situation—and then I made contact. It only took a little pressure to have the desired effect. The black paint began to flake off the surface of the door, and soon the whole W was gone. After a few minutes my entire last name had disappeared. I was sweating from exhilaration and the heat of the day. My former self was disappearing before my very eyes.

My hand was poised above the second L when my office phone began to ring. Habit guided me as I unlocked the door and crossed the room. Then I remembered my decision *to not do this anymore*, to stop being a P.I. I answered it anyway, without bothering to check the call display.

"Ms. Barnow, this is Wayne Sanderson."

I had to steady myself on the edge of my desk to keep from keeling over. My heart was racing, and I knew I didn't have enough breath to speak.

"It occurs to me, Ms. Barnow, that we should meet

and have a little chat. Perhaps you could drop by my office in, let's say, an hour."

The moment he'd announced his name my brain had lost all logic. In its place anger, hate, and a deep desire for vengeance struck with increasing force. I knew the last thing on earth I should do was get anywhere near that son of a bitch, but I didn't care. June would disown me for even thinking about it, but she didn't know how I felt. The thing I suddenly wanted to do more than anything else was to confront Sanderson. I blamed him for Jess's death. If he wanted to kill me now, as he had meant to do in the first place, great. I would welcome it. There was, however, something else I wanted him to do more. For the first time I really understood Sashi's desire for clear answers. I wanted Sanderson to confess, and he had just presented me with an opportunity on a silver platter.

"I'll be there," I said.

Sanderson's office building was much more welcoming in daylight. The door I'd taken such care to lock behind me was ajar, and I could hear movement beyond it. I knocked lightly and a woman's voice answered, "Come in."

I entered to find the receptionist sitting behind her desk, frowning over the top of her glasses at something on her computer screen. She was round and middle-aged and maternal in appearance; not what I expected at all. If what Sashi had reported about her were true, however, her naivety far outweighed whatever was on her résumé, and ensured her ongoing employment. Sanderson was many things, but he was no fool. After what had happened with Maria Pappas, both Sandersons must have taken great pains to hire only people who would fall in line with their way of doing business, or be oblivious to it.

By the time I'd crossed the few feet to her desk, the woman had shifted her attention from the screen to me. "May I help you?" She gave me a sugar smile that dropped ten years from her apple face.

"I'm Calli Barnow. Mr. Sanderson is expecting me."

She ran her finger down a day timer on her desk. "I don't see your name." Her face registered concern, which thinly masked the fear she might have done something wrong.

"It was just arranged," I assured her. "He probably hasn't had time to tell you."

"Oh, I see. Good." She smiled and bustled toward Sanderson's door. Just before she was about to knock, she turned back to me. "What did you say your name was?"

I told her.

She repeated it under her breath, knocked, and then announced my arrival through the wood.

By the time she'd returned to her desk, Sanderson had joined us.

"Ms. Barnow, how nice to see you again." Insincerity dripped from every syllable. "Sylvia, why don't you take the rest of the day off? I won't be needing you for anything."

"Really, Mr. Sanderson?"

"Yes, Sylvia. Go on now." He shooed her away with his hand in an attempt to be playful, but his eyes were deadly serious.

The bravado I'd been feeling flagged. Despite what I had in mind, I didn't relish the thought of being alone with Sanderson.

Sylvia was only too happy to gather her belongs and make it an early afternoon.

The inner office was almost as barren and dated as the outer area, with the exception of Sanderson's leather roller chair, which he occupied as soon as he'd shut the door behind us. "Please. Sit."

I did. Then I wished I hadn't. The chair felt lower than most and put me in a position of inferiority to Sanderson who was enthroned behind his paperless desk.

The window air conditioner hummed and my naked arms sprouted goosebumps at the drop in temperature between the outer office and his inner sanctum.

So far nothing was going as I had envisioned.

"Let me offer my condolences, Ms. Barnow. Tragic. Just tragic."

Instead of the oblique reference to Jess making me weepy, it ignited a slow-burning fuse somewhere in my gut. I made no attempt to extinguish it, but rather nursed it with the bellows of my hatred for the man. "Thank you, Mr. Sanderson." I played along. "As you can imagine, this is a very hard time for me, and I have a lot to do, so maybe you could tell me why you asked me here."

"Of course, Ms. Barnow. Thank you for coming. I wish our conversation could ease your pain in some way, but unfortunately it can't. In fact, it may have just the opposite effect." He leaned on his desk and steepled his fingers. "I know I will only have to say this once, Ms. Barnow. You're going to stop poking your nose into my affairs and my father's."

So, he had asked me here to give me orders and to threaten me. He could have done that on the phone. Maybe he wasn't as smart as I thought he was. He assumed he had the upper hand.

I took a breath, gave my fuse more air, but aimed at neutrality. "Mr. Sanderson, I don't deny that I did make some initial enquiries when I was trying to find answers about the attack on Indira Mehta. All I found out was that your father and Ravi Mehta had a disagreement about something. As it turned out, that disagreement had nothing to do with what had happened to Mrs. Mehta. End of story. End of case."

"Oh, if only you had stopped your enquiries at that point." He removed a whiskey bottle and glass from his desk drawer. "Would you like a drink, Ms. Barnow?"

I shook my head. Much as I wanted a drink, it wouldn't have mixed well with the Xanax I'd taken just before coming over. I also didn't trust that Sanderson wouldn't slip something into it, and I'd been down that road before with someone I did trust.

"I will, if you don't mind," he said, and poured himself a double.

"And what makes you think I didn't stop my enquiries?" I asked.

He laughed so hard he choked. "Surely you're not that naive."

I wasn't, but I wanted to hear what he had to say.

"Well," he struggled to clear his throat, "there's no point in pretending I didn't have your office bugged. That was quite a show you and your friends put on the day you finally figured it out. Thanks for the entertainment."

Obviously my opinion of our acting skills had been way off the mark. "That doesn't prove I continued to investigate you."

"True, but a few other things do prove it."

I longed to slap the smug expression from his handsome face, but instead, I tried for once to use words as my weapon. "Such as?" I asked. I wanted to know exactly how much he was aware of. I needed to get the whole picture from him and lead him down a path where he would end up admitting he had been the one to cause Jess's death.

"I happen to know that not only before, but also after you claimed to have closed the case, you were a very busy little private eye, poking your nose into all sorts of places you shouldn't have been."

"Yes, I figured you knew. Is that why Mrs. Kumar and Maria Pappas are dead? So they wouldn't be able to tell anyone else what they had told me?" The gloves were off.

"Ms. Barnow, please. You're talking as if I were a gangster of some kind. I'm a respectable member of society. An officer of the court. A man who upholds the law, not breaks it. Yes, it was unfortunate that those two ladies perished, but I assure you, my hands are clean. That poor old woman should have retired years ago. She was in no condition to be running around downtown by herself, travelling on streetcars. It was an accident waiting to happen. And Maria Pappas, well, you saw her. It's a miracle she lasted as long as she did with the kind of habit she had. She used to be such a nice, wholesome young woman. I quite fancied her back in the days when she worked for my father. If I recall correctly, so did he, the dirty old man. Poor Maria. I did give her the occasion to turn her life around, but sometimes there's no accounting for the path a person will choose."

"You do know that the police are treating both those deaths as suspicious?"

"It's their time to waste. The cops can't connect me to them. In fact, you were the person who most recently saw them both. Not me." He poured himself another drink.

"But I'm not the one who killed them." I fought to control my breathing.

"Ms. Barnow, I have an alibi for both occasions."

He painted on a satisfied smile.

"I'm sure you do, Mr. Sanderson." My fuse was growing dangerously short. "Just as I'm positive you made sure that you can't be linked to the Chaudharis' fire or tampering with my car." If I hadn't taken that pill, I would have thrown myself across the desk at him.

"You mean it wasn't an accident?" He raised his eyebrows, pretending to be shocked. "Now that is too bad. You must feel so guilty. I mean, it was your car, wasn't it? So it looks like that lovely young woman died instead of you. How dreadful!"

"How did you know it was mine?" I focussed on the painting of a horse that hung just behind him, willing myself not to cry. The booze was starting to have an effect on him, and if I could control myself long enough for it to cause sufficient impairment, it could work to my advantage.

A hint of recognition at his slip escaped before he replied, "I know a lot of people in this city. Word gets around." He gave me another smug smile.

Again I lectured myself about control, but it was becoming harder to remain physically passive. He was enjoying every minute of the torture he was putting me through, but if I wanted any real details, I had to somehow put my personal feelings aside and coax the facts from him. I didn't want to resort to Plan B.

"I'm sure you're right, Mr. Sanderson. No one's ever going to be able to prove you have a connection to any of those deaths. You're a smart man, and you know the law. I'm just a second-rate private investigator, who at the moment is devastated by grief. When you phoned me, I was in the process of taking my name off my office door. I'm finished. I'm packing it in once and for all.

"I found the person responsible for attacking Indira Mehta, but I can't prove it. And like a fool I followed a wild goose chase involving your father. Somehow it ended up with my wife dying instead of me." I stood and went to the door, having convinced myself, if not Sanderson, that I was just going to walk away from the whole thing. "Good bye, Mr. Sanderson. You don't have to worry about my causing you any trouble." I grasped the doorknob.

It was locked.

"You didn't really think I'd just let you walk out of here, did you?" he said to my back.

When I turned to face him, he was calmly pouring himself another drink. "Open the door." I tried to sound as if I still had some nerve remaining. I didn't.

"Calli, Calli, Calli. You don't mind if I call you Calli, do you?"

I didn't answer. I was leaning on the door for support.

"Why don't you come back and sit down. You might as well be comfortable."

"What do you want from me?" I didn't move.

"Well, you seem to think that I had something to do with the death of your wife. And that it was really you who should have been in the crash. Now if what you think is correct, and I'm not saying it is, but if it were, don't you think I'd try again to get rid of you?"

"Of course I think you'd try to get rid of me—again. And I assume that's why the door is locked." So far I was putting up a brave front, but my knees were jelly.

He just shrugged.

"But you see you've already taken away something that is far more important to me than my own life. If I'd been afraid for my safety, I wouldn't have come here in the first place." I was making myself sound far more courageous than I was feeling, but I dared not let slip my true motives for being there. "Besides, what makes you think you can get away with killing me? You're already linked to me through the other deaths. And for all you know, I could have told someone I was coming here. Oh, and don't forget, Sylvia was here when I arrived." I was feeling more secure after my explanation, but Sanderson didn't look worried.

"Very true, Calli. But Sylvia has a terrible memory, and should it suddenly improve, which I doubt, I have witnesses who will swear they saw you leave my office this afternoon, alone, and in one piece. Of course, I don't believe you told anyone, but I'd be able to handle it, if you had."

I didn't doubt him for a minute. "You phoned my office. There'll be a record of your call." I allowed myself a blink of satisfaction.

"So I did. But you see, Calli, even though there'll

be a record of a call to your office, it can't be traced to me." He took a throwaway cell from his desk drawer and waved it at me.

Since I didn't have a lot of options and my knees were beginning to shake, I returned to my chair. "Okay, Wayne, you don't mind if I call you Wayne, do you? You seem to have thought of just about everything. You want to fill me in on what you have planned for me?"

He looked at his watch and poured another ounce of whiskey. "I think we have time. I'm expecting Jerome to join us shortly. We have something…something unimaginative but extremely effective planned for you." He snorted into his glass. "People won't find it hard to believe that you were so distraught you decided to take your own life."

"Jerome from the nursing home?"

"One and the same. He's a bit rough around the edges, but he's very helpful."

Things started to fall awkwardly into place in my grief-stricken brain. Jerome. Of course. I always thought Sanderson would have someone do the dirty work for him. "So Jerome was the person keeping an eye on me, texting and phoning me?"

Sanderson was too busy drinking to speak, but the creases around his eyes gave me my answer.

"So I wasn't just imagining that I was being followed. That means it was Jerome who knew where I parked my car. He fixed the steering. He caused my wife's death. And Mrs. Kumar's. And Maria's. And the fire." I started to shake as the deadly chain of events became clear.

"Congratulations! You're finally starting to put all the pieces together, Calli. Maybe you do have the makings of more than a second-rate private investigator. Too bad you won't be around to find out."

The door behind me might be locked, but I had one big advantage: I was sober. The whiskey bottle had been almost full when Sanderson had taken it from the drawer. In the short time we'd been together, he'd drunk almost half of it, and he was beginning to show the effects. Not only was his tongue loosening, but also his coordination was diminishing. He'd already as much as admitted to his part in three deaths and arson. If I could squeeze a few more facts from him and get out of there before Jerome arrived, my mission would be complete. And I wouldn't have had to resort to anything illegal. Not this time.

"Very clever, Wayne. I should have known that a man like you would never soil his hands. You're the brains. I get it."

"Oh, you don't know the half of it, Calli." His laugh reflected genuine enjoyment. "I met Jerome at the nursing home. He hated his job and was—how should I put this—looking for advancement. I was looking for an associate who didn't mind following orders even if it meant doing a few things that weren't very nice from time to time. Thanks to him I keep my old man in the condition I want him."

I thought I'd misunderstood him. "Your father had

a stroke," I said.

"Oh yes, he did have a stroke. But he was making a good recovery—too good a recovery. That was Jerome's first assignment. He was quite happy to make sure my father remained, shall we say, totally dependent."

I was at a loss for words, but Sanderson was still alert enough to read my mind.

"Come now, Calli, you must know that not everyone gets along with their parents. My father was not a nice man. He made my life hell. I was overjoyed when he had the stroke. At last I would be free of him and all his interfering. And I would have his money. But then the bastard didn't die. Worse yet, he started to recover. If I couldn't inherit, at least I could make sure he didn't have control of his modest fortune."

"Why didn't you just get Jerome to kill him?" I asked.

"I'm not a monster, Calli. He is my father. I never wanted to kill anyone. You probably don't believe me, but it's true. Jerome got a little carried away with Mrs. Kumar. And now…. Well, you know what they say—the first time's always the hardest."

I was deviating from my original plan, but since Sanderson seemed quite willing to condemn his father, I took advantage of the opportunity by asking, "So, if your father was as bad as you say, and since I'm not going to be around to do anything with the information, why don't you tell me about what happened between your father and Ravi Mehta?"

The cellphone on Sanderson's desk buzzed.

"Yeah?" he said into it. "Fine." He flipped it shut. "Jerome's been delayed, so we have some time to kill." He chuckled at his choice of words.

I didn't find it funny, but pushed for an answer to my question. "It was something to do with the adoption agency, and how he continued in that line of work after he closed the agency wasn't it?" I asked.

He looked confused.

"Your father and Ravi Mehta."

"Oh...yeah...that's right. Dear old Dad did everything legit as far as the import business with Mehta went. But the adoption agency was Dad's baby." He took a moment to enjoy his pun.

I was getting tired of them but in no position to complain. At least he was talking.

"Dad was doing a bit of piggy-backing. He'd travel to India to buy items for the store, but while he was there he'd also look for kids to place for adoption."

"I can see that Mehta might not like that, but it doesn't sound illegal," I said.

"It was the kind of arrangements he was making that was the problem. True to form he had managed to find some friends in high places who, for a price, would falsify documents and obtain babies and young children for him in any way necessary. It had very little to do with placing orphans or abandoned children in good homes, and a lot to do with making money."

"And Ravi Mehta found out about this," I said.

"Apparently."

"And that's why your father shut down the agency."

"That and the new government regulations."

"But your father didn't stop, did he?"

"No. He convinced me that we just needed to streamline the operation. He'd obtain babies from within the country for any hopeful parents who contacted me through my practice, and I'd do the legal work."

"And Mehta found out."

"Stupid fool, he should have just minded his own business. He said he had some sort of proof—from when my father had the agency and then from later on. I didn't believe him, but my father did. Once my neck was on the block, I couldn't afford to take chances."

"So you and your father had to find that proof."

"Right."

"How?"

"Dad paid some people. And he got his one and only son to follow orders. The son of a bitch had made sure I couldn't refuse—first by having me do the paperwork for the agency, and then by making me appear to be the main man as the lawyer for the private adoptions. I should have said no. Somewhere along the line I should have told him to go to hell. Sure, the money was good, but it's not like I needed it. It's not like he could still use his belt on me. As far as he was concerned, this was just one more technicality for me to take care of." Sanderson sneered into his glass.

"What was?" I feared the whiskey was eroding his memory, or his ability to logically relate the facts to me.

"Getting the proof. I told him it wouldn't work. He should just pay off Mehta. But Dad said he was too honest. So he hired someone who planned to break into Mehta's house. He even bought off a guy at the bank who would notify us if Mehta accessed his safe deposit box. Since Mehta had given him a time limit, Daddy Dearest figured it would happen soon."

"And did it?"

"No, of course not. I still believe Ravi Mehta was bluffing. He might have been suspicious, but I doubt he had proof. I think he just wanted my father to pay more attention to the import business." Sanderson began to giggle. "But this might interest you." His giggling took over.

I was losing patience. The bottomfeeder who had caused Jess's death was sitting across the room from me, and he was finding something uproariously funny. I had come to his office to get revenge, and although at one point I would willingly have walked away without it, now that I was forced to remain, I'd shown great restraint. I didn't know how much longer I could keep it up. Besides, I would have to make my move soon, or Jerome would arrive and complicate everything.

Finally Sanderson came up for breath. "Where was I? Oh yeah, Mehta's proof. Well, I did get a call from the bank. Not because Mehta had accessed his box, but because his wife had. Since Mehta wasn't well, it occurred to me that his wife might be getting the proof for him, and since the bank was close by, I rushed over.

"I'd do things differently now, but I was new to that sort of thing and I would have tried anything to get my father off my back. So when I got there, our man gave me a nod in the direction of Mrs. Mehta as she came out of the vault. I'd never seen her, and she didn't know me from Adam. The only thing I could think to do was follow her."

I wanted to hurry Sanderson along, but didn't for fear he'd lose his train of thought, or decide he didn't want to tell me after all.

He swirled the liquid around the bottom of his glass and continued. "It was one hell of a long day. I thought I would die of boredom. At one point, after the hair place and shopping, I phoned my dad. I was ready to pack it in, but he made it clear I'd better not. Then I got my first break. She took some things to her car and then went for dinner. While she was eating I went back to it and had a look. Turned out to be just the stuff she'd bought. Stupid bitch. If she really had picked up something important from the bank, she still had it with her. When she was at the movie, I parked my car just down the road from hers and waited. I remember worrying that I'd run out of gas before she came back. It was too cold to sit there for long without any heat."

Sanderson's story was like gold, but the wall clock urged me to act before it was too late.

He looked up at me and continued to drone. "When she returned, she had to walk right past me to get to her car. We were near a construction site, and I picked up a brick that was poking out from the snow next to the sidewalk. I hadn't planned to use anything, but it was there. Once I had it in my hand I only meant to stun her just long enough for me to take her purse and get back to my car."

"So it was *you* who attacked her?" Before Sanderson had started talking, this was a turn I hadn't suspected.

"I'm afraid so. It was against my better judgement, but I was cold and tired and pissed off with my father. I'd had a lot of time to think that day. And the more I thought, the more I realized I would look even guiltier than that bastard, if the proof were real. I didn't enjoy hurting her. And I've made sure since then never to get physically involved."

"Did you find what you were looking for?"

"No. I tried. I couldn't take her purse, because of how she'd fallen, but I opened it. There was only what you'd expect, plus a bit of cash and some old jewellery, no papers, no proof. Just as I was cursing what a fool I'd been, someone turned the corner, so I ducked behind a parked car."

"That's when Anasetti arrived on the scene," I added.

"If you say so. All I know is the guy took one look at Mrs. Mehta, took one look around him, and helped himself to whatever was in her purse. When he went up to the house to talk with the other guy at the door,

I snuck down to my car and took off."

"And the police stopped you for speeding on Davenport."

"So you know about that." He looked impressed.

"Yes I do, as a matter of fact. Anasetti reported a car driving away farther up the street from where he found Mrs. Mehta, but it was never checked out. At least, not until I started investigating the attack. I had a friend do a search of any traffic violations that night in the surrounding area. And what do you know! When I finally got back the list of names, who should be at the bottom, but you."

"Well done, Calli. You know, if I hadn't been shit scared, I would have laughed at the cop who gave me the speeding ticket, when a few blocks away was a woman I'd knocked out with a brick." He laughed now. "And the bloody brick was sitting on the floor in front of the passenger seat."

This was the kind of moment an investigator could only dream of. Not only had Sanderson just confessed to attacking Mrs. Mehta, but he had also managed to nail Anasetti for the theft of the jewellery. I'd come to his office hoping to prove his involvement in Jess's death, and I'd been given so much more—but I didn't care. None of it would bring Jess back. And of course, I was locked in with the maniac, and we were awaiting the imminent arrival of Jerome.

Sanderson emptied the end of the bottle into his glass, and after taking a swig, managed to get himself upright and weave toward the garbage can, where he dropped it with a thud.

I tried to calculate whether I should wait for him to sit down, or try something while he was on his feet.

Instead of returning to his seat, however, he faced me and stood there swaying. Then the corner of his mouth began to creep up. "You know, Calli, you're not an unattractive woman."

I swallowed, not wanting to believe what I was hearing.

"Since Jerome isn't here yet." He took an unsteady step toward me. "And since I obliged you by telling you what you wanted to know." He inched closer.

My stomach heaved.

"You could do something for me. We could pass the time by having a little fun." He began to fumble with his belt buckle.

I filled my lungs, hoping it would stop me from passing out or bringing up. I would rather he killed me than do to me what he had in mind.

He took another halting step as he loosened his tie and slipped it over his head. "Might come in handy," he said, holding it in front of him. Behind the dangling strip of red silk a bulge grew in the front of his trousers.

Every muscle in my body tensed to the point of pain. Although the air conditioner was still spewing out cold air, I began to sweat. Then I heard Pat, her advice as loud and clear as if she'd been standing next to me. "Don't break eye contact. Don't show your fear. Wait till you see a crack in your opponent's resolve or a signal of what's coming. Then make your move."

The reek of alcohol reached me before Sanderson was within a metre of my chair. I fixed my gaze on his bloodshot eyes. He was having trouble focussing and he too was sweating. He struggled out of his suit jacket then tossed it on his desk before he continued his uncertain path toward me.

When we were toe to toe, he dropped his tie on the floor beside me and began to bend over, his hands aiming for the arms of my chair.

Only then did I allow my eyes to disengage his as I lowered my head.

He read my move as submissive, but he could not see my muscles preparing. Just as his palms touched the arm rests, I propelled myself up and forward, the top of my head engaging the bridge of his nose with a crack.

"You bitch!" He staggered back and clutched his face. Blood ran off his chin and stained his white shirt crimson.

My stomach pitched, but Pat's voice urged me on. "When you have the advantage, use it."

Sanderson still held his face, moaned, and cursed me. He collapsed against the edge of his desk and tried to find his balance.

I didn't give him time, but let the fuse ignite the hatred and hunger for revenge that had smouldered in my heart for this man since I first knew he was guilty of Jess's murder. I strode forward, placed my feet, took aim, and launched a sharp jab to his diaphragm. Had Sanderson been fit, my hand might have suffered more from the contact than he did. But the layer of belly fat did little to resist my blow, as his lungs emptied and he doubled over gasping.

Adrenaline and satisfaction wouldn't let me stop. I delivered an upper cut with my left, and decimated his already broken nose.

Enough air had returned to Sanderson's lungs for him to utter a sound so full of primal pain, that had I not inflicted it, I would have quaked with horror.

Instead, it made me stop my assault. It wasn't that I felt pity for the fractured man, but my loathing had waned to dull antipathy. My vengeful attack had given me no satisfaction, no reprieve; the pain and loss and longing still pounded their presence in every cell of my body.

I'd come prepared to torture a confession from him. It hadn't been necessary, but the Flexi Cuffs in my back pocket would still be useful. I slipped them out but then had a more fitting idea. Using his discarded tie, I secured his hands behind his back and pushed him into the chair where I'd been sitting. He hunched forward and still struggled for breath, while blood dripped from his face onto his knees.

Now I leaned against the desk and stared at the pathetic sight before me. I felt in my pocket for my worry stone. Beside it was another object. I withdrew the razor blade container and looked at its innocent shape in the palm of my hand. Then I looked at

Sanderson.

He sat, shoulders heaving, head bowed.

I desperately needed a drink. Although Sanderson had finished off the bottle, I had a feeling there'd be more. I was right. A full mickey of Jack Daniel's sat in the drawer of his desk next to a couple of clean glasses. I helped myself to the bottle and one glass. "I'd offer you a drink, Wayne, but you're kind of tied up at the moment." I took a mouthful, thought of my Xanax, and then swallowed. The liquid burned a path to my queasy stomach and radiated through my body, as it warmed away the crust of my tension. "Of course I could help you drink it, the way your buddy Jerome helps your father. I even have some pills here you might like." I showed him the Xanax I had in my other pocket. "Happy pills. With the amount you've had to drink though, you wouldn't be happy for very long."

Sanderson was now looking at me. Fear had sobered him somewhat, but he said nothing.

I took another drink. "Of course, if you'd like something more exciting, we could always use this instead." I walked slowly and deliberately around the desk and stood in front of him. Then I extracted one dangerous blade from its holder. I held it close to Sanderson's face and tilted it back and forth, so that the edges caught the light.

Sanderson started to tremble, and a pool of urine formed around the legs of his chair.

"Jerome," he managed to say through the swelling.

"The door is locked, remember, Wayne? And I think I could convince you to tell him to go away." I wiggled the blade.

He didn't disagree.

"There's something you could do for me right now, though. I really hope I don't have to get too persuasive."

He waited. And shook.

"You've been very clear about your involvement in the deaths. Now I want an apology. Apologize for causing the death of my wife."

He blinked, but said nothing.

"Let's see, what part of you do I most want to cut?" I examined him, then reached down and began to unzip his fly.

Sanderson began to whimper. "Okay. Okay. Anything you want."

"You know, Wayne, I've changed my mind. That would hurt like hell, and you might eventually bleed to death. But it would take too long. And I'm kind of in a hurry."

The terror in his eyes pushed me on. With my empty hand I grabbed his hair to steady his head. Then I showed him the blade once more before I placed the edge against his jugular.

"Say it!" I spewed spit on his frantic face.

"I'm sorry." The words struggled out.

"I can't hear you, Wayne."

"I'm sorry." It was clearer this time.

"Again!"

"I'm sorry!" This time his apology filled the room.

"And what are you sorry for?" I yanked his hair, and the movement forced the razor blade to draw a droplet of blood from the taut skin on his neck.

"I'm sorry I caused your wife's death," he forced out between sobs.

I tossed away his head and collapsed on the chair behind his desk, panting more from hate and despair than from exertion. I had what I wanted, but I was still empty. I drained my glass.

"It won't do you any good," Sanderson said.

"What are you talking about?"

"My confession." He started to laugh, but the pain from his nose stopped his enjoyment. "It wouldn't hold up in court. I could deny it. It wouldn't even be enough to get me arrested."

"Now it's you who are underestimating me, Wayne. I may be a hick P.I., but I'm not dumb enough to have no proof." I removed my pen tape recorder from my shirt pocket and clicked it off. "I have everything right here. You were too busy drinking to notice me turn it on just before you started to spill your guts."

"You're bluffing."

"I'd have to download it into a computer to prove you wrong, and I'm not going to waste the time. It doesn't really matter if you believe me or not." I kissed the pen and returned it to my pocket.

"Even if you did record it, no one will believe I

didn't make it under duress. Just look at me."

We heard movement in the outer office. Sanderson straightened in triumph, and I struggled to come up with a plan. I'd been so caught up in my aggression toward Sanderson, I'd forgotten about the impending arrival of Jerome. He tried the doorknob. Then banged on the inner office door. Then yelled.

"Calli, open up!" It was June.

Gratitude and relief chased out the panic that had momentarily taken me hostage. I found the key in the drawer where Sanderson had put it and let June in. A man, another homicide detective, was with her.

"Are you all right, Barnow?" she asked, seeing the blood that had made it onto my hands and clothes because of my contact with Sanderson. She reached out to touch me, but stopped herself.

"I'm fine. Thanks for coming." My voice had started to shake.

June's face was a mixture of relief, anger, frustration, and what looked like fear. She shook her head and her blond curls danced. "You idiot," she said, so low that only I could hear.

I allowed myself a private moment with her then I slid my phone from its holder on my belt. "Did you get it?" I asked loud enough for Sanderson's benefit, as I switched off.

June hung up her phone as well. "Loud and clear," she announced.

"You see, Wayne, you did underestimate me. I phoned Detective Sergeant Thompson just before entering your office. I told her you'd asked me to come over here and she might want to listen in on our conversation, so we kept the line open. She heard everything right from the beginning; she knows I didn't force you to confess."

Sanderson grew as pale as the parts of his shirt that weren't covered in blood.

"You did get a little rough," said June. "You'll have to come down to headquarters. But it was clear he was holding you against your will and threatening you with rape."

"What about Jerome?" I asked.

"We picked him up just as he was about to enter the building. If we'd been a few minutes later getting here, things would have turned out differently."

"How did you know it was Jerome?" I asked.

"He was wearing his scrubs. Based on what Sanderson said about Jerome and his father, we took an educated guess. If he'd been in civvies, he would have ended up with you. We'd have heard what was going on and been quick to arrive, but it might have gotten messy first."

Once again June had rescued me. She would be overjoyed to find out that this would be the last time.

The realization that I was physically safe, that this was the final act of my career, and the weight of my grief hit me simultaneously, and using the desk to keep me upright, I returned to Sanderson's chair. As I sat down on the leather seat it began. My hands started to shake, and soon my whole body had taken up the rhythm. Then came the sobs, first dry and silent, then loud and accompanied by tears that splashed on the surface of the desk.

The male detective took care of Sanderson.

June knelt beside my chair and put her arms around me. "It's over, Calli," she whispered. "You're one crazy woman, but you did good."

I let her hold me. For a long time.

CHAPTER NINETEEN

The pen was gold and attached with a matching chain to the tiny wooden lectern. It was heavy and awkward in my hand. How did anyone expect me to sign my name with such a pen? I repositioned it, searching for the right balance between my thumb and fingers, trying to find a place of comfort. Unsuccessful, I moved the tip toward the line at the top of the empty page.

Then I stopped.

The permanent lump in my throat began to grow and made it hard to breathe. My hand shook over the waiting expanse of paper.

"I can't," I said to myself.

Someone had heard, for a strong arm was placed around my shoulders. "Yes, you can." Intense blue eyes mirrored mine, as Ken urged me on. He rested his strong warm hand over my impotent, trembling one, and guided it, until the nib touched the line just under the heading that screamed, "Guests."

What a stupid thing to call us! We weren't guests.

Almost anything would have been better: mourners, bereaved, the decimated, even roadkill. My momentary burst of anger somehow fortified me enough to enable the signing of my name. I dropped the pen with a thunk and spun away from the lectern.

Dr. Chang patted my arm and guided his still-stunned wife to the position I had vacated. One by one our little group of "Guests" filled the first page with reluctant names: Jess's sister and her husband, Dewey, June, my mother. Only after everyone else had finished, did Ken leave my side to add his name at the bottom of the list.

We retired to an anteroom near the main sanctuary. Before long we could hear through the heavy door that separated us from the vestibule that people were arriving. The murmur came in waves, subsiding as each group made its way into the eerie silence of the church. Ten minutes before the service was to begin the mournful notes of the organ reached us, and my throat tightened once again. Dr. and Mrs. Chang had turned to stone on their chairs by the wall. The rest of our intimate number paced, or whispered to one another, while Jess's sister and her husband attempted the hopeless task of trying to keep their two-year-old quiet and occupied.

The door opened and the robed minister slipped into the room. I recognized him from the meeting we'd had to plan the service. He spoke to each of us individually and then called us all into the centre.

I was ready, as ready as I would ever be. My eyes

were dry, I was able to swallow without too much difficulty, and my knees were stable. I just wanted to get it over with—walk into the sanctuary, sit in a pew, try to think of something else, and then leave.

"Let us join hands and say a few words in prayer," the minister said.

No one had mentioned this. I knew there would be a prayer, or maybe even two during the service—out there with all those other people; people who probably prayed on a regular basis. But it had been a long time since I'd prayed, and I knew it would feel like a sham if I tried. Besides, praying wouldn't do any good. I hadn't even wanted to hold the service in a church, but the Changs had, especially since a large turnout was expected. Especially since Jess had wanted to get married here, in St. Clement's where she'd worshipped as a little girl, but hadn't been allowed to marry.

I'd given in. After all, Jess was their daughter. They had memories of her in this building. In the end, it wouldn't matter to me one way or another. It was just something I had to get through.

Dewey took my left hand in his. June grasped my right. I looked from one to the other. Their faces once more threatened to break open the floodgates holding back the tidal wave of my emotions, so I looked at the floor. The carpet was ugly. A pattern of green swirls fought for dominance against a burgundy background. It was the sort of carpet you'd see in the hallways of a hotel, one that wouldn't show the dirt. It didn't look right here in a church. Jess would have hated it.

"Heavenly Father, today we form a circle of sorrow, but also a circle of love and remembrance for Jessica—wife, daughter, sister, aunt, friend."

Shit! My throat seized. The dam shook. I found a spot on the carpet and stared at it.

"Although she is no longer with us in life, she is and will always be with us in spirit."

I couldn't breathe. I began to count the feet in the circle. One, two, three....

"She was a shining light in the lives of those present."

I put my tongue between my teeth and bit down, trying to focus on my physical pain and not on the words, as my dam of denial cracked.

"And although the days ahead will be filled with the agony of loss."

I switched on a recording of "Yellow Submarine" in my head to drown out the minister.

"We will support one another."

Both Dewey and June squeezed my hands and The Beatles stopped singing.

"And we will go forward in the knowledge and comfort that Jessica has achieved life eternal. Amen."

I raised my head to look at the stricken circle, but couldn't see through the wall of salt water.

Someone helped me go where I had to go as we followed the minister down the long centre aisle. The high gothic arches framed the pews filled with mourners. I'm sure I knew most of the people, but I kept my head down and focussed on the blurry backs of Dr. Chang's shoes. "Yellow Submarine" had mercifully returned and was drowning out whichever one of Jess's favourite songs we had chosen for the beginning of the service.

The act of walking and the soundtrack in my head helped me near composure. When we reached the front, I accidentally raised my head before taking my place on the pew. And there it was—laden with a cascade of flowers, a blown up picture of Jess resting against it—the coffin. I collapsed onto the hard wooden seat. This time it was Dewey who put his arm around me. I leaned into him and closed my eyes, tried to shut out where I was and why I was there.

It didn't work.

I could smell the flowers. I could hear the words of the service. I could feel the bump of my niece's legs as she swung her little feet back and forth.

There was something the minister hadn't mentioned in the anteroom. He was still not mentioning it. As everyone else was moving forward supporting each other and being comforted that Jess was somewhere, existing happily ever after, there was something I would carry with me for the rest of my life.

Guilt.

It was my fault that Jess was in the polished mahogany coffin at the front of St. Clement's.

It was my fault that Jess was dead and not getting ready to become a mother.

It was my fault that all of this was happening.

I could have prevented it.

I could have handled the case differently.

I could have been more careful.

I could have said no to Sashi in the first place.

My list of self-recrimination points repeated itself as the service continued.

The minister spoke. An old friend of Jess's spoke. People sang. People prayed.

And then it was finally, mercifully over.

We followed the coffin out of the church. We followed the hearse through the streets of Toronto to Mount Pleasant Cemetery. We followed the minister to the graveside and went through the motions of the interment. Then we were followed to the Changs' house for the reception.

I sat on one of the sofas in the large living room. People brought me tea. People brought me egg sandwiches, which I pretended to be glad of, but didn't eat.

Joe from the coffee shop had been standing awkwardly against one wall. When there was a break in the stream of condolences he walked over to me, his shoes squeaking with each step. I'd never seen him anywhere but in his shop or on Baldwin, coming or going from his shop.

Today his mustache drooped and he paid no attention to his tortoiseshell glasses, which had slipped precariously close to the end of his nose. He sat down beside me. We both watched the people in silence.

Finally he turned toward me and spoke. "Jess, she gone. Nothing can change that."

At last someone had said it. At last someone wasn't trying to sugar-coat what I knew to be true.

"But don't forget, you have friends. Good friends. More than you know." He patted my hand, got up, and squeaked away without expecting or waiting for a response.

I didn't notice Svetlana until she floated into the spot left vacant by Joe. I might not have even looked at her, if her perfume, some spicy scent, hadn't attacked me. Much as I like Svetlana, I wasn't sure I could take her flamboyance right then. She didn't know Jess, so anything she could say to me would be generic and annoying. Maybe this was a good time to stretch my legs or get some fresh air.

"Oh ducky," she cooed and placed her hand on my knee.

It was too late; I was trapped. "Thanks for coming, Svetlana." I attempted to be civil.

"I just can't believe it. You poor dear."

I forced what looked like a weak smile and waited for the platitudes to begin.

"Don't you let anyone tell you that it will be all right. That it's god's will. That Jess wouldn't want you to do whatever it is you are going to do in your grief. Or that she'd want you to do something you can't do."

I took a good look at Svetlana. Her coils of henna hair framed her rouged cheeks. She wore her magenta shawl with the long fringe. The big picture appeared the same. But in all the years we'd shared the upper floor on Augusta, I'd never seen the heartache that her eyes now showed me. And I'd never heard more than a hint of the serious tone her words now carried.

"Oh, I know, Calli. People mean well. But only you really know what you're feeling. Only you know what you must do in order to cope. And it might take a long time. It might not be pretty. There'll be days you think you can't go on. That there's no point. And it's okay to feel like that. You'll be doing your Jess the honour of grieving deeply for her.

"But let me tell you this, and Svetlana speaks from her own experience, there *is* a point in going on. You'll feel worse before you start to feel better. And it will go up and down. It's not a straight journey by any means. But it is a journey. And one day you'll realize that you smiled at something. And then you'll find that you managed to not cry for twenty-four hours. Take the small victories as they come, my love. You'll always carry your grief for Jess somewhere inside." She patted her chest. "But just remember this: you matter. You deserve to be happy again…some day."

I wanted to believe Svetlana, but she didn't know my situation. "It's because of me she's dead," I tried to explain without anyone else hearing.

She furrowed her penciled brows. "People often blame themselves when a loved one dies. Regret is normal."

"You don't understand," I insisted. "I really am to blame. My car was tampered with and it should have been me in the accident. It's because of my job." I was on the verge of announcing this to the house full of people. I wanted their scorn, their derision.

Svetlana put her freckled hands on my shoulders. Perhaps she sensed, as she sometimes does, what I was about to do. "Oh, ducky, you give yourself too much credit."

"Credit?"

"Yes, credit. If you are to blame then you are saying you had the power to stop what happened."

"But I did. I could have stopped it." I had to make her understand.

She looked at me for a minute without speaking. "Are you telling me that you let Jess get into that vehicle knowing that someone had done something to it?"

"No, of course not." Anger started to bubble inside me.

"Was there any time during your case when you suspected that you or Jess was in danger?"

"Yes!" I felt triumphant. Now she would believe me.

"And what did you do about it?" She asked, undeterred.

"I was going to drop the case and take her out of town."

Svetlana looked satisfied.

"But I should have done it sooner!"

"Oh, Calli, so you're not perfect. Dear, dear. You were just doing your best, working at your job, living your life."

"Yes, but—"

"Let me ask you this: did Jess drive your car often?"

"No, almost never."

"And why did she on that day?"

"Because all the company cars were being used, and she thought it would be easier than renting one."

"Ah, I see." She looked at the ceiling while she thought. "So, really whoever is responsible for providing the company cars should have foreseen the shortage. That person holds some blame for what happened to Jess."

"That's crazy," I said without hesitation.

"Oh, well then that makes it clear. If Jess hadn't been too lazy to rent a car, she'd still be alive. It's her fault."

I opened my mouth to scream at Svetlana, but she placed a wrinkled hand over it. "Hush now, love. I was just making a point. Of course it's not Jess's fault, and it's not the fault of the car person at her company. And...it's not your fault either."

When she was satisfied I wasn't going to make a scene, she removed her hand from my mouth. "The only person to blame is whoever did that to the car. And don't you forget it. You're going to have a hard enough time without carrying that kind of load around with you."

I wasn't sure if I believed Svetlana, but she'd given me something to think about, and she hadn't dragged out the hackneyed condolences.

"And when you're ready to come back to work, and you will be ready, we'll have a nice cuppa." She leaned over and smothered me with a hug before floating off into the crowd.

It had been a day of following, a day of blocking out, a day of reality striking through hastily erected defences. A day I would like to forget. A day I would remember in every sandpaper, broken glass detail until it was my turn to be ushered into life eternal, or wherever we all go. Or don't go.

CHAPTER TWENTY

So far, Svetlana's words of wisdom hadn't transformed me from a guilt-riddled widow into a new woman ready to get on with her life. I hoped that someday they might, but it hadn't happened yet, and I doubted it ever would. I was living in the granny suite in June's basement with Sherlock. I was popping pills and not eating right and watching too much TV. Some days I forgot to brush my teeth, and I couldn't remember the last time I'd worn anything but pyjama bottoms and a t-shirt.

Dewey came over as often as he could and brought food and news of his life. Pat dropped by from time to time and gave me a pep talk, and Mrs. Chang phoned occasionally and cried.

I'd come home with June after the funeral, and I'd never left. The thought of going back to my empty apartment over the bong shop on Baldwin made me physically ill. June had fetched Sherlock and whatever else I needed for a few days. Neither of us had anticipated that my initial inability to be alone there would develop into an ongoing state of inertia.

I hadn't been back to my office either. Since my work for Sashi had finished and I had no commitment to other cases, I had the perfect excuse to take a break. The only thing that had stopped me from formally calling it quits was the fact that I didn't know what else I would do. At the moment I was in no state to try and figure out a new career path.

"Barnow, open up. I've got my hands full," came June's voice from the other side of the door that separated my living quarters from the laundry room and the basement stairs.

I shuffled toward the voice, not sure I wanted company, not sure I didn't.

June did indeed have her hands full. She was carrying a tray crowded with steaming dishes. "I decided you need some good home cooking, so I made my famous stew." She carried the tray to the little table that snuggled up against the wall under the high window. "Besides, I've been craving it. And I didn't feel like eating alone."

"Thanks, June." What else could I say?

We took our places at either end of the table. The stew was thick and delicious and the chunks of bakery bread were warm and fresh.

"You know, Barnow, some people are missing you."

I gave her a feeble smile and kept eating.

"Including me." She gave me a look that lasted

too long for comfort.

"But you see me all the time. I'm living in your basement."

"You're hiding in my basement," she said. "And it's the old Calli I miss."

"I can't help that," I snapped.

"Well, maybe I can." June tossed another piece of bread on my plate. "Eat."

I did as I was told. It was easier than resisting.

"In all the time you've been here, you haven't asked me about any of the people you were investigating in your last case."

"That's because I don't care. I don't want to know." I moped into my stew.

"Well, I'm just going to sit here and talk to myself about it then." She glanced at me to see if I was going to respond. When I didn't, she continued. "Borisav Belic is still in custody. His sister was as good as her word, and refused to help him in any way. In all likelihood he'll be convicted and sentenced to another jail term."

The stew was warming my stomach, and I was starting to picture Belic as he had been during the interview June and I had conducted with him. I'd been quite proud of myself that day.

"Anasetti was arrested based on what Sanderson said he saw him do when he found Mrs. Mehta. Although we all know he's as guilty as sin of taking the jewellery, finding solid proof is another matter. It also looks as though he really did just accidentally find her that night. Of course he's hired the best legal counsel available and he's out on his own recognisance. He won't spend a day behind bars."

"That's too bad," I mumbled.

June smiled and continued, "His business has suffered, however. This was one instance when the media was our friend." She stopped talking and paid more attention to her food.

I waited for more information. When it didn't come I asked, "What about Sanderson?"

June gave me an even bigger smile. "I thought you'd never ask. Well, Jerome was happy to tell us anything we wanted to know about Sanderson, and then some. Wayne Sanderson was indeed the mastermind behind everything. Jerome was just a willing henchman. They've both been indicted on three counts of first-degree murder. As long as Sanderson doesn't manage to pay off the jury, which quite frankly isn't going to happen, they'll be incarcerated for a very long time."

"Good," was all I could squeeze out. The talk of Sanderson was making me sick to my stomach, as any thought of him always did.

"And you might find this interesting," June added. "Since Jerome is no longer looking after Sanderson senior at the nursing home, the old man's health is much improved. If we had any evidence on his adoption agency escapades, we might even be able to go after him."

I'd finished eating and I had nothing to contribute to the conversation. The P.I. in me was glad of the update, but the rest of me wanted to forget it all. "Thanks for the food," I said.

"You're welcome," said June. "Now go and have a shower, while I take the dishes upstairs. We're going out."

"Oh, June, I don't really feel like it," I whined.

"Well, I do," she insisted. "Just for a little while. We'll go for a walk in the park or something. Anything to get you out of this basement and into the open air."

I knew she was right, and I knew I couldn't win, so I headed for the shower. Before I'd made it halfway across the room, my phone rang. It was Sashi. I hadn't seen her since the day of the funeral. She'd called a couple of times, but we didn't have much to talk about, since our only connection was based on the source of my misery. Yes, we were both carrying a lot of guilt, but I was too consumed by mine to help her cope, or to give her absolution.

"Calli," she said, "how are you doing?"

"Okay, I guess," I lied through my teeth.

"That's good. Listen, I don't know if this is important, or even if you're interested in hearing about it, but I found something."

I flopped into an old armchair.

June was finished with the dishes, but she waited. She could already tell it was more than just a social call.

"What is it, Sashi?" I wasn't interested, but I stopped short of being rude.

"Well, you know how my dad said he had something incriminating on Sanderson?"

"Yes, but that turned out to be a dead end. It looks as if neither Sanderson will ever answer for the adoption crimes."

June sat down. With the mention of Sanderson, she was not leaving.

"That would be too bad," said Sashi. "But maybe what I found will help."

"What are you talking about?" I asked.

"Well, I was finally going through some old boxes of things from my parents' house. One of them was full of my father's papers, all sorts of things, you know, but there was this file. It has Sanderson's name on the front and inside are some official looking photocopies."

June could tell from the change in my posture that something was going on. "What is it?" she hissed.

I waved her silent and said to Sashi, "We'll be there in half an hour."

We'd taken the Gardiner Expressway across the bottom of the city as far as Etobicoke. Although June is a skilled driver, I didn't enjoy being a passenger with nothing to do but watch the frenetic pace of the traffic. June just laughed at me as she wove her little yellow Mini in and out of the other speeding cars.

I only relaxed when we parked under the maple tree on the street in front of Sashi's two-story brick house in The Kingsway. Although winter was just around the corner, the sun was shining, and as we walked up the driveway I felt more alive than I had in ages. I'm not sure if it was being outside or the nail-biting drive that had lifted my spirits, but I was anxious to see what had prompted the phone call.

Sashi must have been watching for us, because she opened the front door as soon as we reached it. "Calli!" She held me in a hug. "Nice to see you again, June. Come in."

June and I were no sooner settled on the sofa with our backs to the big front window, than Sashi presented me with the file she had found. It was a standard legal-size file folder, a little worn at the edges. One word was handwritten on the label: Sanderson. Even the sight of the name made my skin crawl, but I took a deep breath and summoned any professional objectivity I still possessed. As I opened the file that old feeling of excitement bubbled up—that and the fear I might find nothing. Inside were several legal sized photocopies. I didn't have to look twice to know what they were.

I passed the folder to June. "Look familiar?" I asked.

She examined each sheet. "These look like some of the same documents you photographed."

"They do," I agreed. A strange feeling had started at the top of my head and was working its way through my whole body. It was something I hadn't felt for a long time. Excitement.

"Check the back," said Sashi.

June flipped over the top sheet. On it was a handwritten message—the same handwriting that had labelled the folder. She had a look then showed me.

There was a date, September 2002, and below that was an explanation of how Ravi Mehta had come into possession of the adoption documents. Prabhakar Sanderson had accidentally left a file folder containing the originals in the import shop on Gerrard. When Mr. Mehta looked inside he knew something was going on that shouldn't have been, so he made photocopies, signed and dated the back of each, put them somewhere safe, and then confronted Sanderson.

At the bottom of the folder were two pieces of paper stapled together. The top sheet was a print-out of an email from Prabhakar Sanderson to his son saying that the merchandise was set for pick-up in Sudbury on the twelfth. It gave some names, dates, and times in reference to documents that needed to be prepared. Stapled to the back of the email was a photocopy of a newspaper article detailing the abduction of a baby boy from a Sudbury hospital on January 9th, 2008. On the back of the article was another handwritten explanation.

Ravi Mehta had overheard Prabhakar Sanderson in the back room of the store as he was leaving a phone message for his son. During the message Sanderson had made it clear that they were involved in an adoption deal involving a baby that had been obtained illegally. The elder Sanderson had then used the store computer to send the email to his son in which he gave details of their scheme. He stopped just short of giving an address where the baby was being held.

Since Sanderson had used the company email account, Mehta had been able to print the message. He then searched for and found the article about the baby and confronted Sanderson. Because of the attack on Mrs. Mehta and her husband's quick decline and death, this information had been boxed up until now, ensuring that the Sandersons would not be brought to justice.

When I looked up at June, her smile rewarded me before her words. "This might just do it. I'll take them in tomorrow."

By the time we drove to High Park, the trees were casting long autumn shadows across the dormant grass. Although the temperature was starting to drop, June convinced me to walk with her along Grenadier Pond. I'd become used to following June's suggestions, so we headed down the hill to the water.

We didn't say much. June was quieter than usual and appeared to be caught up in her thoughts and in her enjoyment of our surroundings. That suited me, for I was thinking about our visit with Sashi. If only she'd found that file a few months ago how different things might be. My life had become a list of *if onlies*, and the weight of them was threatening to permanently immobilize me. I knew I couldn't continue down that path, not if I wanted to have any sort of real future. Other people go through horrible things and have to deal with *if only*. There must be a way...a way to cope.

"Come on," June said, and headed back up the hill away from the pond and past the withered maple leaf flowerbed.

I followed.

The park was quiet. We weren't alone, but due to the time of day and the time of year there were few people around, and we could hear the splash of the fountains as we reached the top of the hill and headed toward the fern-filled arbour. Thanks to a late fall there were still some blooms in the hanging planters, and the sweetness in the air accompanied us as we walked beneath the canopy of wood and vines. Any night now we would have the first frost and everything would change.

I trailed behind June as she crossed the road and down a set of steps made from wood and dirt and surrounded by trees. I was sweating from exertion and realized just how out of shape I had become in the last couple of months.

We emerged onto another road, but directly across from us was a chain-link fence and behind the fence were some small deer. "June, why did you bring me to the zoo?"

"I didn't. We're just passing through on our walk."

"Maybe we could sit on a bench for a minute," I suggested. There were several available.

A piercing, raucous laugh answered me, and I jumped.

"My sentiments precisely," said June. She turned and headed off toward the noisy peacock's cage.

Once again I followed. My breathing had levelled off and my neglected muscles were starting to sing. I watched June's back and tried to keep up as she quickened her pace. Only when the pungent stench of dung hit me did I bother to look behind the fence, then I wished I hadn't. The dejected bison looked more like sad statues, than the once noble creatures they were. They all seemed to be waiting for something—death, deliverance from the hell of their pathetic lives in their tiny unnatural home. I hurried after June.

Just past a parking lot June stopped short and I almost slammed into her. "Sit," she ordered and nudged me onto a bench.

The wood was cool, even through my jeans, but it felt good. I closed my eyes and inhaled to the bottom of my burning lungs. I could feel June sit down beside me, but I didn't move. Each breath became less laboured, as my heart rate returned to normal.

At length I opened my eyes. Because my head was bowed I could see that the ground around my runners was covered with wood chips. I lifted my face and there stood a wooden fence, only a few feet in front of us. Names were carved on each narrow picket. The sight beyond the fence struck me in the chest: a set of swings, the seats hanging idle. Swings had always reminded me of my father, the prince of my childhood, the demon of my youth. But that was in my past, locked away in a room I rarely visited.

The last time I'd seen a swing was with Jess, the evening she'd told me she wanted a child. What struck me now with such force was the realization that I had lost not just my present with Jess, but my future. Our future. We would never take our child to the park to play on the swings. We would never do anything together again. I turned to June, the horror of my thoughts an ugly mask of accusation on my face.

She put a hand on my shoulder. "Relax, Calli. I brought you here on purpose. Not to be cruel, but because I wanted to show you something."

I chose to let her continue, rather than leaving her alone on the bench.

"Did you ever come to the park as a kid?"

I nodded, not wanting to speak for fear of what I would say.

"So did I. My parents used to bring us to the playground at the other end of the park. This one hadn't been built yet. Well, not this one exactly. Did you ever see it? The original?"

"Yes," I squeezed out.

"Wasn't it great? I would have had a ball in all those rooms and turrets."

I nodded again, picturing what the playground had looked like until half of it had burned down thanks to a fire-happy teenager.

"You know, I'll never understand how people can just destroy something so wonderful, something that does so much good and gives so much pleasure." She stood up and began to walk toward the other end of the play area. "Come on, Calli," she said over her shoulder.

I fought my reluctance and joined her. We walked together down the paved path past what had been saved from the fire. I was glad to see the weathered wood of the entranceway still stood, decorated by the paintings of children long since grown. At the far end was the new structure, the most impressive in the whole playground.

"Look at that." June said.

"It's nice," I said. "They did a good job."

"Yes, they did," said June. "They designed it well to fit in with the rest of the playground. It's similar to what was there before, but not exactly the same. It couldn't be the same, of course, even if they'd tried to make it identical, because of the past—its history. Lots of people will have fond memories of the old castle, but now there's a place to create new ones. Yes, it will do just fine."

We walked slowly back toward the roadway in silence. Dusk was deepening. When we reached the bench where we'd been sitting, I turned back. The darker details of the old play areas were fading into the shadows, but behind them higher and clearly visible, the wood of the strong new turrets glowed. If nothing befell the playground overnight, it would be here when the sun rose. The children would come. They would climb and play and laugh. They would grow stronger as they built memories.

"I think I'm ready to go home now, June," I said across the growing darkness. "To my own home. I have some things to do."